The Early Pohl

The Early Pohl

FREDERIK POHL

DOUBLEDAY & COMPANY, INC.

GARDEN CITY, NEW YORK

Acknowledgments

Contents

Introduction

Autobiography is a form of dissipation that should not be permitted to mortal man. It inflames the ego and wrenches the organs of nostalgia. I love it.

Since this whole book is in a sense an introduction I will be brief here, but I do want to express gratitude to a number of people:

to the cousin (I have forgotten which one) who gave me a copy of *Wonder Stories* when I was ten, and started the whole thing;

to Dirk Wylie, the first fan I ever met other than myself, who showed me I was not alone;

to George Gordon Clark, Science Fiction League Member No. 1, who started the Brooklyn Science Fiction League chapter and introduced me to organized fandom;

to T. O'Conor Sloane, Ph.D., editor of *Amazing Stories,* magnificently white-bearded and imposing, who was the buyer for my first sale;

to F. Orline Tremaine, editor of *Astounding,* who rejected every story I showed him but bought me a lunch for every bounce and tried to tell me what magazine publishing was like;

to John W. Campbell, Jr., his successor, who also rejected (almost) everything, but by example showed me how to be an editor;

to Robert O. Erisman, editor of *Marvel* and *Dynamic Science Fiction,* who told me how to get a job as an editor;

to Rogers Terrill, bright, kind man, brilliant editor and long-time friend, who hired me;

to a thousand or more fellow fans and fellow writers, who reinforced my enthusiasm for science fiction and showed me how to write it; and, above all,

to Sharon Jarvis and her masters at Doubleday, for permitting me these unwholesome pleasures.

FREDERIK POHL

Red Bank, New Jersey

January, 1975

The Early Pohl

In the winter of 1933, when I was just turned thirteen, I discovered three new truths.

The first truth was that the world was in a hell of a mess. The second was that I really was not going to spend my life being a chemical engineer, no matter what I had told my guidance counselor at Brooklyn Technical High School. And the third was that in my conversion to science fiction as a way of life I Was Not Alone.

All of these new discoveries were important to me, and in a way they were all related. I had just started the second semester of my freshman year at Brooklyn Tech. It was a cold, grimy winter in the deepest depths of the Great Depression. There was not much joy to be found. Men were selling apples in the streets. The unemployed stood in bread lines and prayed for snow—that meant there would be work shoveling it off the sidewalks. Roosevelt had just been elected President but hadn't yet taken office—Inauguration Day, still geared to the stagecoach schedules of 1789, had not yet been moved up from March 4. Banks were going broke.

There was not much money around, but on the other hand you didn't need a lot. Subway fare was a nickel. So was a hot dog at Nedick's,* which was enough for a schoolboy's lunch. You could go to the movies for a dime or, sometimes, for a can of soup to be donated to the hungry.

Brooklyn Tech was an honor school, which is possibly why I decided to go to it in the first place. Like many of my colleagues, I regret to say that as a kid I was always something of an intellectual snob. (I do not wish to discuss what I am now.) Tech had been born in an ancient factory building, next to the entrance to the Manhattan Bridge in the grimiest part of Brooklyn's industrial riverside district. It had outgrown that and was now spread around a clutch of decrepit ex-gram-

---

* I bought one of those nickel hot dogs at Nedick's the other day and it cost fifty-five cents.

mar schools in the same area. We commuted from building to building, class to class. I found myself walking from my Mechanical Drawing class in P.S. No. 5 to my Forge and Foundry class in the main building in the company of a tall, skinny kid named Joseph Harold Dockweiler. Along about the third time we crossed Flatbush Avenue together I discovered that we had something of great urgency in common. He, too, was a Science-Fiction Fan, Third Degree. That is, he didn't merely read the stuff, or even stop at collecting back issues and searching the secondhand bookstores for overlooked works. He, like me, had the firm intention of writing it someday.

Six or seven years later Joseph Harold Dockweiler became Dirk Wylie (I'll tell you about that later on). Later still, he and I went partners in a literary agency and later, but tragically not very much later, he died, at the appalling age of twenty-eight, of the aftereffects of his service in the Battle of the Bulge in World War II.

Dirk was the first person I had found like myself. Having learned that we were not unique, we contemplated the possibility of finding still others who would be able and anxious to compare the merits of *Amazing* vs. *Wonder Stories* and discuss the galaxy-ranging glamour of E. E. Smith's *Skylark* stories. In a word, we went looking for science-fiction fandom.

The bad part of that was that fandom did not yet quite exist.

The good part was that it was just about to be born.

A year or two later *Wonder Stories* started a circulation-boosting correspondence club called the Science Fiction League. We joined instanter, and began attending club meetings as soon as a local chapter was formed. We met others like ourselves. We worshiped at the feet of a few who had actually been published in the professional sf magazines, and we learned the answers to the two key questions that confronted us: How do you become a writer? and, How do you get published?†

The Brooklyn Science Fiction League met in the basement of its chairman, George Gordon Clark. He was an energetic fellow. When *Wonder Stories* announced the formation of the SFL Clark did not waste time, he sent in his coupon at once and consequently became

---

† "How do you become a writer?" You write. That is, you put words on paper until you have completed one or more stories. There is simply no other way to do it. "How do you get published?" You send those stories to someone who, if he likes them, can publish them—as for instance the editor of a magazine you read, whose name and address you get from the contents page of the magazine. That is the Whole of the Law.

Member No. 1. When the SFL announced it was willing to charter local chapters, he acted instantly again, and so the BSFL was Chapter No. 1, too. We outgrew Clark's basement pretty quickly; there was only room for about four of us, in with his collection of sf magazines. We moved to a classroom in a nearby public school. What I mostly remember about those meetings is surprise that I couldn't fit into the grammar-school desks any more—after all, it was only a couple of years since I had been occupying desks just like them every school day. I remember we talked a lot about how to interpret Robert's Rules of Order and spent quite a lot of time reading minutes of the previous meeting. If anything else substantive took place, I have forgotten it entirely.

But, ah, the Meeting After the Meeting! That was the fun part. That was when we would adjourn to the nearest open soda fountain, order our sodas and sundaes and sit around until they threw us out, talking about science fiction.

It was always a soda fountain. Not always the same one; over the years we fans must have staked out and claimed dozens of them, all over the city. But we were addicted to ice cream concoctions, so much so that a few years later, in a different borough of the city, after the meetings of a different club, we finally designed our own sundae, which we called the Science Fiction Special, and persuaded the proprietor of the store to put it on his menu. We were a young bunch, as you can see. Except for Clark, who must have been in his early twenties, the old man of the group was Donald A. Wollheim, pushing nineteen. John B. Michel came with Donald; and a little later, down from Connecticut, Robert W. Lowndes; the four of us made a quadrumvirate that held together for—oh, forever, it seems like—it must have been all of three or four years, during which time we started clubs and dispersed them, published fan magazines, fought all comers for supremacy in fandom and wound up battling among ourselves. The fan feud is not quite coeval with fandom itself, but it comes close. None of the clubs seemed to live very long. The BSFL held out for a year, then we moved on to the East New York Science Fiction League, a rival chapter of the parent organization which seceded and renamed itself the Independent League for Science Fiction. That kept us engaged for another year, then it was the turn of the International Scientific Association (also known as the International Cosmos-Science Club). The ISA was not particularly scientific, and it certainly wasn't all that international; we met in the basement of Will Sykora's house in Astoria, Queens. (The ENYSFL-ILSF had met in a basement, too, the one belonging to its chairman, Harold W. Kirshenblit. I do not know what science-fiction fandom would have done in, say, Florida, where the houses didn't have basements.) It didn't much matter what the name of the club was, or where we met. We did about the same things. We held meetings once a month, mostly devoted to arguments over whether a motion to adjourn took precedence over a point of personal privilege. We got together between times to publish mimeographed magazines, where we practiced our fledgling talents—for writing, and also for invective.

The fan mags‡ were sometimes club efforts, sometimes individual. I managed to wind up as editor of the club mags a lot of the time, but that wasn't enough; I published some of my own. The one I liked best was a minimal eight-page mimeographed job measuring 4¼″ by 5½″ —a standard 8½″ by 11″ mimeo sheet folded twice—called *Mind of Man*. Since it was my own I could publish anything I liked in it. What I liked best to publish was my own poetry, which at that time was highly sense-free, influenced in equal parts by Lewis Carroll's *Jabberwocky* and some of the crazier exhibits in *transition*.

. . . Oh, why not? I will give you one sample from *Mind of Man*. It is meant to be read aloud. If I remember correctly, I wrote it in a single blinding flash of inspiration immediately after learning that the "&" mark on my typewriter was called an ampersand.

```
           ?
      .  .   &
     ! my frand
      ;    $
     - - . . . . . .
```

I will leave the exegesis to any interested Ph.D. candidates, but I would like to observe that the proper title is not *Question Mark* but *Interrogation Point*. I mention this for the benefit of any coffeehouse artists who wish to include it in a poetry reading.

I don't know what kind of a writer I would have been if I hadn't met Dirk and, through him and with him, the whole world of science-fiction fandom. Much the same, I imagine. I almost certainly would have been a writer—I'm hardly fit for anything else. And I had been

‡ Now they are called "fanzines," but the term hadn't been coined then.

trying to write sf at least a year before I met Dirk, in idle moments in classes in the eighth grade. But it would have taken a lot longer. I owe a lot to fandom. From Wollheim, Michel, Lowndes—later from Cyril Kornbluth, Dick Wilson, Isaac Asimov and others—I learned something about what they were learning about writing; we all showed each other our stories, when we weren't actually collaborating on them. In the fan mags I acquired the skills necessary to prepare something for public viewing—and the courage to permit it.

What I am not as sure of is whether all the things we learned were worth learning.

Science fiction was purely a pulp category in those days. Sometimes the emphasis was on gadgetry, sometimes on blood-and-thunder adventure; when it was best the high spots were vistas of new worlds and new kinds of life. In no case was it on belles-lettres, nor was it a place to look for fresh insights into the human condition. What we learned from each other and from the world around us was the hardware of writing. Narrative hooks. Time-pressure to make a story move. Character tags—not characterization, but oddities, quirks, bits of business to make a person in a story not alive but identifiable. So I learned how to invent ray-guns and how to make a story march, but it was not for a long, long time that I began to try to learn how to use a story to say something that needed saying.

In fact, when I look back at the science-fiction magazines of the twenties and the early thirties, the ones that hooked me on sf, I sometimes wonder just what it was we all found in them to shape our lives around.

I think there were two things. One is that science fiction was a way out of a bad place; the other, that it was a window on a better one.

The world really was in bad trouble. Money trouble. The Great Depression was not just a few million people out of work or a thousand banks gone shaky. It was *fear*. And it was worldwide. Somehow or other the economic life of the human race had got itself off the tracks. No one was quite sure it would get straight again. No one could be sure that his own life was not going to be disastrously changed, and science fiction offered an escape from all that.

The other thing about the world was that technology had just begun to make itself a part of everyone's life. Every day there were new miracles. Immense new buildings. Giant airships. Huge ocean liners. Man flew across the Atlantic and circled the South Pole. Cars went faster, tunnels went deeper, the Empire State Building stretched a fifth of a mile into the sky, radio brought you the voice of a singer a continent away.

It was clear that behind all this growth and acceleration something was happening, and that it would not stop happening with the *Graf Zeppelin* and the Empire State but would go on and on. What science fiction was about was the going on. The next step, and the step after that. Not just radio, but television. Not just the conquest of the air, but the conquest of space.

Of course, not even science fiction was telling us much about the price tag on progress. It told us about the future of the automobile; it didn't tell us that sulphur-dioxide pollution would crumble the stone in the buildings that lined the streets. It told us about high-speed aircraft, but not about sonic boom; about atomic energy, but not about fallout; about organ transplants and life prolongation, but not about the dreary agony of overpopulation.

Nobody else was telling us about these things, either. A decade or two later science fiction picked up on the gloom behind the glamour very quickly, and maybe too completely. But in those early days we were as innocent as physicists, popes and presidents. We saw only the promise, not the threat.

And truthfully we weren't looking for threats. We were looking for beauty and challenge. When we couldn't find them on Earth, we looked outside for prettier, more satisfying places. Mars. Venus. The made-up planets of invented stars somewhere off in the middle of the galaxy, or in galaxies farther away still.

I think we all believed as an article of faith that there were other intelligent races in the universe than our own, plenty of them.* If polled, I am sure we would have agreed that wherever there's a planet there's life—or used to be, or will be.

Now, alas, we know that the odds are not as good as we had hoped, especially for our own solar system. The local real estate is pretty low quality. Mercury is too hot and has too little air; Venus is too hot and has too much, and poisonous at that. Mars is still a possibility, but not by any means a good one—and what else is there? But in the mid-thirties we didn't know as much as we do now. The big telescopes hadn't

---

* I still believe it! What puzzles me is why we haven't seen any of them as visitors. I wish I could swallow the flying-saucer stories—I can't; the evidence just isn't good. But the absence of hard facts hasn't shaken my faith that Osnomians and Fenachrone are out there *somewhere*.

yet been completed, and of course no spaceship had yet brought a TV camera to Mars or the Moon. So we believed.

The first sale I ever made came out of that general belief.

It wasn't a story. It was a poem. I am afraid that I don't think now that it is a very good poem, but it contains the first words I ever put down on paper that I actually received real, spendable money for, and so I am going to include it here.

People sometimes ask me when I made this first sale. That's harder to answer than you might think. I wrote it when I was fifteen. It was accepted when I was sixteen. It was published when I was seventeen—in the October 1937 issue of *Amazing Stories*. And I was paid for it ($2.00) when I was eighteen.

That's how things were in those days.

Elegy to a Dead Planet: Luna

Darkness descends—and the cluttering towers
Of cities and hamlets blink into light.
The harsh, brilliant glitter of day's bustling hours
Gives place to the glowing effulgence of night.

The moon—that blanched creature—the queen of the sky
Peeps wistfully down at the life-forms below,
Thinking, perhaps, of the eons rolled by
Since life on her bosom lapsed under the snow.

A dead world, and cold, this satellite bleak,
Whose craters and valleys are airless and dry;
No flicker of motion from deep pit to peak;
No living thing's ego to ask, "Why am I?"

But once, ages past, this grim tomb in space
Felt bustle of life on her surface now bare,
Till Time in his flight, speeding apace,
Swept life, motion, thought away—who can know where?

I just now noticed for the first time that T. O'Conor Sloane changed the title on me. I had called it *Elegy to a Dead Planet: Luna*. But Luna isn't a planet, and so he changed *Planet* to *Satellite,* which, to be sure, is correct . . . but I'd rather have it my way, and so I have changed it back. A thing I would never have dared when he published it. Sloane was a magnificently white-bearded patriarch, looking a lot like Boris Artzybasheff's drawing of God in the guise of George Bernard Shaw. As far as I was concerned he *was* God. He could say "buy" or "bounce."

When *Elegy* appeared, it was under the by-line of Elton Andrews.

Who was Elton Andrews?

My pseudonym, that's who. You have to remember that I started writing very young. I not only had not reached the age of mature wisdom* when I began, I was barely into puberty. I had a lot of romantic, immature ideas.

One of these notions was that using a pen name was glamorous. Every one of the stories in this book appeared under some other name when first published. So did everything else I wrote for pay—with the single exception of a poem, where there was a change of editors and the new man didn't know about my quirks—until I was past thirty, by which time I had been writing professionally for nearly fifteen years. Fan mag stuff I signed my name to. Professional stories I did not.

It isn't altogether a bad idea to publish one's early work under an assumed name. It takes some pressure off. If things go badly, you can always lie out of it. But that wasn't the reason I did it. What appealed to me was the romance of the thing. I remember the fantasy very clearly. I would be sitting at the soda fountain of some candy store with a newsstand. Next to me would be somebody—some pretty girl, if possible, although in those days there weren't many pretty girls who read science fiction. She would be thumbing through the latest *Wonder Stories* or *Astounding.* Her attention would be caught by a story and, fascinated, she would read it through, while the ice cream melted in her black and white soda and the bubbles went flat. Then she would look up, still entranced, coming back slowly to the real world.

And I would call for the check, smiling, and say, "Liked it, did you? Yes. That's one of mine."

There was another consideration affecting whose name was signed to a story, and that is that there was often some doubt about whose name belonged there.

One thing we young fans did a lot was collaborate. Don't think

---

* Any day now, right? Please God?

badly of us. It was a long time ago, in a different world. We were crazy kids, with no real roots; if from time to time we wrote with somebody else, what was the harm? I'm not ashamed to say that I collaborated with at least a dozen other persons, both male and female. It didn't seem wrong. I didn't feel that I was being promiscuous. And certainly I didn't take part, or at least very rarely took part, in the Futurian Group Writing sessions, where as many as four, five, even six or seven people took turns in writing a single story. I'm not criticizing their life-style; what goes on between consenting adults is their own business. It is simply that that sort of thing never attracted me except, oh goodness, possibly two or three times, at the most.

As a result of all this collaboration there exist a fair number of stories of which the authorship was in doubt, and may remain so to this day. There wasn't much to do but put pen names on them.

After a lot of thought, I have decided against including any of those collaboration stories in this book, but there were a lot of them. I collaborated with Dirk Wylie; with Doc Lowndes; with Dirk *and* Doc; with Cyril Kornbluth; with Cyril and Dirk, and with Cyril and Doc; with Isaac Asimov; with Leslie Perri—I do not remember all the permutations; and there was at least an equal volume of material in which I did not happen to take part involving some or all of the others.

The first actual stories I published were collaborations, with a young fan torn between music and physics as a career, named Milton A. Rothman. The stories appeared under the name of Lee Gregor. Milt did most of the writing. In fact, he wrote the whole story in first draft. Our arrangement was that he would write them, I would rewrite them and sell them and he would take the bulk of the money. We sold two stories that way, in 1938 and 1939, both to *Astounding*—and for nearly a quarter of a century, those were the only stories I had any part in writing that ever appeared in *Astounding*. I was not part of the Campbell revolution. I was in the opposing camp.

In fact, John Campbell and I were competitors. By the fall of 1939, when I was nineteen years old, I had discovered how to be sure there was at least one science-fiction editor who would look with favor on my stories: I became one.

The first story I bought from myself that was all my own was *The Dweller in the Ice*. I published it in *Super Science Stories* for January 1941, under the pseudonym of James MacCreigh.

The Dweller in the Ice

JAMES MacCREIGH

"My dear woman, it's *always* snowing here. Well, maybe not really always, but it certainly seems that way. This weather may seem bad to you, but—well, I've been on this sort of work for thirty-five years. They didn't have any Salts to take the place of fur parkas and bonfires when I started. There were times then when a man who walked outside the ship's port, or who stepped out onto the ice for a second, could have got lost immediately, and frozen to death within the hour. And, even now. . . . WHUP!"

Captain Truxel broke off his flow of chatter voluntarily for almost the first time in four days, as he grabbed the helm of the speeding ship. With a quick flip he slammed the manual control over to starboard; the rudder motors whined angrily into action, twisting the ship's course to the right. For a second the vessel careened crazily to the left, until the tiny, odd-shaped screws of the vortex-keel also hit their speed and once more straightened the ship.

"Iceberg," Truxel explained briefly as he returned the ship more leisurely to its course. "No danger, of course, but it could have caused a lot of annoyance if it had stripped the speed-sheathing from the hull —or if we had climbed right up onto it. I've heard of ships that . . . ."

"I think we'd better get below," Kye Whalen interrupted impatiently. "We've got to pack up a lot of things before we land. Don't we, Beatta?"

"I'm afraid so," his wife smiled, taking all the sting out of their departure for the Captain. "When will we land, please?"

"Oh, about half an hour from now, I guess." The Captain didn't *like* to have listeners walk out on him, but long experience had got him pretty well used to it. "And stay away from the heated sections while you're below. The Salts will burn you to a pair of frizzled cinders if you don't."

That was an exaggeration. And yet it was dangerous to go anywhere where there was what might normally be called bearable warmth when one had the heat-producing Hormone Salts in the bloodstream. The germ-produced fevers were nothing compared to the inferno produced in the body of one who disobeyed that vital rule. Wonderfully valuable though the Salts were in such things as Antarctic exploration, their use was limited for that reason.

Kye was moody as they descended. As soon as they gained their cabin, he slouched down on the side of the bed, not looking at her.

With quick understanding, Beatta stepped to his side and threw an arm about his shoulder. "I know what the matter is, darling," she said. "You're still worrying about the transfer. Aren't you?"

Kye stiffened. "Why shouldn't I be?"

Beatta groaned mentally. They had been over this a hundred times. Kye was so maddeningly sensitive about his ability to provide for her. "Dear," she said. "After all, this isn't so bad. This wave of carelessness or whatever it is has to be stopped, if the drill-jewels are to come out of the ice. And they send *you* down to make sure of it!"

Kye glared at her. "Beatta, that's all very fine. But what gets me is, they don't need a mining engineer here at all; they need a psychiatrist. The machines are working fine, according to the reports. It's the people that are at fault. They've had fifty accidents here in one month! What can I do about that?"

Out of her woman's wisdom, Beatta said, "You'll do something, Kye. You'll see, dear, you'll feel a lot better about it when we get to the mine." She stood up and essayed a smile, to which Kye responded, weakly. "Now let's get packed!"

Beatta was wrong. Even when they had been at the mine site for a full week, and more, Kye's mood was still with him. The mere fact of his presence hadn't been enough to stop the wave of accidents.

The "mine" wasn't anything at all like any ordinary mine. Kye's company—International Milling Machines, Inc.—manufactured all sorts of machine-tool equipment, needed semi-precious and precious stones for drill-points. Intermill, as the company was called, had sponsored for publicity an astronomical observatory near one of their plants in the Andes.

The observatory had detected a brand-new comet, a wanderer, approaching the Solar System in an orbit almost at right angles to the plane of the ecliptic; had followed the comet's tortuous course, spectro-analyzed it, and seen an unusual display of meteorites strike the Earth's Southern Hemisphere at about the time the main body of the comet was heading sharply in for the sun—with which it collided.

It took no great deductive ability to realize that the meteorites had been part of the comet's body, and to see further that they must contain a large amount of the carbon that the spectrograph had shown in the comet itself. So Intermill had sponsored an expedition, found some of the stones, and been delighted to find their utility as industrial gems. For the Earthdrawn meteorites were shot through with every manner of jewel!

Kye's routine, at first, had been simple. A top-notch mining engineer, he had checked over all the equipment; visited the mine-shafts; slid himself on a cable down the slick and unutterably frigid tubes in the ice made by the heat-borers. Everything was in perfect order.

He reported as much to Beatta.

"Of course there's nothing wrong with the diggings," she said. "You knew that before you came here."

"Well—yes, I knew it. In a way. But I have to make sure for myself. I'm going to tackle the generators next, and see if they're working all right. Five of the accidents were there, after all. Maybe . . . ."

Beatta stamped her foot. "Maybe nothing!" she cried. "You know there's nothing wrong with *any* of the machines here. It's the people! Remember what you said on the ship, Kye? —that they didn't need an engineer here, but a psychiatrist? Kye, I think that *you* are the one who needs a psychiatrist now!"

Kye stared at her woodenly. His lips shaped words, but were stopped before the words came out. He turned on his heel, walked out as though on stilts. "I'm going to look at the generator," floated back to Beatta as she gazed, startled, at his departing back.

Beatta sat erect. "Kye! *Kye!* Come back!"

But he was gone.

Beatta sat on her hard chair for three hours and more, trying to think the thing out. What had happened to Kye? To every man she knew? A schoolboy could see that Kye was terribly wrong in looking for mechanical trouble to explain the slowing of production. No, it was a mood that had gripped the men at the camp.

And—her brow unconsciously wrinkled in perplexity—why was *she* unaffected? Except for the contagion from Kye, her spirits were normally high. So, it seemed, were the spirits of the half-dozen other women at the mine site . . . .

Suddenly the house-lights flickered and went out. The radio, which she had left playing away in another room, died also.

A fuse burnt out?

She whispered a mild oath, fumbled a flashlight out of a drawer, and sought the fuse-box. She put a new fuse in place and snapped down the contacts.

But the lights did not spring up.

Had something happened to the power-source?

If the generator had temporarily gone out of order, a very possible thesis, the batteries should have cut in immediately.

As if in answer to the unspoken thought, the lights came on again, noticeably dimmer than before. Beatta salvaged the fuse she had removed and thrown away, and went back into the bedroom.

Kye was there, sitting on the bed, gazing at the wall.

"What happened to the lights, dear?" asked Beatta.

"One of the bearing-mounts had a flaw. It split, and the generator stopped. They'll fix it pretty soon."

There was something odd—odder, even, than had become usual—about Kye's listless speech. "Did Preston call up to tell you about it?"

"No," said Kye, stirring restlessly. "I saw that it would happen when I was there. The flaw had opened up to the surface, and it was only a matter of time until it was bound to split right off. I should have taken it down then, I guess, but . . . ." His voice trailed off and he shut his eyes, stretching back across the bed. "It would have been such a lot of trouble. It doesn't matter, really, dear. They'll have it all fixed, sooner or later."

"Kye, I've got to talk to you. There's something—oh, I've said that a hundred times. But it's true. Kye, what makes you act like an irresponsible *baby?*"

A hunted look crept into Kye's eyes. "I don't know, Beatta," he said slowly.

"The way things are—it's just too much trouble to do anything. Oh, I knew what I should have done when I saw that flaw. Everyone there —Preston, and Argyle, and the rest—they all knew it was there too."

"Well then! Why didn't you—"

Kye raised a restraining hand. "I know. But . . . . Beatta, do you know how it feels to be utterly *alone?* Lost, away from every person you can talk to? Like Hale's 'Man Without a Country.' That's how I feel, Beatta; as though I were exiled and an outcast. As though I never would see my home again, or see you again, darling,—even when I'm right in the same room with you I feel that way. I can't explain it."

Beatta sat down beside him, her hands clasped in her lap, not wanting to disturb him by touching him sympathetically. His utter dejection made him unapproachable. "Why don't we women feel it, Kye?"

"I don't know." His eyes closed; he withdrew into himself.

Beatta sat regarding him for a while. She tried to get him to speak, but he would not be cajoled.

Then she got to her feet and walked out into the snow.

Christine Arbrudsen was at home. Nominally the Recreations Director of the little mining colony, her job had no duties at all now—for none of the men had left any interest in recreation. Christine was a friendly girl, and Beatta had liked her from the start. In the week they had known each other they had become the best of friends. Beatta spoke directly:

"Christine, you've got to help me. I'm going to try to find out something about this—this craziness that's got every man in the field. I think I know just about what to do and where to go; and I want you to come along. I may not be able to do everything alone."

Christine nodded in quick understanding. "I know," she said. "You want to investigate that borer, don't you? The one that turned aside?"

"How did you know?" gasped Beatta.

"I observe things too," Christine smiled. "I tried to talk some of the men into looking into the matter, but you know how they are. I was going to make the trip tomorrow, alone. But you're right—it's better that two of us should go."

Among the mishaps of the mine had been a minor one when a heat-borer had deflected itself from the normal, almost vertical course, melting through the ice on a long diagonal and coming perilously close to a "bubble"—a sort of inverted pit in the ice where submarine currents had hollowed out a cavern. Had it actually penetrated the bubble it would have been the last ever heard of that borer—but one of the men, making a routine checkup, had discovered the one that was out of its place, and stopped its power in time to rescue it.

After Beatta had left him, Kye lay in a stupor for a while. Several hours passed; it grew "dark" outside as the sodium lamps were extinguished and the pale violet, fluorescent night-time lamps took their place. Naturally, there was no such thing as night or day in the Antarctic, where six months passed between the rising of the sun and its setting. An arbitrary period of eighteen hours, based on the needs of the body for rest with the use of the Salts, had been chosen for the "day"; the life of the colony was regulated accordingly.

Eventually Kye got up and prepared himself some food. Beatta was not home; without much interest he wondered what had become of her.

Having eaten, he went back immediately to bed. . . .

And when his phone buzzer sounded thrice, and the sodium lamps went on again to indicate morning, Beatta was not in the bed yet. She hadn't been home at all.

He ate again, hurriedly and without enjoyment. His increasing anxiety was cracking away the armored shell of apathy. Unable to contain himself, he got up in the middle of the meal and phoned all the places she might possibly be. She wasn't at the Prestons', he was assured; no, they hadn't seen her at the Dispensary, but thought she might have stayed with Christine Arbrudsen, who had been asking for her the day before.

There was no answer to Christine's phone, though.

He made call after call, till he had almost exhausted the score or so of other phones on the line. But when he called the generator plant, the phone suddenly went dead in the middle of the conversation. Simultaneously, the sodium lights, which had been growing dimmer, went out completely. The entire camp became black as the night sky above.

The fault in the generator hadn't been repaired, he realized, and the emergency batteries had been drained. The camp was powerless.

Suddenly it came to Kye, where Beatta was. The borer! She had wanted him to look into it; he'd refused, so she'd done it herself.

He hastened out, in the direction of the airplane hangar.

When the two girls got to the runaway borer, they suddenly realized they'd no actual plans made. They held a hasty conference.

The upshot of the debate was that they'd send the borer down once more, as far as it would go before making the slant; then follow it down, hand-over-hand, on the cable.

They hooked up the borer to its cable; tuned it in on the radio power-beam. It slipped through the ice very rapidly. The hole was there already; all that the borer had to do was to eat away the tiny bit of ice that formed since it last went in; widen the tube where the rheological movement of the ice had, with all its titanic weight and force, crushed its walls together; and remove the snow that had drifted in. (The water formed by the passage of the borer through the ice was automatically pumped to the surface, where it immediately solidified.)

Beatta was watching the cable as it paid off the winch. When it reached the eight-hundred foot mark—the point where it had suddenly swerved off before—she cut off the power. She rose and looked at Christine.

"Well—how shall we work it?" she asked. "Draw lots, or both of us go down together?"

"Draw lots," Christine said immediately. She rummaged through her pockets. "Here," she said. "I've got a quarter and a dime in my hands. Pick one hand. If you get the quarter—you go down. The dime —I do."

Without hesitation, Beatta touched the right hand. The quarter!

"Help me put on the armor," she said, not a quaver in her voice. "And let's decide what I'm to do. As I see it, I'll slide down. When I reach the bottom I'll let you know. Then you turn on the power. I'll try to steer the borer straight at whatever seems to be drawing it. And I'll tell you whatever I see. Right?"

"I guess so," said Christine uncertainly. "Don't let anything happen to you, Beatta. Please!"

Slipping the band of the asbestos coolie-hat under her chin, Beatta lay flat on her stomach at the entrance to the tunnel; slowly eased herself forward, gripping the cable. Then she swung herself into the tube, and slipped rapidly out of sight.

Christine flipped on the phone speaker. "Are you all right?" she asked anxiously.

There was no answer but labored breathing for a few moments, then a sudden soft thud.

"I made it all right, Christine," Beatta's voice said. "I'm standing on the borer now. I'm going to lean against the wall of the tunnel and try to kick the back of the borer around. I'm ready, Christine. Turn the power!"

With a determined motion, Christine spun a dial attached to the base of the winch. "Power is on!" she called.

There was a sound of muffled struggle from below. "I'm—moving it," Beatta's voice came through, between gasps. "It's a little bit hard. I—ugh!—I haven't got anything solid to—to push against. I keep slipping on the ice."

"Better save your breath," Christine interjected. "I can hear you moving around all right."

There was a long period of silence then, while Christine strained her ears for every sound. Then:

"I've got it going almost straight to one side," Beatta panted. "But I have to keep pushing it along, or else it tries to go straight down. It's a pretty tough job." Abruptly she was silent again, while slithering, rasping sounds came through the diaphragm.

"Beatta!" Christine said tautly. "Maybe you'd better come up. We'll get one of the men to help us, somehow. Maybe we can sink another shaft right over the place you're aiming for. But this is too hard, Beatta. Come up!"

She waited for an answer. There was none. She listened more intently, her brow deeply furrowed.

There were no more sounds of movement from below.

"Beatta! *Beatta!* Can you hear me? Please, Beatta, *answer* me!" Abruptly she ceased calling. That was worse than useless.

Indecision and stark fear for Beatta were in her face. Should she pull the borer up on the winch? Without having consciously decided on that course, she put her hand on the control,—

And saw that all the meters read at zero.

No power was flowing through the winch. The radio-beam, dependent on the emergency batteries, was dead; the batteries had given out.

There no longer was any doubt in Christine's face. She knew precisely what she had to do.

Just as had Beatta, she lay on her stomach and wriggled into the tunnel.

Behind the controls of the little scouting plane, Kye's face was grim. The borer he was looking for was two miles—say, three—from the camp. The plane's cruising speed was two hundred miles an hour. Three two-hundredths of an hour was fifty-four seconds.

And he had been flying for nearly twenty minutes.

The trouble was the utter impossibility of recognizing landmarks in the dim starlight, which was all he had to go by. The plane went too fast to make ground objects more definite than shadows. He reversed the plane in a wide arc; sped back to the camp again, and started over. At the expiration of precisely forty seconds he stopped the propeller and switched on the heliscrews. Hanging on their vertical thrust, he was able to use the forward movement of the plane to whatever degree he desired.

And yet the borer was as evasive as ever.

Just as he was making up his mind to go back to the camp, leave the plane and look for it on foot,—he saw it, a gleam of metal just below him.

The whine of the vertical screws lowered in pitch as he cut their speed. Slowly the plane dropped; Kye saw a more or less level spot about a hundred yards from the jumble of metal that was his objective, and dropped the plane onto it. He cut the switch and scrambled out, racing to the machinery.

The borer wasn't on the surface, he saw with a sinking feeling. It was, in fact, very far down. Every last inch of cable attached to the winch had been paid out. That should be a thousand feet, he realized.

But where was Beatta? Had she been here?

There simply was no way of telling.

Holding to the cable for support, he peered into the ice-tunnel. The borer was out of sight,—of course. He had thought he might see a light from a handflash there below. But there was nothing.

Was it his imagination? Or was there a faint, thin fog of vapor rising from the tunnel?

The cable, he suddenly saw, was taut. It had been paid out as far as it would go, and there was dead weight swinging on the end of it.

The Bubble!

It was horribly clear to him now. Beatta, and possibly Christine with her, had followed the borer down. It had retraced its previous route—but this time gone all the way! It had broken through the last thin crust of ice and fallen into the deep Antarctic Ocean, wisps of fog from which were rising to the surface.

And Beatta? . . .

Kye flipped over the winch-control. Though it was dead now, if the power should come on while he was down there, he might have warning enough to grab the borer as it was drawn to the surface.

And even if he didn't—if Beatta were down there, Kye would find a way to bring her back to the surface. If not, if he found that she had been drowned, he himself would never return.

As had the two before him, he swung himself easily into the tunnel.

His feet kicking wildly against the slick icy walls on the tunnel, Kye swung himself painfully on down, down. He had long ago lost count of the distance he had descended; all he could know now was the recurrent agony in his torn hands; the stubborn weariness of his muscles. There was no way to stop and rest. If he relaxed his grip for even a second, he would fall. And he could not know how far such a drop might be.

Hand over hand, hand over hand. After what was long hours to Kye, there came a time when a separate effort of will for each muscle in his hands and arms was required to make them obey. Though he couldn't see, and his hands were too numb to feel, he could tell by the warm drops that trickled down his arm that his hands were fiercely cut and bleeding. Beatta and Christine had been equipped for the descent; they had had tough, thick gloves, and lights. Kye's gloves were paper-thin, and he had no light.

In the end, it was Kye's inability to see that caused him the most trouble. For his swinging toe caught in a little niche in the wall of ice: frantic for rest, he wedged his foot into it and leaned back across the tunnel, bracing his back against the opposite wall. His tortured hands he pressed to his mouth; he began to feel the pain, now.

But Kye's body temperature was of the order of more than a hundred degrees. Ice could not long resist that; his foothold melted a little and he slipped; clutched for the cable—*and missed*.

The drop was not great; thirty feet at most. And what he struck seemed to give under him; he found himself *sliding* down the slanting tunnel the borer had made just before it was stopped the first time.

And then he plunged into water, frightfully cold even to him. He went down ten feet or more, came struggling to the surface.

Water. *Beatta was drowned!*

His despondency closed in on him again like a thick black shroud. There was no object in life; only the commands of his subconscious made him continue to flail the water.

And then the light returned to the world. He was swimming in *fresh* water. He tasted it again; it was—not salt, not the ocean.

His reason told him that Beatta could drown in fresh water as easily as salt, but he disregarded it. His theory was wrong; the borer hadn't broken through. Therefore all of his theory must be wrong, and Beatta still alive.

But where was the borer?

He fumbled for the cable. It wasn't there.

There was one inescapable conclusion, and it brought joy to his heart. They had made a side tunnel, somewhere up above. They were there now, waiting for him to rescue them.

He had to get to them.

Disregarding the pain of his hands, he pressed one of them against the side of the sloped tunnel, as far above him as he could reach. The ice melted a little, enough to give him a fingerhold. He drew himself up, stabbed the other hand against the ice a little higher, kicked his feet into the ice too. Over and over he repeated the agonizingly slow process, gaining a few inches each time, going as fast as he could to avoid melting the niches away under him and slipping all the way down.

A foot, ten feet, fifty feet he gained that way, when suddenly he felt the light swing of the cable strike his head, and simultaneously a strong draft of air blew on his back. He clutched the cable, swung himself around,—and saw, less than a hundred yards away, down a horizontal ice-tunnel, the faint gleam of a handlamp!

Progress through that passage was child's-play, though he could not walk erect. Curiously, the light was not constant; it was as though someone were walking about in front of it. He shouted at the light: "Beatta! Christine! Beatta! I'm here!"

There was a cry from ahead; Beatta's voice. If Kye had been crawling rapidly before, that pace was slow compared to what he produced when he heard the cry.

"Kye! Oh, my darling—I was sure you'd come!" Welcomings were short. There was no real need for words.

Abruptly Kye realized that Beatta was alone. He said: "Isn't Christine Arbrudsen with you?"

Beatta was suddenly quiet, though she hugged Kye as fiercely as ever. "I think—I think Christine is dead, Kye," she whispered. "I'd forgotten—Kye, we must be quiet. There's something awful here. Look!" And she moved aside to let Kye see beyond the light.

At first he could see nothing. Then he realized that there was a vast cavern before them, hundreds of feet high and wide. And in it—

There was a shape that he couldn't quite define. He strained his eyes; it seemed to be faintly phosphorescent. It looked like some sort of a statue, or an animal.

But it was alive! He saw it stir, saw what was now visibly the head of a living creature move, and a great, luminous eye blink open. Red it was, and brilliant as a cat's eye is brilliant. It stared at Kye, without passion, and he felt that overwhelming torpor creep back into his brain. And a horrid feeling of pain came with it; soul-killing pain that made him forget the physical hurt from his hands. Then, abruptly, the eye closed again.

"What is it?" gasped Kye.

Beatta shuddered. "I don't know, but Christine went down to investigate it—hours ago, Kye—and she hasn't come back. I'm afraid!"

There was a quick, jerking movement of the cable. With one accord, they scrambled to the ledge, looked down. Christine Arbrudsen was climbing the cable!

Kye reached down, helped her up into the tunnel. She appeared to have gone through a terrific ordeal. Her clothing was disarranged; her face was a mask of strained lines. There was hysteria in her voice as she spoke.

"Kye! Thank God you're here!" she gasped as soon as she saw him. She clung to him for support as they sat in the tunnel; there was no strength in her. She began to chuckle to herself, but without humor. In the light of the fading hand torch they could see tears streaming down her face even as she laughed.

"Christine! What's the matter?" whispered Beatta.

The girl threw back her head and screamed laughter. "The matter? Nothing! I'm alive again!" She abandoned herself to her hysteria, rocking back and forth in spasms of throat-tearing laughter. Kye grasped her shoulder roughly, shaking her; slapped her face.

"Christine," he said intensely. "Tell me what you mean!"

Abruptly she sobered. Her voice was quiet, with overtones of immense awe as she answered. "Kye, *I have been dead*. That monstrous, terrible, frightening thing out there—it killed me and brought me to life again!"

"Why? Christine, why?" Horror was in Beatta's whisper.

"I don't know! Because it's dying, and can't move, and it's in frightful agony. I diverted it for a while—that was all! Oh, Beatta, it's awful to be dead! You can see things and hear them, but you can't move or speak. I tried to answer you, Beatta, when you were calling me—but I couldn't! I was *dead!*" Her voice trailed off in a whimper.

Hysteria, only hysteria, Kye's rational mind was telling him over and over again. You can't die and then come to life again. The girl was hysterical. You can't die and . . . .

But Kye couldn't believe his rational mind, for his rational mind had no explanation for the creature out there in the cavern.

"What is that thing?" he asked. "How did it come here?"

The question seemed to restore Christine to normalcy. "It came from the comet. It lived there, Kye, and when the comet broke up in Earth's gravitational field, it was on a section that was drawn to the Earth. It is an incredible creature. It fell, Kye, fell all the way to the surface of the Earth. And it's still alive—though it is dying. It told me that. It read my mind, and it spoke to me. And it made me a promise, too. A promise—that it would kill itself! Because it's a highly rational creature, and it found in my mind that it was interfering with us. It's going to die soon, anyhow,—it just won't fight death off any more."

"That explains the apathy of the camp," said Kye slowly, trying to comprehend an immense thing. "This vast mind, right by us, in horrible pain, dying. And worst of all—cut off from its home—because its home is eternally gone, part of the flaming gases of the sun!"

"But why didn't Christine or I get that feeling?" Beatta asked.

"I don't know," Kye said helplessly. "I can't understand any of this —I don't think any human being can, really. But I have an idea . . . which is probably wrong. But it might do till we find a better explanation. This—emotion that that creature has been spreading is a longing for the homeland. That's a basic feeling of every human being. But— women are not as subject to it as men. A woman is trained to cling to a man; a man, to support his country. And . . . ."

Kye never finished that speech. There was a sudden bright sweep of motion in the cavern, as though some shining thing had swooped, comet-like, up and away, through the walls of ice. In the same moment, the dull phosphorescence of the figure paled away; the huge red eye opened as the figure stirred in soundless agony, then dimmed to extinction.

It had kept its promise. Obviously it was dead.

But a few seconds later, before the three awed witnesses had dared to break the spell with words, there came a sudden new motion in the cable; a quick jerk, then a steady rise.

The power was on!

Silently, still gripped by the drama of the strange creature's death, the three forced their rebellious limbs to clutch the cable, and slowly were drawn to the surface, where was waiting a settlement, bright with returned power, and brighter with the lifting of the dismal cloud of despair.

Milt Rothman was not my only client as agent-cum-collaborator. Milt needed me badly, of course, because his home was too remote and out of touch for him to deal with the New York editors. (He lived in Philadelphia.) But there were others. I trotted the rounds of *Wonder Stories, Astounding Stories, Weird Tales* et al., offering my wares. Real agents don't usually do this, I found out later. They either employ messengers or use the mails. I couldn't afford either. Two-way postage on a story was as much as thirty cents or thereabouts. Subway fare to the editor's office was only a nickel. Sometimes I saved the nickel and walked. All this took a lot of time, but I had the time. As soon as I was legally old enough I had quit high school, having concluded there was nothing I was learning in the classrooms that interested me as much as what I was learning outside. All this running around to editorial offices didn't earn me much in the way of cash, but it taught me that editors were, after all, human beings. Not only that, most of them didn't seem to know any more about science fiction than I did.

Moreover, I reasoned, the trickiest part of getting a story published was finding an editor who would accept it. If you *were* an editor, that problem disappeared.

So I cast about for a likely editorial job. The editor of *Marvel* and *Dynamic* was a likable man named Robert O. Erisman, and one day I asked him for a job as his assistant. No, thanks, he said, but why didn't I go across town to 205 East 42 Street, where Popular Publications had its offices? They were already one of the largest of the pulp chains, and he had heard they were thinking of expanding.

So I took the crosstown trolley and called on Rogers Terrill, managing editor of the chain. He hired me. It was as simple as that.

. . . Well, not really as simple as that. When I got the job so easily I took it as a natural tribute to my talent. It was only a lot later that I realized they would have hired Mothra or Og, Son of Fire, just about as readily right then, because they were *very* interested in expanding.

Popular Publications was run by a man named Harry Steeger, an intimidatingly polished Princeton sort of person who skied and owned a yacht and entertained callers who conducted long phone conversations in idiomatic French. He had some fancy Princeton ideas. One of them was that he should pay writers a decent rate—a penny a word, sometimes even more.

That may not seem like much now. The reason for that is that it wasn't really much even then. But all the same it was more than some other pulp publishers were paying. Steeger was under pressure from the other people involved in his empire to cut his costs by lowering his word rate.

He didn't like to do this. What he did do was start a mythical other publishing company—it was called Fictioneers, Inc.—which would bring out a whole new line of pulps at a base word rate of half a cent. 205 East 42 happened to be the address of a building that went clear through the block and came out the other side. 210 East 43 was the address of the other entrance, and that became the official address of Fictioneers. The switchboard girl, Ethel Klock (dear, lovely lady who couldn't bowl for sour apples but kept us all company every Friday lunch hour at the alleys), was given a new telephone line, and was instructed under pain of death not to put through any calls to anybody connected with Popular Publications in the Fictioneers number. Well, that drove them all crazy. They tried. But it was tacky to call up an agent as Loren Dowst, editor of *Fighting Aces,* and buy some stories for Popular Publications at a penny a word, hang up and then call back a minute later as Ray P. Shotwell, editor of *Battle Birds,* and in a quavering assumed falsetto attempt to buy half-price stories for Fictioneers.

What Fictioneers obviously needed was at least one or two real, flesh-and-blood, actual people to be editors; and I happened to hit the place at the right time.

So there I was, nineteen years old from head to feet, and editor of two professional magazines. I had my name on the masthead. I was listed in the writers' market magazines.

To be sure, Popular didn't pay me very much. It was $10 a week for the first six months or so. That wasn't so bad. They hired another editor at the same time, and he had to work three months for nothing before they *raised* him to $10 a week.

The art director was a wonderful man named Alex Portegal, who doubled as a lending agency. You could get five dollars from Alex any time, provided that on payday you gave him back six.* And we needed it. Without Alex, I don't think any of us would have made it through the month, not even the senior editors who were making as much as $35.

---

* It spoils the story, but is true, that at the end of each year Alex took the spoils of his usury, bought drinks for all his clients and gave the rest to charity.

We weren't really expected to live on that kind of money. What we were expected to do was write stories and buy them from ourselves, and somehow piece together enough to survive.

I did so. *The King's Eye,* from the February 1941 issue of *Astonishing Stories,* is one of them. At 5,900 words, at my premium rate of ¾¢ a word, it came to $43.50 that it fetched me . . . equal to a month's editorial pay, just about.

The King's Eye

JAMES MacCREIGH

Chester Wing shoved the cards away from him and rose with a snarl on his lips. "Damn you and your sleight-of-hand, Farrel," he lipped. "Cut it out!"

"What?" innocently asked Farrel Henderson, Wing's partner in exploration.

"Dealing from the bottom—that's what. I know we aren't playing for money, but I still don't like the idea of losing every hand."

"Oh, calm down," suggested Henderson, rising himself. "I was only joking. We'll quit playing if you feel that way." He sauntered over to the quartz viewplate, stared at the fetid swamp that was dimly visible through the steamy fog. The scenery was pretty uninspiring, being nothing better than a steam-shrouded tangle of vegetation, mostly dull greying white. All Venusian landscapes were much alike; all revoltingly wet and unpleasantly hot. "What a place to blow a rocket-tube," he muttered, less than half to Wing.

Wing nodded vaguely, no longer angry. "Hope to Heaven we get out of here soon," he said fervently.

"How much longer do you suppose it'll actually be before the tube's ready?" inquired Henderson.

Wing cocked a thoughtful ear at the faint humming sound that told of the automatic repair-machines at work, extracting isotopic beryllium from the constant flow of swamp-water that passed through its pipes, plating it in layers on the steel core that was the mold for their new rocket-tube. "Maybe two days," he pronounced finally. "At least, the tube ought to be ready then. Whether or not our fine-feathered friends will do something to keep us here is something else again. I don't feel very happy about that—though there isn't really much that they could do, once we get the new tube in place."

It had been a bad day for the Earthmen when they'd been forced to land in this particular section of Venus. The local tribe of natives had developed a positive allergy to Earthmen, the result of a fracas that had occurred years before, when planetary pioneering had been newer. Wing had never got all the details from the reticent tribesmen, but it had had something to do with the great *Venustone* that was now on exhibition in the Hall of the Planets, back in Washington on Earth. The Stone was really a huge red diamond, but its great size and unusual coloring had made it highly valuable. Wing couldn't blame the chief for regretting its loss to the tribe. Probably the Earthman who had taken it had "paid" for it with trumpery beads or colored cloth—at gun's point. That sort of trade dealings was all right, of course, for the more ignorant Venusians, but the chief hereabout—he was really a king, and "Ch'mack" was as close as Terrestrial lips could come to reproducing the verbal click and splash that was his name—was no less intelligent than the average Earthman.

"Hey!" Henderson's cry broke in on Wing's absorbed reverie. "Who's pounding on the lock?"

Certain enough, there was someone scratching on the airlock, obviously desirous of attracting attention. Wing refocused his gaze, saw, just visible at an angle through the quartz port, a hideously furred, troll-like creature, manlike in face, resembling most nearly a web-winged caricature of a kangaroo in body.

"It's one of Ch'mack's boys," said Wing. "Suppose we're in trouble again?"

"You don't mean again," Henderson shrugged expressively. "You mean yet. Ch'mack is about the touchiest living thing I've seen. I don't know why—*we* never did him nothing. Let's find out what he wants anyway. Go talk to the messenger."

"Me? Why me? Go yourself!"

"All right," Henderson sighed, contemplating the mucky terrain. "Let's both go. Here!" He tossed a wire-coiled sort of helmet at Wing, who caught it deftly and slipped it over his head. Henderson donned one also, and stepped into the airlock. The wire helmets were perceptors—what you might call telepathy-radios, allowing the explorers to converse mentally with the Venusians. No human could have spoken the Venusians' native tongue.

A touch on a button closed the inner door, sealing off the ship; as soon as that was closed, the outer door of the lock opened automatically. Henderson and Wing grabbed at their nostrils, and stepped out on to Venusian soil.

Humans could breathe Venus' air indefinitely, providing they didn't overexert themselves. The CO_2-rich atmosphere contained enough oxygen for life, though not as much as did Earth's. But it also contained a variety of rank, hot odors, most of which resembled decaying fish.

Wing marvelled at the fact that so disgusting a smell wasn't actually poisonous, and turned to the Venusian waiting. "What do you want?" he inquired, ungraciously but without attempting to give deliberate offense.

"Ch'mack wishes to see you," the Venusian thought back, hostility in his tones. "Come with us." The Earthmen might have refused, but they suddenly discovered that there were more Venusians than one present. And all of them were armed.

They went.

"Why will you not admit your purpose here?" bellowed Ch'mack suspiciously. The Earthmen shrugged and didn't answer. They had been asked that question, or a variant, a dozen times since that quiz began. And Ch'mack had refused to tell them just of what they were suspected. Nor had their perceptors been able to penetrate his will-shielded mind. "I know what you want," he went on vindictively. "Don't think that I do not. I know almost everything. But admit it to me!"

"Modest cuss," thought Wing "below the threshold"—i.e., without sufficient intensity for the thought to be telepathed. Aloud he said, "I don't know what you mean."

"Fool! Do you think you can hide things from me? I know what you are after," repeated the king. "And you won't get it!" With a furtive movement he stuck his hand into his pouch, the only article of clothing he wore. He seemed reassured at what he found. "No, you won't steal it," he continued. "I won't let you! But you must be punished for wanting to steal it. I will see that you are punished."

"Steal what?" inquired Wing, annoyed.

"Steal what! As if you didn't know. My Eye, of course!"

Wing and Henderson exchanged puzzled glances. The king had two perfectly good eyes, that was true enough, but certainly neither of them had any intention of stealing one. The king glared at them heatedly. For a second it seemed he would actually walk over to them, violating the tribe's eon-old custom and actually setting his feet to the ground, to strike them. Then he looked away, a cunning smile spreading over his face, seemingly plunged into deep thought.

"Ah," he said finally. "I have been trying to think of a punishment for them, but I cannot. My mind is too subtle, too delicate, to think of a fitting doom. Besides, we must make absolutely sure that they are guilty, must make them confess. I shall refer the matter to the Tribune!"

The Tribune! The hapless two knew what that meant. The Tribune was an old institution in all Venusian tribes, apparently a relic of the laws that had governed Venus when it was a unified, planetwide democracy. It was a group of a dozen or so of the leaders of each tribe, the most powerful men in them and generally the oldest and bitterest as well. To appear before a Tribune was akin to appearing before a highly refined and super-deadly Spanish Inquisition. It was a rule of the Tribune that confession must precede punishment. But any kind of a confession would do, and the Tribune was perfectly willing to use torture to obtain it. Often the "questioning" was worse and more to be feared than the punishment itself—for the worst punishment was merely death, and death is always too abstract a concept to be feared with the heart, only with the mind.

Henderson felt his companion nudging him. He looked—Wing had flicked the switch that turned off his perceptor, was motioning to him to do likewise. "Listen," spoke Wing tensely as soon as Henderson had prevented the transmission of the words, "we'd better give in to them. Time works for us; it'll be a while before they can summon the Tribune. Maybe we can stall them off until the tube's ready. If we make a break for it now we can probably get away all right—but what'll we do then?"

Henderson comprehended. "Okay," he said. "But we better hang onto our guns—Hey!" His surprise was justified; before his very eyes, Wing stiffened and fell heavily to the ground. Then he felt a sharp sting in his own thigh and realized, as he collapsed in his turn, that they had both been shot with paralysis darts.

And as he lay there rigid, he cursed himself. For a smirking Venusian face bent over him and took away the gun he'd just determined to retain at all costs.

Wing had no clear idea of how long it was before he felt the first muscle-twinges that indicated that the effect of the dart had begun to work off.

The first thing he did was to move his eyes. The particular sector of the wall on which they had been permanently focused had become boring.

He discovered that he and his companion were in a sort of cage; bars of Venus fern-wood, floor of some rocky, cement-like material. It had a door, and the door was standing invitingly open. But Wing could only look longingly at the door, and not pass through it, for he and his partner were very securely tied with rope twisted from the "veins" of the fern-wood leaves, as strong as cobalt-steel, and tougher.

They were alone in a large room, their cage only one of a dozen or more, but all the others empty. Beside the cages the room held a good many seats and benches, and a lot of equipment at which Wing looked only briefly. Its purpose was too plain for his nerves. It was torture tools, and all ready for use.

Wing kicked and rolled over, touching his companion, who was also back to normal. "What do we do now?" asked Henderson, carefully keeping fear from his voice.

"Wait. That's all we can do."

That was true enough. Wing knew their bonds were amply secure; there was no chance of immediate escape. To make plans now would be stupid, for they had no idea of what chances the future might offer.

So they waited, passing the time in desultory conversation. In twenty minutes or so one of the Venusians peered in the door at them, widened his eyes when he saw they'd regained the power of movement, and went away again. "This is it," said Wing, and Henderson nodded in agreement.

It was it. In a moment the door was flung open wide and in solemn procession, entered the Tribune.

Wing thought they were the toughest-looking representatives of their kind he'd ever seen. They were every one members of the nebulously defined aristocracy of their tribe.

The two Earthmen were unceremoniously unbound and yanked from their cage. Dragged to a brace of high-backed fern-wood chairs, they were bound again, to the chairs. That was no pleasure, for these chairs had been designed for the different Venusian anatomy—and, being for the exclusive use of the Tribune's prisoners, hadn't been intended for comfort anyhow.

The Tribune took seats, all but one. This one, apparently the Chairman, advanced threateningly toward the Terrestrials. He reached out to touch Wing's head. Wing feared the beginning of the torture and strained desperately against the ropes, but the Venusian merely wanted to turn on Wing's perceptor. When he had done the same to Henderson, he lanced a thought at them, menace implicit in his manner.

"Earthmen," he thought, even his mind-vibrations coming ponderous and slow, "confess to us and save yourselves pain!"

"Confess what?" Henderson flashed. "We told you—we came here only because our ship was wrecked. We had no intention of harming you, or of stealing your king's 'Eye,' whatever that may be. As soon as our ship is repaired, we will go away."

The Venusian's next thought conveyed an impression of sardonic laughter. "Go away! Earthmen, you will never go away from here. Not alive." His demeanor had been hostile; now it became aggressively menacing. Like a scourge the thought came: *"Confess!* We know that you came here to steal the Eye. We know that your pretended ignorance of the nature of the Eye is a bluff. Let us end all bluffs and lies. The Eye—I shall say it to keep you from using this line of evasion anymore—is a great, red, sacred gem, the twin of the one that was foully stolen from us forty years ago. Now that I have broken down that veil of lying—*confess!"*

The Venusian stepped back, panting with the vigor of his thoughts. He eyed his two prisoners intently. Seeing that they had resolved not to answer, he angrily motioned toward a pair of guards stationed near the door. Together they lugged up a heavy, squat metal basin, in which burned a fiercely hot flame.

The two Terrestrials realized that the torture had come, and braced themselves for it.

But they weren't to be tortured just then anyhow, it seemed, for, before the torture could commence, there was a disturbance at the door and a new Venusian burst in. "The King is dead!" he screamed, the thought beating on the brains of the Earthmen while the gibberish of his voice resounded in their ears. "His body has been found on the throne. He was murdered!"

Wing and Henderson had suddenly become secondary matters. The

Tribune left the room in a flurry—though not so fast but what the guards returned the pair of Earthmen to their cages, retying them. In a moment the hall was empty again.

"This is not going to help us at all, Farrel," Wing said with dark foreboding. "Of all the things I didn't want to happen. . . . I don't care who killed the king. I know who's going to pay for it. Us."

"Shut up," growled Henderson, who knew that. His eyes were fastened on his own wrist, where he was fighting the ropes with his fingers. "Let's think about getting out of this place. The monkey that tied me up was in a hurry, and I know a couple of things about ropes, anyhow. He didn't notice the way I kept my arm poked a little away from my side. I've got a little slack here. If I can find something long and narrow, I think I can pry that knot open."

Wing flopped painfully to his side. "In my pocket," he grunted, contorting himself so that Henderson could get at it. "It's a fountain pen. Will it do?"

"No," said Henderson, extracting it. "But I'll make it do!" Holding it in his teeth, he slipped it into the precious inch of slackness he'd created, pried, and stretched the inch to two. A moment later his arm was free; he shed his own bonds and quickly got to those of his companion.

"Let's get from here," muttered Wing when they were both standing, trying to massage the pain from their hurt limbs. "If we use our perceptors occasionally, just flip them on and off, we'll be able to catch thoughts and see if anyone is looking for us."

They moved quietly to the door and stood in attitudes of intense concentration as they "listened" for sentries. Their questing minds could find no trace of anyone watching, so they slipped out the door and broke for the surrounding jungle at a quick, space-consuming walk. Their perceptors they continued to use at intervals. For their purposes, the things had a great defect; they broadcast thoughts quite as well and as far as they received them. . . .

The uniformly grey Venusian jungle, with its toadstool plants and fern-like trees, offered no pleasing prospect to the two explorers as they slogged their way along as quietly as possible. They had to take immense care that the apparently dry spots they stepped on were really what they seemed. Bogs and swampholes freckled the Venusian terrain.

Wing shoved an overhanging creeper out of his way and stood

straight, panting. Suddenly he stiffened. "Look!" he whispered, piercingly. "Just ahead."

There was a glint of metal through the trees. Wing and Henderson stared at it intently. It was a metal building, as unlike those of the town behind them as the Coliseum is unlike a Twentieth-Century baseball grandstand. The degenerate Venusian architecture with which the two were familiar, stacked up against this new building, would have seemed unbearably shoddy.

The building was metal, some sort of steel, apparently, but obviously rust-proof. The corners of it were weathered to soft curves, they saw as they slipped closer. It was *old*.

Octagonal, it had no windows at all, as far as the two explorers could see. The structure was thirty feet or more in diameter, about the same in height.

"This is no place for us, Chet," whispered Henderson. "That place is probably crawling with Venusians. Let's go!"

Wing nodded agreement and turned.

But didn't go far. He spied a flicker of motion in the underbrush not far away. He tugged at Henderson's sleeve, pointing silently.

Henderson looked first at Wing's face, then at the indicated spot. Fern-trees, he saw, and the toad-stool growths, and the vines and sinkholes.

And something else. He couldn't quite . . . yes! He saw it clearly and grabbed Wing's shoulder. "It's a *snake!*" he whispered hoarsely, panic in his voice.

Wing nodded, silently pointed toward the tower. A "snake"—really a lizard, fast and deadly poisonous—was nothing to play around with. Their only hope of life was to get away before it spied them.

The snake, it seemed, wasn't especially hungry, though there was never a time at all when a Venusian snake wasn't willing to take just a little bit more food. But it wasn't actively *looking* for a meal. Consequently, it didn't see them right away.

But eventually it had to—and did. When they were less than fifty feet from the tower, having progressed a hundred away from the snake, there was a sudden commotion in the undergrowth and it came slithering with immense speed toward them, its great, cone-shaped head waving from side to side, the horizontal jaws opening and closing as the rudimentary, clawed hands flailed the air.

The two adventurers caught sight of the monster coming at them and rapidly decided what to do. Together they broke for the building, then dashed around it, searching for a door. Luckily, there was one, and it was unlocked. They flung themselves inside, slammed the door and braced their backs against it just as the snake rammed it.

A glance around made them wonder if they had done right. The Tribune tortured, agonizingly, before it killed; the snake, at the worst, would eat them alive, a matter over with in a few minutes. For, though no living thing was visible, there was no dust or rust—and the place was lighted with several burning torches.

Wing headed silently for the only visible doorway, Henderson following.

They emerged into a huge room. What they had been in before, they realized, had been only an anteroom. This new auditorium comprised almost the entire structure. They had entered at the very front: just before them, on a dais, was a sheeted recumbent figure. The dead king, Wing thought swiftly, but thought no more about it.

For occupying the room with them, their heads bowed in mourning, were half a hundred armed Venusian natives!

The confusion that followed was terrific. They were seen immediately, and a babel of voices arose.

Wing thought with frantic speed, and evolved a plan. Before the Venusians could recover from their shock, he stepped quickly to the side of the dais, and screamed at Henderson:

"Snap on your perceptor! Tell them to stay back! If they take one step forward, I'll turn the table over and dump his immortal majesty on the ground!"

Henderson shouted joyously as he comprehended the plan; and immediately did as he was bid. There was sudden consternation among the Venusians as his sacrilegious words smote them to a standstill. The person of the King was inviolate! Never was he allowed even to walk on the bare ground or floor, was carried from place to place in a palanquin, could stand or sit only on a specially consecrated throne or dais. To have his corpse desecrated horrified them beyond words.

One of the Venusians, the leader of the Tribune, stepped forward.

"What do you wish of us?" he asked.

Henderson spoke for both of them. "A guarantee of unhindered passage to our ship; and freedom to leave in it as soon as we can."

"That is impossible," said the Venusian flatly. "You killed Ch'mack. We cannot permit the king's murderers to live."

Henderson swore, gazed vainly at Wing. Wing took part in the discussion. "We didn't kill Ch'mack," he said. "How was he murdered?"

"As you know, he was stabbed."

"We were in a cage when that happened. How could we have killed him?"

The Venusian laughed sardonically. "Fools!" he cried. "Do you think to deceive us as simply as that? Ch'mack was killed while you were supposed to be paralyzed. You escaped from your bonds—do not deny it; we know you were able to do it, for you did so a second time to make your escape—killed him and returned to the cage, knowing that you would have a better chance of escaping for good in the confusion after his body was found."

Wing cursed without hope. "What can you do with people like that?" he murmured to himself.

Henderson said, "Why not let us go? We swear, by any oath you ask us to take, that we had nothing to do with the death of Ch'mack. You cannot harm us, for if any one of you makes a suspicious move, we'll dump his corpse on the floor. Better that his murderers—even if we were his murderers—go free, than that the soul of Ch'mack be refused admission to the special heaven of royalty because its body has touched the unhallowed ground."

"You are still a fool, Earthman," thought the Venusian heavily. "You cannot remain on guard forever. Sooner or later you may fall asleep, or even look away for a second. If not, then you will starve to death in a few weeks, or die of thirst, agonizingly. We can afford to wait. . . . Earthmen, we will make you an offer. Step back from the body of Ch'mack, and we will kill you where you stand, for you must die. If you do not do this, you will die soon anyhow . . . but slowly. If not of thirst, it will mean that you have fallen into our hands. And *that* death will not be pleasant."

Wing's stomach wrapped itself into a tight hard knot: There was one hundred per cent of truth in what the Venusian was saying. Death he really did not fear—but the slow wait for death, or the absolute certainty of its coming if he accepted their offer, was infinitely horrible to him.

"Chet!" Henderson's urgent cry brought the faint flicker of new hope to Wing.

"What is it?" he asked, looking up to see Henderson removing his mind-reader, which he had already switched off.

"I have an idea. While they were talk—wait a minute," he interrupted himself sharply. "Forget that. I—um—I think if I go down and mingle with them, maybe I can grab a gun and we can get away. You stay by the body, and dump it if anything happens."

That was why Henderson had removed his mind-reader, thought Wing; he didn't want the Venusians to know what he was doing. Henderson was already moving toward them as Wing assented, "Okay," cheerfulness in his voice for the first time. He prepared to transmit to the Venusians the order not to move; then realized that they'd know it already because it had been in his mind, and—

His heart dropped again, and his stomach screwed up even tighter than before. Oh, what a fool Henderson was, he thought agonizedly. Henderson had told him the plan; therefore, it had been in Wing's mind; therefore, by courtesy of the efficient perceptor, the Venusians knew all about it. He swore, dully.

But what was Henderson doing? He was gesturing to one of the Venusians—the one who had spoken, the head of the Tribune.

"Chet," Henderson called. "Tell this guy to stop running away. I won't hurt him. I just want to talk to him. Tell him to let me put the perceptor on him. And *don't argue!*"

Though puzzled, Wing complied.

"And you are still fools," the Venusian sneered. "This one thinks he can surprise me, take my rifle. But look!" and he loosed his weapon-belt, handed it to another Venusian. Now openly contemptuous, he said, "Tell him he can put that thing on me!"

Wing relayed the statement in English. Very carefully, Henderson slipped the mind-reader on the Venusian's forehead, and snapped the switch on. Then he shouted to Wing, "Chet, for God's sake, *repeat what I say!*"

With blinding speed, he grabbed the Venusian's pouch away from him, ripped it open, and held on high—the Eye!

"Tell them that here is the murderer of their king!" he screamed to Wing. "Tell them!"

But Wing didn't have to. For the Venusian was wearing a perceptor; surprised by the lightning attack, for a moment his defenses were down, and every person, human or Venusian, in that chamber felt the cold impact of the thought,

"Of course I killed him. But YOU will die for it!"

He was wrong, and comprehended his error immediately, as he saw the staring faces of his compatriots around him. He saw how he had been tricked—but too late. He ripped the mind-helmet from his head, dashed it full in Henderson's face, leaped for the door.

Henderson fell, hurt and unconscious, to the floor. So great was the turmoil caused by surprise that the criminal made good his escape from the building. But the others followed him, drawing their weapons, shouting and screaming as they ran.

Wing leaped to the side of his comrade. Henderson wasn't severely injured, he found; merely unconscious, and cut about the forehead. As Wing was chafing his wrists to revive him, he heard a great babble of shouts and a volley of rifle fire from outside. In a few moments the Venusians began to trickle back, very grave in appearance.

"Earthman," thought one of them, "you are free. Please leave as soon as you can. You have brought us enough sorrow."

More cheerful instructions than that Wing never hoped to hear. "Did you kill him when you shot at him?" he asked.

The Venusian stared at him. Ponderously he replied, "We were not shooting at him. We killed a snake. It had been lurking just outside, and *it* killed him. Now . . . go." And he turned away.

Henderson had lost a lot of blood, and was pretty weak. Still, he had regained consciousness in time to help Wing replace the rocket tube, now all repaired. They were all set to leave now; without formalities, Wing touched the firing keys, timing the rockets to thunder in sharp, staccato jerks, "rocking" the ship free of the hole it had dug for itself in the mud.

In a moment the powerful suction of the mud was broken. Wing slammed down an entire row of keys; the ship creaked and groaned; the mighty rockets shoved them forward with immense acceleration, and in a moment they were roaring through the atmosphere, their ship ripping the air to shreds as they sped for the high vacuums where they could really make speed for the nearest Earth colony.

Wing cut half the rockets, and touched the lever that brought out the tiny, retractable stubby wings. Even in the stratosphere, where they were, their immense speed made wings useful. It saved fuel, for one thing, and, more important to Wing, it made conversation possible by cutting down the noise. Wing had been too anxious to get away from the Venusian town to bother with questions; now he succumbed to his curiosity, turned to Henderson, and said:

"Now spill it. How did you work that little trick?"

Henderson smiled weakly, but with triumph.

"Well, I knew that neither you nor I had killed Ch'mack. It had to be one of the Venusians. Which one? That I had to find out. . . .

"But there was a logical suspect, if you followed the detective-story pattern, and looked for the motive. Someone stood to become King after Ch'mack died. I thought that might be a powerful inducement to killing. . . .

"And while you were talking to them, *I* was trying to read their minds with my perceptor. I couldn't make a great deal of progress with any of them,—but one of them had me stopped cold. He was very intently *not* thinking about the murder. I figured that was sort of suspicious, and I saw that he was the guy who'd inherit the king-ship, so . . . I took a chance. It worked."

"Good for you," applauded Wing. "You got us out of a pretty damned tight mess." He sat complacently at the controls, smiling into the black sky ahead as the ship sped along. Suddenly his smile clouded. "If you couldn't read his mind, how did you know that he had the Eye?" he asked.

"Oh, that," said Henderson proudly. "I didn't. I mean, he didn't. I knew that he *didn't* have the Eye, because I did. I found it on Ch'mack's body, and planted it on the other guy for effect. I knew that it would take a real shock to make him think 'out loud' about the killing, so I provided one. And that," he said, hastily pursuing his advantage, "is all due to my 'sleight-of-hand' that you're so fond of criticizing. I hope you'll be a little more respectful about it in the future."

"I will," agreed Wing happily. "In fact, soon as we land I'll let you play cards with me again."

"For money?" particularized Henderson.

"Well—" Wing hesitated, then grimly agreed. "Yes, for money. I guess I owe you something." He resumed his sunny smile at the sky. "Well, it's too late to do anything about it now, but I wish I could have got a closer look at that Eye," he said a moment later. "Seemed to me that Ch'mack was a lot more worried about keeping it than even its value warranted. I wish I had it to find out why."

"Do you really wish you had it?" grinned Henderson.

"Uh-huh. It ought to be. . . . Say! Did you—?"

"You bet I did!" Henderson cried. He took the object in question from a pocket and tossed it at his colleague. "Here—catch!"

When that story appeared, around the end of 1940, I had been an editor for a year and, among other things, I had gotten married.

The girl I married was a slim, pretty brunette named Leslie Perri. Well, she wasn't really named Leslie Perri. That was her writing name. The name she was born to was Doris Marie Claire Baumgardt. She wrote, she painted, she knew about music and, in the ego-busting environment of the Futurians, she held her own.

The way I met Doë was that an old school friend—a civilian, no connection with science fiction—was dating a girl he thought a lot of, and brought her around to show her off. That was a serious miscalculation on his part. He had not stopped to think that I had been living a pretty depressingly monastic life. Brooklyn Tech was an all-boy school and fandom, where I spent most of the rest of my time, was wholly male, not out of choice but because no girls ever seemed to show up at our meetings. Doë was about the first girl I had ever met who wasn't either some sort of a relative or an old family friend, and I suddenly perceived what nice creatures girls were and how fine it would be to have one. So I moved in. Very hard, very fast. I was maybe seventeen when we met. We dated for three years and then got married as soon as I had a job that looked like lasting for more than a week.

This had immense implications for science fiction.

See, I had all these male friends, who had little contact with girls.

Doë, on the other hand, had vast resources of female friends, and apparently they hadn't had too much experience of men, either. We brought them together. Instant critical mass was attained. In the fall-out my friend Dick Wilson married Doë's friend Jessica Gould; my friend Dirk Wylie married Doë's friend Rosalind Cohen; my friend Don Wollheim married Doë's friend Elsie Balter,* and of second-order effects and liaisons that did not quite reach matrimony there was no end. Such a flowering of instant romances had not been seen since Jeanette MacDonald and the rest of the *paquet* girls reached New Orleans and the arms of Nelson Eddy.

Women had a civilizing influence on us. We began to think in terms of lifetime careers and Making a Buck. We also began to think in terms of nest-building.

So a few of us decided to rent a house, to serve as a sort of primitive commune. Doë and I were slated to be house-parents. The occupants were to be Dick Wilson, Don Wollheim and Joseph Harold Dock-

---

* Donald and Elsie still are married, and jointly run the sf publishing firm of DAW Books.

weiler. In the event Doë and I didn't move in, but the other three went ahead and, with that innate sense of concinnity so characteristic of science-fiction writers, at once perceived a pattern emerging: DW, DW and—JHD? No, that would never do. So on the spot Joseph Harold Dockweiler rechristened himself Dirk Wylie.

The house episode lasted a couple of months, and the survivors fled to an apartment on Bedford Avenue, Brooklyn, which they named the Ivory Tower. Cyril Kornbluth had turned up by that time, an evilly bland, precocious fifteen-year-old. So had Robert W. Lowndes, migrating to the big city from Connecticut. Some of us lived there, some only visited, but one way or another the Ivory Tower was our center of activities for a couple of years. It was where we talked and partied. It was where we put together fan mags and plotted strategies against other sf fan groups. It was where Dick Wilson and I kept our common car. (We used a common driver's license for a couple of years, too. His. We matched up almost exactly on height, color of eyes, weight and everything else on the license.) And it was where we kept our still.

That was Cyril's contribution. I did say he was precocious? He took up a collection, went off to a chemical supply store and returned with a glass water-jacketed distillation rig that turned cheap, bad red wine into cheap and even worse brandy at the rate of about ten drops a minute. With half a dozen Futurians waiting their turn at the business end of the still, it rationed our liquor consumption better than A.A.

The Ivory Tower is where we began to do our collaborative writing in earnest. I was a market for much of it. A little later, Wollheim and Lowndes got their own magazines, and then the typewriters were kept smoking. It wasn't all very good science fiction—some of it was pretty terrible—but it was better than we could buy on the open market at the rates we were paying.

It was not, however, the best we could possibly write. I think we all began to be aware of that at around the same time. In my case, when I began seeing the fan mail that came in to my magazines I perceived that Being a Writer was not enough. Even Being a Published Writer was something short of the ultimate. What I really wanted was to be a published writer of whom the audience wrote enthusiastic letters to the editor.

So I resolved to try to write better stories.

I didn't resolve to write masterpieces. Heaven knows, I was simply neither mature enough nor skillful enough as a writer to be Great. But I was capable of writing better than I had been doing. Capable of writing something that was uniquely my own, and not a piece of yard goods that any hack could rattle off as fast as he could type. And the story that came out of that resolve was *It's a Young World,* which appeared, under the James MacCreigh pen name, in the April 1941 issue of *Astonishing Stories.*

It's a Young World

JAMES MacCREIGH

1

In the Enemy's House

I don't think there was anyone in the universe that shot better than my Tribe, but I brought down the average a lot. Though I'd been a hunter all my life, I never became really proficient. Even the babies of the tribe were better than I when it came to shooting at a moving target with a light bow, and I was never allowed to participate in the raids on enemy camps for that reason.

Hunting was all right. There my natural gifts for being inconspicuous and very quiet helped me. I could be more motionless than even the rocks I sat upon. When the wood's life came close to me I didn't have to be a good shot to kill more than my share of marauding animals.

Not that most of the animals we ever saw were really dangerous: of course not. But there was a species of lizard we had come to fear. It was big and powerful, and it moved almost without sound, but those were not the worst things. Being a lizard, akin to the fish of the streams more than to us, it actually ate the flesh of the animals and men it killed. When it could get no living thing to eat, it chewed and swallowed leaves or grass, or the flowers and fruits of the trees. It had to. If it did not eat, it would die. It was too low in the evolutionary scale, it seems, to live as all warm-blooded creatures do, on the fresh water and fresh air that are free to all.

Because of this vile habit of eating, it always gave me a feeling of pleasure to kill these lizards whenever I could, almost like what the others boasted of when they came back from a raid and told of the fun of killing the members of the Enemy tribe.

Four times in every year I was sent out to kill a lizard—we called them Eaters—and each time I remained away until I caught one. Though it might take me days or weeks to track one down and slay it, I dared not come back without at least one skin on my shoulders. Though they became increasingly scarce, I always managed to trap one eventually—always, that is, but once.

For there finally came a day when, look where I would, use whatever arts of searching I knew, there was no Eater to be found. I ranged a hundred miles and more, over a period of nearly a month, utterly without success. In our own area of the planet, at least, the Eaters seemed completely extinct.

As I trudged into the village of my Tribe I saw that something was up. I had no wish to attract attention, since my quest had been fruitless, so I did not quite enter the village, but stood within the shelter of the trees and watched for a little while. The warriors were stalking around importantly in a bustle of scurrying women and hunters like myself, each warrior lugging a twelve-foot war bow.

A raid?

It had to be that. Little Clory, my favourite girl friend, spied me before anyone else and came running up to me with a finger on her lips. "Stay back, Keefe," she warned. "They're going out to lick the Red-and-Browns and you'd better not get in the way."

I picked her up and sat her on my shoulder. She was a little thing, even for her seven years of age, but her long yellow hair covered my face. I blew it aside, and said, "When will they have the Affair, Clory?"

"Oh, right away. Look—they're building the fires now."

They were. The warriors had gathered and were seated in the triple-tiered Balcony of Men, while the youths and women built a tottering little shack of firewood. I should have helped them, being a non-military, but I wasn't needed, and I preferred to keep as much as possible out of anything connected with raids.

The whole Tribe was in the little clearing on the outskirts of the village by now. The House of the Enemy—that was the little jerry-built shack that would be burned—was nearly completed. The four braided vine ropes that would serve as fuses were already laid out, and the musicians were tuning up with an ungodly din.

Corlos, Chief of the Warriors, and Lord of the Tribe of the Blues, strode into the centre of the cleared circle, and raised his bow. A ten-foot arrow, hollowed at the point, was in it; he drew it back in the string until I could almost hear the wood of the bow creaking, then released it, aiming at the tiny red disc of the sun, setting on the horizon. The arrow screamed up and out in a flat arc—literally screamed, because the pitted point caused it to whistle in flight.

That was the signal. The musicians, who had been silent for a few moments, waiting their cue, screamed into their instruments, slapped their drums, sawed their stringed gourds. The noise was frightful—but almost beautiful, I had to admit. Maybe the beauty lay in the unusualness, because we heard this ceremonial music only just before a raid, not more than once in a year.

To the tune of the tempestuous music, a group of the younger girls of the Tribe came pacing in to the centre of the ring, bearing a closed palanquin on their shoulders. In it, presumably, was the Enemy, the animal—sometimes, the person—which would be burned alive, representing the members of the Tribe against whom our warriors would soon be marching.

Corlos strode up to the car and halted, raising his arm peremptorily. The music stopped. In a savage, deep guttural he declaimed: "Who is our Enemy?"

The antiphony rose in unison from the benches of the warriors: "He who does not serve the Tribe—he is our Enemy: he must die! That which kills one of our Tribe—that is our Enemy; it must die! He who profanes the Name of our Tribe—he is the Enemy; he must die." I repeated the familiar words of the Three Evil Acts with the warriors. I knew them by heart. Corlos went on with the ritual.

"How dies our Enemy?" he bellowed.

"By the flames of our fire," rolled back the response.

"Where seek we our Enemy?"

"In the woods; in our Tribe; on mountains or plain; wherever he may flee, there we shall go."

Corlos was working himself up to a frenzy. As the echoes of the warriors' shouts died away, he signalled to the musicians. A drum then boomed to accent each syllable, as he shrieked, "Behold our Enemy!" He ripped open the door of the palanquin; four warriors ran up and dragged out the Enemy.

I stared hard, then stepped back a pace and clutched a vine for support. The Enemy, this time, was human. It was a youth, slight, shaking in a hysteria of fear. It was Lurlan, my sworn blood brother!

Lurlan! Except for Clory, I had rather see anyone of the Tribe perish in the flames, even myself, rather than him. Clory clutched my arm, and a tiny whimper escaped her. It was a surprise to her too, it seemed.

I dismissed the thought that I was on ground none too secure myself, and my mind spun as I tried desperately to think of a way of saving Lurlan from the flames. But there was no time for thinking, for in a matter of minutes the fire would be lighted and Lurlan's corpse would roast in its embers.

If he had to die, he would die. Certainly I could never hope to save his life. But—need he die in the horrible agony of the flames?

He did not, I decided agonizedly—and found that while I had been painfully thinking it out, my body's reflexes had come to the same conclusion. My bow was in my hands, and an arrow was notched. I took hasty aim and released the bowstring. The arrow fled from me and cleaved straight to its target—the throat of my blood brother, Lurlan.

Consternation! The entire Tribe was in an uproar. I saw proven then what I had always known—Corlos, though a beast and a braggart, was no coward. He whipped around like a pinked Eater, and peered directly at me, his slightly nearsighted eyes blinking in the smoke of the smaller fires. I could have slain him as easily as I had Lurlan, and he must have realized that. But he stood his ground, though his swarthy face turned pale and he fingered his arrowless bow.

"Keefe!" he bellowed as soon as he identified me. Then he spun back and faced the warriors. "This man has slain the Enemy!" he howled. "He has profaned the Tribe—he is our Enemy! Let us burn him!"

They had every intention of doing it, too. The warriors rose, howling with rage. Though none of them loved Corlos unduly, they were all hogtied with respect for the sacred traditions of the Burning of the Enemy. I had violated them. I was the Enemy.

I plucked at Clory and backed away, as unobtrusively as I could. I had my bow still in my hand; I notched another arrow and held it ready. I wanted them to see that I wasn't going to burn without a fight.

The bush was pretty thick, and within twenty feet we were hidden. Then I slung the bow over my shoulder and made speed with Clory.

"Where are we going, Keefe?" Clory murmured in my ear. She was obviously being as brave as she knew how. I didn't have to tell her that we were in serious trouble. Maybe if her own father hadn't been dead, killed in a raid while unsuccessfully trying to protect her mother, she would have made a fuss about going away with me. But the only person she was really close to in the Blues was myself. She trusted me, and that was a powerful incentive, because her own life might not be entirely safe if we were captured.

I could hear them shouting back in the clearing, howling for my blood. Then Corlos's bullish yowl sounded over the others; I couldn't make out what he said, but it seemed to quiet them.

I set Clory down on the ground and led her along. It was growing late. If the warriors were to raid the Red-and-Brown tribe this night, they must leave soon, too soon to try to capture us—until they returned. That gave us a certain period of grace.

We stood statue-still for a second, listening for sounds of pursuit. There weren't any. Apparently the Tribe had decided to let our punishment wait until the raid had been completed, for I could hear the chant of the warriors resume their deep-voiced promises of catastrophe to the Enemy tribe.

Distantly Corlos's yowl came to me. "So burns the Enemy!" he shouted, over the thin pounding of the drums. "So dies their tribe! Burn, Red-and-Browns! Burn with the House of the Enemy!" And there was a blood-freezing screech from fifty throats, as the warriors echoed, "Burn!"

Then the drums rolled up to a bleak crescendo and stopped. I wondered what they had substituted for us in the House of the Enemy. Lurlan's corpse, probably. Well, better than his living body, or ours. I strained my eyes in the direction of the village, and saw the trees weirdly black and orange in the flickering of the burning shack. Then the cries died down and there was no sound we could hear, for a long time.

2

The Glider

I woke up with a start and clutched at my bow. Some sound had awakened me. Voices!

We had slept for hours, much longer than I'd intended. As I looked at Clory I realized that, for there was light to see her sleeping form. Dawn was near.

I rose cautiously without waking her, and peered around for the source of the voices. It was a party of warriors swinging along the trail, not twenty feet away.

Were they pursuing us? I saw they were not. They were pilots, the men who, secure in the speed of our gliders, would fly over the village we were to raid, shooting into the forces of the enemy, dropping blazing torches if they could, causing disorder in a hundred ways. They were on their way to the hill where our gliders were kept, there to launch them and be on their way to the enemy town.

I knew how to pilot a glider, that was one of the things for which I had been indebted to Lurlan. If we could steal one of those ships . . .

The men had passed out of hearing. Quickly I woke Clory and explained to her what I had seen, and the plan I'd made. Most wonderful of seven-year-old girls that she was, she understood immediately and followed me cautiously through the underbrush to the clearing where stood the catapults for the gliders.

We were noiseless—literally—as we wormed our way towards the clearing. We moved slowly, and as we approached we heard the dull "dwang-g-g-g" of the released catapult as the first glider took to the air. We hid under a tree as it soared down the slope of the hill to gain speed, directly overhead. Luckily, the initial effort to gain altitude made it necessary for the pilots to cover a good deal of territory; they couldn't, therefore, wait for each other and proceed to the enemy village *en masse*. If they had, our hopes of escape would have been ruined, for we would have been spotted immediately, and shot down.

I've never stalked an Eater as soundlessly as I led Clory, crawling, to the catapults. The sky was already showing colour, and the ground was wet with pre-dawn mist. I heard the catapult drone its fiddle note again—that was the second glider. Two gliders, each carrying two men, were gone; three gliders and eight men, if I'd counted correctly, were left.

A third glider had taken off before we gained the position I wanted, commanding the catapults. I counted the men in the clearing. There were five; I'd made an error before, but it was all to the good—it meant one man less to take care of later.

It seemed hours before the fourth glider was off and the time it took the three men remaining to wind the catapult again was weeks. But finally it was done.

I have said that I am a good marksman. Though I had always had a horror of killing men, the thought of what would happen to Clory and me if I weakened strengthened my resolve; as fast as I could speed the arrows, the three men dropped, one after another, and Clory and I broke for the glider. We fastened ourselves securely and I yanked on the release cable. There was a dizzying surge of motion and the loudest sound I ever heard, as the catapult arm threw us far out and up into the sky. We were free and away!

Clory had never been in the air before—few women or girls had. Her exuberance was unbounded as we skimmed on our way. I felt joyous too. It was a wondrous morning.

Morning is the best time for gliding, because there are all sorts of convection currents caused by the rising of the sun. I pushed over the lever arm to send us down in a flat glide for the river bank. There was a small formation of cliffs there, big enough to send us a needed up-current. We reached it easily, and I spun the glider in a slow spiral as we climbed. We gained hundreds of feet of altitude before I levelled out, and headed in a straight line for the mountains to the North.

The flight was uneventful. Almost automatically I took the lift from every up-draft under a cloud. We weren't going really fast—I've run faster—but we were making steady progress over forests and swamps and rivers. There was only one fly in my ointment. I was tired —had had no sleep to speak of, and I certainly couldn't sleep while we flew. Yet we could land only one way: permanently, since we had no catapult.

My drowsiness grew and grew, as the miles slid by us. I had no particular destination; I steered by my shadow in front of me, cast by the morning sun behind. Though I kept reminding myself to stay awake, I drowsed again and again, each time coming a little closer to falling completely asleep and thus losing control. If only we could have landed for a second . . .

I suddenly realized that Clory was tugging at the back of my coat. "Keefe!" she was crying urgently. "Look!" I thrust off my sleepiness and turned to her smiling.

But there was a real alarm in her eyes as she pointed out over the forests, and my smile died when I saw what she had seen.

It was another glider and it was flying straight for us.

In my amazement I nearly lost control. One of the other ships from our Tribe—it had to be that. Though it was a mile away or more, between me and the sun, it was much higher than we were and was coming at us impossibly fast, faster than I'd ever seen a glider go.

I had only one course—to flee. Cursing savagely, I dipped our craft until it was just skimming along the surface of the trees, fast as we could go.

But not nearly fast enough. The other glider was catching up with us as easily as we were overtaking the motionless trees ahead.

I wondered briefly how it had attained the altitude that gave it such speed from its initial dive, then turned all my attention to the controls.

Clory was holding to my coat with fervour. I could feel her body shaking with sobs as we both leaned forward, trying to cut down air resistance. I hung on to the controls tightly, fighting with all my energy for an extra foot of altitude, a trifle more speed.

A peak of green whipped up at us—crack! The ship jolted and faltered. I darted a glance below; we'd struck the top of a tree. Our landing skids had been wrecked.

But that had been the last of the tall trees; the land ahead sloped gently down. As far ahead as the eye could see was this gentle slope, the valley of an immense river bed. I tilted the controls and we picked up a few precious feet of speed in the shallow dive.

But our pursuer was faster yet. I glanced behind for a split second and saw it ominously close, close and huge. Much larger than our ship, it seemed . . .

"Clory!" I cried tensely. "Can you fly this for a minute?" She didn't answer, but twined her arms around my neck and grabbed the levers. "Good girl," I muttered, unlimbering my bow. "Just hold them that way for a second."

I twisted under her arms and took careful aim at the plane which followed us. I strained the bowstring back as far as I could and released it.

But Clory moved, just at the wrong moment! The cord struck her arm, the arrow was deflected far to one side. She gasped and winced from the cutting blow of the cord, and she must have jerked involuntarily at the controls.

For the ship's dive became abruptly steep and we spun crazily, whirling rational thoughts from my brain. I clutched at whatever I could reach; it turned out to be the control lever, killing our last chance of keeping to the air. The ship careened and fell off on one wing, diving directly into a giant of a tree—the solid trunk of it, this time. I had time to realize before my face smashed into the hard, rough wood that little Clory had been thrown out of the glider. Then I struck!

I don't know how long I was stunned. I was cut and bleeding and my face felt raw when I came to, lying sprawled on a grassy mound. But no bones seemed to be broken. I leaped to my feet, crying Clory's name. If we could find shelter somewhere! The glider wouldn't dare to make a landing to scout for us. We might yet escape.

Clory did not answer. I dashed madly about, peering into the undergrowth, searching behind every bush. Then I spied her slight, white form lying motionless on the ground. I raced to her, fell to the ground beside her and shook her roughly.

She was unconscious—but not dead. My ear pressed to her heart convinced me of that. I tugged her to a sitting position . . .

And a shadow swept over me. I stared up. It was the other glider. We were seen.

Shaking Clory to bring her back to consciousness wasn't much use, though I tried it. The only thing I could do was to leave her there and run. The pilot of the glider, I hoped, would think she was dead. If I could hide long enough to make him give up hope of shooting me from the air . . .

The glider had whirled away; I could see its tail twist as the pilot banked it in a long curve, planed smoothly back towards us. I gaped no longer. I jumped to my feet and raced for cover.

I don't think I've ever run any faster than I did that dozen yards to shelter, but it seemed slow. Time passes slowly when you are expecting a five-foot arrow to feather between your shoulder blades.

But I made the cover, which was a long thicket of flower-ferns. Their broad leaves over me were perfect protection.

I knelt and glared up at the glider which was continuing its swooping back and forth. The sun was high now, and pouring into my eyes, so I had difficulty in seeing through the gaps in my roof. But I could see well enough to know that the flier was something out of the ordinary.

It had seemed huge when we were fleeing from it, larger than I had ever seen a glider before. But now, when I could sit back and stare at it, I found that it was something brand-new to me. It was no glider of our Tribe's, that was certain. Too large by far, designed much differently, with wings little larger than our own, but an immense fuselage slung low between the wings, twice as long as an ordinary glider.

It was made of something that shone and glistened in the sunlight. And it had a curious whirling contraption on each wing, something I'd never seen before, and could not understand. It flew low overhead, and I stared up at it. The pilot's face was visible over the side of the ship; so close that I could make out the features. It was no member of the Tribe. The face was surmounted by a headdress whose pattern was also unfamiliar to me.

I slumped back on the ground to think this over, and . . .

. . . Rose again much more rapidly, clutching a stung rump. I spun around and peered to see what had stung me. It was an arrow! I looked again and saw my bow, just outside the cover, lying temptingly exposed in the open.

I shot a quick look at the mysterious glider. The pilot was completing another arc, about to return. I leaped up and scuttled out from the flower-ferns, clutching the arrow. The bow was unharmed by its fall; I fitted the arrow to it, drew it back and took aim. The glider was sweeping closer, travelling at great speed, difficult to hit. But I'd never get a better opportunity—I stretched the arrow back as far as I could—released it!

There was a sharp note from my long bow, and I saw the new glider waver ever so slightly in its course. I'd hit it. I heard the voice of the pilot in a shout of pain and anger, saw him rise from the seat and try to leap clear as the ship sliced through the air in a whistling wingover, turned and plunged out of sight. I heard a loud splintering sound of breaking branches, and the crash of the ship, and a scream.

The hunter had been snared!

3

The Two from the Boat

Even after Clory had come to again, and was perfectly fit for travel, we two remained in the neighbourhood of where the strange ship had crashed. Somehow, in its fall, a fire had been started. How, I had no idea. Possibly there was a fire in the ship all the time, though that seemed unlikely. But there it was, an immense column of white-hot flame, almost invisible in the sunlight, shooting high at the heavens.

Clory and I watched it for some time without saying a word. We wanted to come nearer and investigate, but the flame was hot as well as bright. We sat on the banks of a river nearby and stared at the column of fire.

"What is it, Keefe?" whispered Clory, but all I could do was shake my head.

The ship twisted and moved in the heat of the pyre. Odd noises, almost human, came from it; they could have been the cries of the trapped pilot, but I thought that unlikely—they continued too long. Cracklings and sighings were to be heard for hours.

The sun began to set while we were still there. Luckily the ship had crashed in a clearing so there were no branches overhead to catch fire: the oddly long-lived flame expended its heat and light harmlessly in the air.

But not too harmlessly, I realized swiftly. Though it was still not completely dark, we could see the light of that hundred-foot flame reflected from every tree in sight. What a beacon it was, visible for miles around.

I touched Clory's shoulder, and she followed me back, down the sloping banks of the stream and into the water. We waded as far as we could, then swam the hundred yards or so of the width of the stream. Just within the woods on the other side I spread small branches and grass on the ground, and covered the mass with my jacket. We would camp there for the night—it was as good a place as any.

All I had been able to salvage from our glider, except for my bow and arrows, was a short hunting knife. And I had only three arrows left. I determined to try to make some.

Clory fell asleep while I stripped the bark and leaves from a pair of straight, thin branches, then proceeded to whittle them down with the knife. I was no weapon maker, I discovered ruefully, but I managed to get the shafts smooth and straight as an arrow need be. I had yet to feather them though, and that wouldn't be easy. Nor would the job of getting bone or rock points for them.

I stopped whittling suddenly and cocked an ear. What was that? A whirring noise, faint but clear.

Without awakening Clory, I rose and stole noiselessly over to a point of better vantage, a knoll on the river bank.

The origin of the muted sound was difficult to trace in the warm, dark night, particularly with the crackling of the huge flame across the river interfering. But it seemed to come from the river itself, at some point downstream from me.

The river was not broad, but it was straight as a lance, almost as though man-made. I could see a long way up and down it, at least a mile.

But I didn't have to see nearly that far. Much less than a mile away —a fifth of that, at most—was a group of moving lights, speeding up the river in my direction. As it approached I could see a dark hulk surrounding the lights, the shape of a ship. The whir became louder.

But how did it move? Already it was close enough for me to see that it had no sails or paddles, nor was there a rope connecting it to anything on the bank which might be towing it. And it was moving much too rapidly for any of those methods to be responsible.

The connection was obvious, and alarming. Whoever had been in the glider had friends—friends who, seeing the flame of its crash-pyre, had come to investigate.

Possibly they would not be inimical. I couldn't afford to find out. The thing for Clory and me to do was to get away from there.

But it could do no harm to linger for a while and see what would happen; we were safe, across the river.

Clory awoke and stole up beside me, slipping her hand into mine. Together we watched the strange craft dip in towards the river bank next to the still blazing ship.

The boat must have been of very slight draught, for it swung in within five feet of the beach before it halted. Light flared briefly on the shore as a door opened on the side away from us. The door closed again, and we saw two figures limned against the light of the fire as they climbed towards the ship.

They seemed scarcely human in the firelight, those two men. Certainly their dress was unlike that of any Tribe I knew. As they strode up the hill, all I could see was their backs, each wearing what seemed to be a species of bow slung athwart his shoulders. There was a crisscross affair of belts on their backs, from which depended small objects that I couldn't quite define.

Clory's fingers gripped mine fiercely. "Keefe!" she whispered piercingly. "In the woods—over there. Look."

I looked—and my shoulder blades crawled to meet each other. There was something huge and dark moving in the woods, shambling slowly towards the fire. It was an Eater—but a monster. Twenty feet long? More, much more.

The men did not see the approaching beast. They were regarding the blaze intently. One of them drew something out of a pocket—I could not see it clearly—and hurled it into the fire. Immediately the flame shrank; it was going out.

The Eater had come into the open now, but behind the two men. They could not see it. Should I shout and warn them, exposing myself if they were inimical? Or should I keep quiet and thus possibly condemn them to death?

Clory settled the question. Impulsively she raised her head and shrieked a warning to them across the stream.

The two men whipped around—and saw the Eater. I had to admire them for their quickness of thought—there was only a split second of hesitation before they recovered, and advanced on the Eater. Advanced on him—those two tiny men, unarmed as far as I could see.

Although, if their weapons were of as high a standard as their gliders and their boats, they might not be in any danger at all.

Their smooth efficiency was joyous to behold. In unison they unslung the short sticks I had thought to be bows and held them as you might a javelin. They were not more than four feet long—did the men hope to get close enough to run them into the huge animal?

They did, for they ran towards the Eater, divided, and as though following a carefully rehearsed programme, ran around the slow-thinking Eater. He turned to snap at one of them with his immense jaws—the one farthest from us. I could not see what happened, but I heard a yell of a man in agony which told me the story.

But the other man gained the position he wanted. He stabbed his javelin-like pole into the Eater's side. This time it was the monster that screamed in pain. Immense, fat sparks of light shot from the pole where it went into the creature's flesh. There was a high ripping sound, audible even at this distance, and I could feel for the Eater—that pole was deadly!

The squall of the wounded Eater drowned out other sounds, but the man must have cried out too. He had reason to, for the wounded monster, shuddering in unbearable agony, curled its huge length back upon itself and lashed out with its mighty tail. The tiny tip of it alone hit the man, but it was enough to flick him into the still burning ship.

I think the man was dead before he began to burn. I hope so.

The Eater was dying too. As Clory and I watched, it staggered weakly off into the darkness, but could not even make the edge of the little clearing. It slumped to the ground, trembled all over once more, then lay quiet.

We watched, but nothing more happened. The two men had failed in their mission. They were as dead as the man they had come to save.

We decided, Clory and I, to reswim the river and see if there was any sign of life in the two men. With the death of the Eater, there was no other danger there, unless another beast had been attracted by the sounds of combat. That seemed unlikely, for an Eater as big as this would surely have killed or driven off all lesser ones.

We emerged dripping wet and walked quickly up the gentle slope. The men were dead—very. I reached the bodies before Clory, and I shooed her away. Every Tribe girl had seen death, Clory as much of it as any, but no seven-year-old girl had any need to see a corpse as ghastly as that of the man who had been slashed in two by the fierce jaws of the Eater.

The light of the fire was dimming—that little object the man had tossed in the flame was slow, but it did the work. As we watched, the fire grew less and less.

But it was not owing exclusively to the work of the man. Clory called my attention to that. "Can we get somewhere out of the rain, Keefe?" she asked, shivering.

I started and looked around. Sure enough, it was raining. Pouring. It was out of the question for us to remain exposed to that downpour—already the fierce flame of the ship was out, though the wreckage was still too hot to approach. The question, of course, was where to go.

There was a dull booming crash from afar. Thunder. I could see the play of lightning flashes off in the distance. If the rain had already arrived, the lightning would soon be overhead. It would be very unpleasant to be near trees then.

Clory pointed—I followed her gaze. The boat! A very good place to be, undoubtedly. It had a roof—that was all we could ask. We ran down to it, tugged open the door, and stepped right in.

We closed the door tight behind us before we looked around.

And the first thing we saw was—them.

A man—and a girl. Dead, it seemed, for they lay unmoving, not even breathing. I stared at them. Neither was dressed in the odd garments of the two we had seen die. Their garb was much like our own, the everyday dress of Tribespeople.

"They must have been nice people," Clory said aloud, and I found myself agreeing with her.

The man had as open and honest a face as any I've seen, and the girl was beautiful.

I stepped around them to get a better look at the girl's perfect features. They were lovely from any angle. I knelt to touch her pulse, and as my hand touched her wrist I felt a numbing tingle in my own fingers. I drew back my hand quickly.

There was a pale, bluish light falling on the two bodies from a lamp of sorts that hung over them. From the lamp extended a cord, which ran along the ceiling, then down the wall, terminating in a pedestal-like affair at the front of the boat, on which were dozens—hundreds!—of mysterious levers and dials. I moved over to examine it.

The levers were of all shapes and colours. I knew the purpose of none of them, but what harm could they do?

There was a temptingly small, red lever set into the very base of the pedestal. So small, and so far down, it could not be dangerous. "Don't touch it, Keefe!" Clory's terrified voice begged as I stooped to finger it.

But I had already moved it.

Without result.

Emboldened, I moved another, then several more.

And with a lurch, the boat shuddered underfoot! The whirring sound again became audible, and it began to move. I had started it!

"Oh, Keefe! Why . . ."

But Clory stopped—words were of no use. I'd done it.

Together we raced for the door, staggering with the motion of the ship. It wouldn't open. Somehow, the motion of the ship also controlled the door; I couldn't budge it. I leaped to a window and hammered on it. It just would not open, nor could I shatter it, though I shouldered it with all my weight behind the lunge.

Could I stop the ship? I turned back to the pedestal and stared anxiously, tempted. But which lever was the right one? I had no way of knowing, and I dared not experiment again.

I glanced out of the window fearfully. The angular prow of the ship divided the water into two neat curling crests, one on either side. The lightning had come, was striking at the taller trees all around. The black water ahead and the fierce play of light in the sky made a frightening combination.

"At least," I said to Clory with a confidence I did not feel, "we're going someplace. See how the boat stays in the middle of the river—something must be directing it. We'll be all right." How could the boat be steered? I didn't know; certainly we were not steering it, nor was anyone else in the ship. Just one more mystery to tuck away in our minds.

I half heard a rustle of movement behind me, and turned to see that the "dead" man had come to life again—dangerously!

He was creeping up to me, preparing to spring. If he had, it would have been a hand-to-hand fight, which I might have lost; he was powerfully built, and I had no time to draw my knife. But when he got a good look at me he faltered.

"Who are you?" he whispered, relaxing his menacing attitude. "You're a Tribesman!"

The girl was alive too, I saw thankfully. She had been close behind him, backing him up.

4

The Mad Tunnel

Yes, we were Tribespeople, and so were they. We were all equally ignorant of the nature of the owners of the vessel in which we were. We exchanged stories.

Their adventures were interesting, but not very helpful. They, with all of their Tribe, had been asleep one evening. (Their Tribe was called the Greystripes—I'd heard of it, but it was too far away from my own village for us to have had any dealings, commercial or martial.) The girl's name was Braid; the man's, Check. Their individual huts were at almost opposite ends of the village; how they came to be together they did not know. They had gone to sleep in their own huts, and wakened, for a brief period, in a dimly lighted cell, together with dozens of other Tribespeople, all in an unnaturally deep sleep. They'd tried to arouse others, and failed. But their activities had drawn the attention of a guard dressed like the men Clory and I had seen, who had come in, found them awake, and pointed something long and tapering at them. They'd gone back to sleep, quite involuntarily, and awakened in the ship.

Our own story, which we then told, took more time. In fact, before we'd finished it, it was halted by an outside event. Braid had been keeping watch on the progress of the boat, and she suddenly cried out, pointing. The river forked off ahead, one branch continuing on into the distance, the other ending in what seemed to be the side of a mountain. Closer inspection revealed a hole, a tunnel, in that cliff wall; into it the boat unerringly sped, not abating its speed.

And a few seconds later the ship halted. The subdued whir of the motors diminished and died altogether. There was a soft jar from outside and we were motionless. I seized the door; it opened freely.

The four of us crowded around the door and peered out cautiously. Not a living soul was in sight. After a moment, we stepped out, timorously at first, then more bravely, as it became evident that we were in no immediate danger.

Unless we wanted to entrust ourselves to that boat again, allowing it to proceed as it would back down the river—if, indeed, we could get it to move—we were trapped here. We might have been able to swim out, but it was a considerable distance; just how far, the darkness made it impossible to say. And there was no way at all of walking back through the tunnel, for the water lapped precipitous walls, except at the landing where we stood.

Set into the face of the rock there was a door, ajar. With one accord, we entered it.

We found ourselves in a long tunnel, which swept in a broad curve away from us in either direction. No human was visible, even now, though the place was brightly lit. Too brightly lit. It showed things that I could not understand, that drove me almost to the sharp brink of madness.

Picture a tunnel, a long one, and high and broad as well, descending in a shallow slant into the ground, as far as you can see. Fill it, in your mind, with a tremendous number of strange and eerie machines of some sort, each in motion. Make sure that every machine is different from the one next to it, and remember that each gives forth some tiny sound all blending together into a low, sustained chord, in which you can nevertheless distinguish individual tones.

Imagine that you are part way into the tunnel, that no human being is visible save three as ignorant as you, that the motions of the wheels and cams and levers of the machines are totally incomprehensible; see with amazement that in some cases there are wheels revolving in thin air, without an axle; that occasionally a piece of one machine will detach itself, float unsupported through the air to another, where it joins on, then recommences its spinning, twisting, gyrating activity; that more than once a wheel will roll completely through what appears to be a completely solid machine, leaving no hole or mark to show where it had entered.

Add to all this the fact that the machines are constructed of strange materials, some transparent, almost invisible, others seemingly transparent but curiously reflective; most of glistening metals—which, you must remember, you have seen comparatively seldom in your former life.

To our left, the tunnel sloped up, and downwards to our right. Up would mean the surface—but the entrance of the subterranean canal was in the direction of our right. Which way would take us out?

We spent minutes in debate, and could not decide. Braid settled it finally. "When you cannot follow your head," she said, "you must follow your heart. We can try the left. If it seems the wrong way, we'll come back."

So the four of us executed a broad left-wheel, and marched down that glittering action-filled tunnel. The machines—as I should have said—lined the walls only. The centre was a broad, flat path for us to walk on.

We walked mostly in silence, all of us gaping at the mad activity that surrounded us. For some distance we walked, until I tore my attention from the machines long enough to note that Check was acting strangely. He was twisting around to stare back, then forward; then tilting his head to peer at the ceiling overhead. A frown of puzzlement was appearing on his face.

"What is it?" I asked.

"I don't know—listen." We listened, but heard nothing more than the constant machine-drone; the same drone we had been hearing all along.

But with a difference? Yes, surely. There was a new, growing note in the symphony. A deep buzz, something like the whir of the ship's motors.

Check peered over his shoulder, and his face changed. He cried out and shoved my shoulder, spinning me around. I looked—and staggered.

Bearing down on us faster than any Eater ever ran was an immense, wheeled metal shape. The noise was coming from it, from the sound of its huge wheels on the flooring, and from the hidden motor within. The thing was large—it almost filled the tunnel from top to bottom, though it wasn't wide enough by far to interfere with the machines that whirled along at the sides.

Leaving Check to look after Braid, I dragged Clory by main force into the maze of machinery at the side of the tunnel. We dodged spinning wheels and bars and climbed behind the pedestal of one of the machines.

Braid and Check were quick to do the same, but on the other side of the passage. But not quite quick enough, it seemed. Before they were well concealed, the metal monster was upon us. And it became evident that we had been seen.

For the thing squealed to a halt fifty feet beyond us, then rolled back to where we were and stopped.

5

The Subterranean City

I shouldn't have been surprised at the black cloud of sleep that descended over us all just then, because Check and Braid had told me about it before. I knew the people in that car were the same as the people who had abducted my two friends, but in the shock of that swift blotting out of consciousness, I didn't connect their experience with the present one.

Clory awakened me, and I found myself in a pleasantly light and cheerful room, lying on a luxuriously soft couch. We might be prisoners, but we were being treated well enough.

All four of us were there. For no reason except, perhaps, that she was youngest and best able to throw off the effects of the sleep ray or whatever it was, Clory had come to first, and immediately roused me.

Together we woke Braid and Check.

The oddest feature of the room was its very curious windows. As we looked out of them from the interior of the room, we saw a blue sky with occasional puffy clouds. But as we approached, and tried to look down, the apparent transparency of the glass clouded. By the time one reached the window, it was almost opaque; only vague formless shadows could be seen. And as one walked away, the sky slowly reappeared.

The door, we found, was locked.

The style of the room's furnishings was far less strange than we might have imagined. Except that each item was so beautifully made, it might almost have been a Chief's home of any progressive tribe.

But we didn't have too much time to investigate it. Some signal must have been given of our awakening, for the door flew open, and a man entered.

He seemed friendly enough, but when we besieged him with questions he said nothing, just stood there looking at us. There was no malice in his stare, but neither did he seem particularly interested.

He just stood there, regarding us. He was dressed like those of his kind we had already seen: the abbreviated divided trousers, tunic, belted back. In his hand he carried a smaller version of the rod we had seen used on the Eater; on his head he wore a flat-topped pillbox hat.

As moments passed without a movement from him beyond his shifting glances, Check edged over to me, darting meaningful stares at the man and at me. I didn't comprehend his meaning at first, but the stranger did.

"I wouldn't do that," he said smoothly, and raised the rod a trifle. (Check and I both noticed for the first time that we were unarmed.) He continued his easy stare as Check brought up sharp, flushing.

"No," said the man after a space, reflectively, "I don't think you'll find it necessary to gang up on me. Certainly"—he gestured with the rod—"you wouldn't find it safe. If you are all comfortable, we had better get started. There has been a special meeting of the Council to consider your problem. Come with me." And he stood aside. But he would not answer questions even then, just gestured wordlessly with the rod.

You might think we could have overpowered him. Certainly it would seem that we could have—and should have—made some objection to going so freely with him. I thought so. I even attempted, in passing, to clutch at the door and slam it on him as he stood in the threshold, barricading ourselves in until we could make more definite plans.

But I couldn't. Just couldn't. My muscles would not obey the orders from my brain. It was like a complete paralysis, though I was perfectly free to walk, to look around, to do anything that did not conflict with his orders.

It was his pillbox hat that did it. There was a tiny instrument in it which acted to amplify his will, to force his commands upon others. Our thoughts he could not control, but our actions were his to command.

So we went with him quite obediently. We had not far to go, just out into a door-studded hall, and along it for a few feet until we came to an empty door. We entered, the door closed and we looked around perplexedly. We were in a tiny room, scarcely large enough for us. There was no furniture save a row of studs set in a wall by the door. This could not be our destination.

Nor was it. The man with the helmet stabbed one of the buttons with his forefinger and an inner door whirred shut. There was a muffled click, then the floor surged up under us, and the whole room shot up into the air.

There was a frightened squawk from Clory, who grabbed me and hung on. I was nothing much to cling to, having left my stomach below when the room swooped up, nor were the others in a better state. The man took it calmly enough, grinning at our discomfiture, though, so I concealed my apprehension as much as I could.

The motion lasted only a few seconds. Then it stopped smoothly and the door opened. We were escorted out and into a large, handsome hall.

The man with the rod escorted us in, then stepped aside. "This is the Council Chamber," he said. "Go forward and answer the questions of the Council."

We stepped forward timorously, and he made his exit. The Council Chamber was vast—larger, even, than the big ceremonial field back in the village of the Tribe, the field in which I was nearly burned to death. How long ago that seemed!

A triple-tiered balcony ran around the wall. It reminded me of the Balcony of Men back in the ceremonial field, though the crude wooden balcony there was not to be compared with this ornate structure of metal and fabrics. The seats were occupied, with some vacancies, by perhaps fifty men and women. They eyed us with much the same friendly unconcern that had characterized the man with the rod.

We were brought up before this impressive audience and seated in chairs as comfortable as their own. The questions began almost immediately.

The oldest of the Council—they were a youngish lot—rustled some papers on the flat arm of his chair and glanced at us piercingly. "Have you any objection to allowing Check to act as your spokesman?" he asked suddenly. Check asked us with his eyes; we all nodded.

"None," he said. "But how did you know my name?"

"I know a great deal about you—all of you," laughed the judge. "Braid and Keefe better than Clory, and you best of all, but even Clory is familiar to me. We have heard of her from her father."

"Her father!" I gasped as Clory squealed in surprise. "Her father is dead!"

"No. Clory's father is not dead. He is—elsewhere, just now, but he is alive. Perhaps Clory may see him soon, when he returns. At the time of his 'death' he was injured by a blow. He did not die, but he would have, had not one of our patrols found him. When he was well again we examined him, as we are examining you now, and decided favourably. . . . But we will do the asking here, just now. You, Check, tell me: how did you come to be here?"

Check told what he knew, and I supplemented the account with Clory's history and mine. The interrogator appeared to be satisfied; when he had finished, he held a low-pitched conversation with those around him, which we could not hear. For a few moments all of them talked among themselves, then apparently a decision was reached.

The one who had questioned us signed to a guard standing by the entrance, who opened the portal and admitted three men trundling a large, flat box on wheels, from which depended flexible tubes of varying descriptions. The guard, who was wearing one of those hypnotic hats, accompanied them up to us, ordering us to do as they said.

We submitted perforce to having a tube wrapped around the wrist of each of us, various other gadgets clamped to other parts of our anatomy, and our eyes bandaged so we could see nothing. As soon as all the equipment was adjusted to their satisfaction, one of them commenced to question us.

But what questions! Nothing we could have expected—at least, not in our right minds. Apparently they had no desire to learn facts, to discover what we wanted to do here, or anything about our backgrounds. To the accompaniment of ominous buzzings and clickings from the machine, we were asked such questions as, "If you were to be imprisoned in a dark room for twenty-four hours, what would you do?" and, "Would you prefer to witness a pageant or take part in it?" and others even less rational. I could hear a stylus scratching the answers on a pad, and wondered what type of persons these might be.

Then I heard a cry of alarm from Braid and tensed my muscles to rip off my blindfold and see what was happening. I couldn't, of course; the hypnosis of that helmet forbade any resistance. But I felt a gentle pressure in my arm, and then a stinging jolt of mild electricity. I leaped, and I think I cried out too. A squeal from Clory and a grunt from Check showed that they had received the same treatment.

Our blindfolds were removed, but the tests continued. They detached all the gadgets from Clory and sent her away to sit in the corner, while Braid, Check and I were quizzed in a new fashion. A string of such words as "read," "learn," "sleep," "eat," and other verbs of varying meaning were spoken to us, and one of the men noted the readings of a leaping dial needle attached to the bands on our wrists.

But that was all. We were released from the apparatus and conducted out of the room by the same man who had brought us. As we left, the head man of the Council called to us, "You will return tomorrow, and everything will be clear. Have patience till then."

We were returned to our room, where we found ourselves unaccountably sleepy. Though we had been awakened not more than four hours before, we could not stay awake. We sought couches and lay down. Just as I was dropping off, I thought I saw the door open, and a man enter and fasten something to Clory's head. It appeared to be a helmet, but I could not force myself to awaken and make it out. As he approached me, I dropped off into deep slumber.

6

The Dream

My sleep was full of dreams—odd ones. I saw myself in a thousand impossible situations.

Quite naturally, I dreamed of the scene in the Council Chamber. But in the dream I was not the object of the Council's attention—I was a member of it. In fact, I was chief of the Council. Before me, in one fantasy of sleep after another, were brought dozens of persons to be asked the questions I had been asked that day; thousands of other persons with other problems to be settled. I could not understand the tenth part of those problems, but in my dream I knew all about them; I solved them all, to the complete satisfaction of everyone. I was not supreme among the Council, but I was its co-ordinator, the one finally to resolve each knotty problem according to the suggestions of the others.

As the dreams grew in clarity, an immense amount of background material began to fill it. I saw a teeming, populous world, many times the size of my own. Almost completely underground, it was, but it filled millions of square miles on a hundred different subterranean levels. In this new world—which I came to identify with the underground city my sleeping body was in—was a complete civilization, vaster by far than all the Tribes put together, of a culture and depth of understanding that bewildered me.

The surface of this world, I saw, was given over to relaxation. No one died, either on the surface or below, save by accident, but the swift pace of the underground life aged its inhabitants, made them old in mind while still young in body. They needed refreshment, refreshment which meant a complete relaxation, complete forgetting of all of the cares of the world below. Forgetting, even, that there was a world below . . .

At which point I awakened. It was morning again—according to the elusive sky on the window—and the others were awakening too.

They had had much the same sort of dream, with individual differences. Check had dreamed of himself, not as leader of the Council, but as a worker in a sort of "large room, with funny pieces of machinery spread all over," as he described it. He seemed to have been engaged in some sort of research, but he did not know any more about it. Clory had not seen herself in any of the dreams. Braid hesitated, looked fearfully disturbed about something, then finally said she couldn't remember, and stuck to it.

Eventually the guard came once more and took us out again to go to the Council.

In the elevator, I saw something that took me a moment to comprehend. The guide carried the force rod, and seemed as supercilious, as free from worry about our actions as ever—but he did not wear the mind-compelling hat! I stared again to make sure, then nudged Check to a position behind the man and pointed. Check saw, widened his eyes, then together we whirled on the man and bowled him over.

Our muscles obeyed us! The man cried out, then lashed at us with arms and legs, but our first leap had knocked the rod from his hands. It was two against one, and Check and I were strong. The man toppled to the floor, Check upon him; I secured the rod and turned it on him.

Just then the elevator door commenced to open quietly—we had arrived. And as it slid open, we all saw just outside a full dozen of armed men walking along the corridor!

I was staggered, but had presence of mind enough to level the weapon at the foremost of them. "I'll kill the first one to move," I yelled, and meant it—it simply never occurred to me that I didn't know how to operate the thing!

The men outside didn't know that. It was an impasse.

Braid caught Clory to her instinctively and said, "What shall we do, Keefe?" I didn't know, but I could not afford to have either her or the men know that.

I asked a question. "Do you think you can run that car?" I didn't take my eyes off the men, but I could see her shadow at the little bank of keys.

"Maybe—not very well," her voice came. "At least I think I can start it."

That was not so good. "Check—come here," I called after a space.

He stirred suddenly, as though my command had jolted him out of some deep thought. He stepped slowly forward, still with puzzlement at something in his eyes, and looked a question at me.

"Take the rod from one of them," I ordered, stabbing my weapon at one of the men. He hesitated. "Go ahead," I cried with irritation. "There may be more along in a minute."

He hesitated for only a second after that. Then, with a swift swoop, he snatched a rod, stepped back a pace—and snatched my rod!

Swinging it to cover all of us, Clory and Braid and me as well as the men, he wrinkled his brow. "Now, wait a minute, all of you," he muttered. "I want to think—" He stared at the men, and at us, then shrugged. "Get up!" he cried to the original owner of the rod. "I'm going to see this through. We're going to the Council Chamber!"

The man rose, smiling. "You are coming along very well," he observed cryptically, and led the way along the hall. Nor did he say anything more.

The man who, in my dream, I had replaced as leader of the Council, widened his eyes in surprise as the lot of us entered. "Weapons?" he murmured questioningly. "There should be no weapons in here."

But Check said, "I am not sure of that, yet—though I am beginning to believe it. But I shall keep this until you explain things to me."

The man smiled. "There is no need to explain," he said, seating himself. I saw with a start that he had not taken the seat of the day before, but was in a small, less conspicuous seat to one side of it and below. That was how I had dreamed it!

"No," repeated the old man, "there is no need to explain any more. We have explained already. Did you not have dreams last night? . . . Yes. Those dreams, then, were fact. We induced them, hypnotically, to tell you what words could not tell as well.

"If you had accepted them as fact, they would have told you that this city is your home. Your real home, more so than the Tribes from which you came. Even, it is Clory's home, though she was born in a Tribe. Her father and her mother lived here."

"This snake hole?" ejaculated Braid.

The man laughed gently. "This is not all of the world. This city here, which houses a paltry few thousand people, is only one of a hundred thousand such; the others all on other planets. This world is merely the sixth satellite of the fifth planet circling one sun. And each of the other planets is inhabited, and many planets of other suns. On the third planet of the sun is the home of our race, from which we all stem, but there are a thousand times as many people of our race now as the planet could hold—even were there still Death."

"But why—" I began, and then stopped, for the man had raised a hand.

"I shall tell you the 'whys' in a moment," he said. "And when I have told you a few of them, to prepare you for the shock, your minds shall be returned to you."

Check quickened his breath at those words. His rod dropped unnoticed to the floor; one of the men picked it up and slung it over his shoulder. Before we could ask another question, the old man went on.

"As I have said, there is no more Death, save by accident. You know that; you know that, though many disappear, few die. Those who disappear come here.

"For immortality brings age. The fine blade of the mind dulls from constant use. The body does not sicken nor age, but the mind grows old. It must be rested.

"And for that are these rest planets—one in every System—established. All knowledge, save of the simple art of language, walking, and the others, is taken from a man when he is discovered to need rest. He is given an artificial, hypnotic memory, and sent to join a Tribe. For a dozen years or more he lives with the Tribe, while his mind grows younger. Then he is brought back, as were Check and Braid, or finds his way back as you did. And he takes up his place again, refreshed."

He paused and looked sharply at the door. It was open; a man was entering, bearing a shimmering bright gem in his hand. "You have all been examined," he continued slowly, "and found to be completely rejuvenated. Then you were given the sleep-teaching treatment, to prepare you, and then this little speech. You are now ready to have returned to you your full minds, with all the memories of your long, long lives!"

The man with the crystal stepped forward, looking from one to the other of us. "Keefe will be first," said the older one. "Simply look into the jewel."

I looked—I heard the man who carried it commence to speak, a droning voice that compelled sleep. In seconds the voice faded away, and the lights dimmed and the entire world was dark. Then there was a sound like thunder, and I heard the word, "Awake!"

My eyes opened, and I felt a maddening, dizzying swirl of thoughts into my brain. I reeled and clutched at the man as my brain, stung into swift activity, sorted and filed the knowledge it had taken me a long lifetime to acquire.

I stood there, swaying. Then there was a sudden feeling of released tension, and I opened my eyes.

Everything suddenly was familiar. I knew my life, and what I had to do.

And with a sort of joyous gravity I had never known in the life of the Tribe, I stepped forward and, with the ease of long experience, slid quietly into the seat of pre-eminence among the Council.

There are two things I've been meaning to talk about, because they seem to me relevant, but I haven't found a place for them—so I'll arbitrarily put them in here.

One is Futurian games.

We were a competitive bunch, all arrogant individualists. When we played games we played for blood. We started with the usual games everyone knows—all the card games; all the board games; parlor games like Twenty Questions and Ghosts. Then we improved on them. Instead of Twenty Questions we played Impossible Questions, the point of which was to ask a question to which no one else knew the answer. It had to be fair. It had to be something that any highly intelligent Renaissance man could have been expected to have come across in the course of a lifetime's study. Ideally, it should also contain an item of information interesting in itself, because of its oddity or its significance. (Example—from the last time I played it, shortly after World War II: "What did Wernher von Braun say when the American rocket experts asked him what the aerodynamic reason was for having such small tail fins on the V-2?" Answer: "Wernher von Braun laughed and laughed and said, 'Aerodynamics, *nicht*. We had to make them small because we shipped them by rail, and the German train tunnels were so narrow.'") The end of the game was when anybody present could answer any question. Sometimes that never happened.

Ghosts palled after a while.* So we began playing Tsohg (Ghosts backward), then *Le Spectre,* which was Ghosts in French. (What made it hard was that none of us knew any French, except for the occasional word like *tiens!, alors, merde* and so on.) When that began to run out of steam we invented a whole new game, or way of life, called *Djugashvili.* Superficially this resembled Ghosts, but every player said whatever he felt was appropriate (Reverse! Foot fault!—whatever), and the loser was whoever the other players could brainwash into admitting he had lost a point. The rule was there were no rules.

Then there was the Piece of String. That was not a game we played with each other, we played it *on* people, in parks, on warm summer nights, when there were plenty of strollers and the light was not too good. Two of us would stand in the middle of a path, gazing expectantly at approaching strollers. Then, as they came close, we would back away into the underbrush on opposite sides, paying out nonexistent cord with our fingers; when it was all out we would lower it to shoetop level and wait to see what happened.

What happened was never, for some reason, that people killed us, or even chased us. Some people would feel with their feet. Others would stride right through, glaring at us, daring us to trip them. Now and then somebody would say something, either hostile or now and then amused; but usually they would just walk away.

Jack Gillespie and I went hitchhiking to Washington one weekend, not for any particular reason, just to have something to do. On the way back we decided on a detour through Hagerstown, Maryland. Sf fan Harry Warner lived there; we had corresponded with him, but never met him. So we had a pleasant visit, and then moved on. But not very far. On the way out of Hagerstown toward Chambersburg, Pennsylvania, we realized we had made a mistake. We were off the well-traveled roads. There just wasn't much traffic to hitch from, and what there was wasn't stopping for us. Along about three o'clock in the morning it stopped being fun, but we were committed by then. There was nothing. No diner, no filling station, not even a house with lighted windows. It was getting cold, a damp, dreary night that did not make the idea of sleeping in the open attractive. We got to hate the occasional driver that zoomed past without picking us up, and along about 5 A.M. we invented a variation on the Piece of String to get even.

*You know what Ghosts is—every player says a letter, and the one on whom a word ends gets a letter G, then an H, then an O until he himself is a Ghost and cannot be spoken to by any other player without the penalty of a letter.

We heard a car coming. We bent down together in the middle of the road, struck a match, held it to the concrete long enough to be sure it was seen and then ran like hell. The driver decelerated from an easy eighty to zero in five or six car lengths, nearly popping his tires in the process and winding up with one wheel in the ditch. We watched from behind trees while he got out of the car, stamped around for a while, looking for a bomb and talking to himself, and then drove away. We didn't play that game any more.

And then on Monday morning I would put on a clean shirt and a tie and go in and be an editor.

The other thing that I've been meaning to put in was a rather major aspect of my teen-age life, and that of some other fans of the late thirties: A number of us, myself most certainly included, got involved in Communist groups around then.

For me it began in 1936, when a fan friend took me to a meeting of the Flatbush Young Communist League. It was a sort of wide-angle loft over some stores on Kings Highway in Brooklyn. I don't know what I expected, exactly. I don't think I got it. No one talked about throwing bombs or destroying capitalist oppression. To the extent that what went on was political at all, it had to do with trying to get Franklin D. Roosevelt re-elected President by drumming up votes for him on the "third party" Farmer-Labor ticket. There was a lot of talk about the evils of Hitlerism, about how desperately the legally elected government of Spain needed help against the Fascist invaders and about how collective security for all democratic peoples was the only way to ensure world peace. It all sounded pretty good, especially since everybody there seemed open, friendly, joking and caring with each other. We listened to the talk, sang a few lefty songs like *Joe Hill* and the *Internationale* and chatted over coffee. The Flatbush YCL was just planning to publish a club magazine, mimeographed. Well, that was right down my alley; at sixteen I already considered myself a world expert in how to edit, lay out and produce mimeographed magazines, and by virtue of my experience with fan mags, I pretty nearly was. So before I left I was signed up as editor.

There was, to be sure, a certain amount of lip service paid to the works of Marx, Engels, Lenin and Stalin. Pamphlets by all of them were on sale. After a time I did, in fact, try to read some of them. I gave up. I am a person who will read almost any book on almost anything, any time. But I drew the line at *Das Kapital* and the Little Lenin

Library. Nothing in them seemed to relate to what I perceived as happening in the Communist movement in America—i.e., boycotting Japanese goods, trying to get Hitler stopped, helping the newborn C.I.O. organize the underpaid workers and so on.

The head of the c.p.u.s.a. was an intelligent, humorous, decent man named Earl Browder. I heard him speak several times, actually met him once; I liked him. The pamphlet of his I remember best was called *Communism Is 20th Century Americanism.* It seemed reasonable enough to me, and Browder apparently believed it; while he was running things the C.P. and its satellite groups like the Y.C.L. acted it out. When the party line changed in Russia Browder was unceremoniously fired and, of course, systematically reviled as a revisionist traitor and Fascist by his successors.

The Y.C.L.ers I knew over the next three years were a smart, likable, incredibly moral lot. I was quite disappointed about that. I had had some hope of free love, if not actual orgies. There were plenty of parties—fund-raisers, every one; there was never enough money. They would play records, or someone would have a guitar. Sometimes there was dancing. But I don't remember seeing even wine served, and there sure wasn't much sex. Not *none.* But not much; about, I guess, like any young people's church auxiliary.

The majority of the Futurians stayed clear of the Y.C.L., not so much because they seriously objected to the politics of it as because it just didn't interest them, I think. Me, I liked it. At first I was desperate to graduate into the Communist Party, but they would have none of me because I was too young. By the time I was old enough I didn't want it any more. After the Stalin-Hitler pact in 1939 I found myself less and less able to stand the about-face from people I had liked and trusted; the ones who had been most passionately against Hitler now being equally virulent against Roosevelt. And the cut-off date, when I decided once and for all that, whatever else happened, I would not ever be able to belong to the American Communist movement again, was six or eight months after that. I can give the exact date, maybe even the hour. It was the fifteenth of June, 1940, somewhere between three and four o'clock in the afternoon.

I had lunch with a friend of mine, both a fellow sf writer and a Y.C.L. member. He proposed we have a glass of wine. "Why?" said I. Wine was maybe twenty cents a glass, which would put the cost of our meal well over a dollar apiece. "To celebrate," said he; and when the wine came he raised his glass in a toast: "To the liberation of Paris from the decadent bourgeoisie by the forces of the people's socialism."

Well, sir, that took me aback. Paris had fallen to the Wehrmacht the day before. I took no joy from that, and it really had never occurred to me that anyone I thought of as a friend would, either.

To my eternal discredit I drank his lousy wine. Then I went back to the office and spent the afternoon deep in thought, and at the end of that time I knew I had had it, forever.†

Anyway. Something puzzles me about this whole business and that is that, try as I will, I can't find much trace of my boy-Bolshevik orientation in any of the stories I was writing around that time. A certain amount of loathing is visible, aimed at government and power structures in general; well, I still feel that; Lord Acton was right on. But that's all I can see. The science fiction I was writing was much more concerned with the glamour, the color, the excitement of the field—what Sam Moskowitz calls "the sense of wonder." It had not yet occurred to me to poke fun at power concentrations by science-fiction satire. It was not that the form didn't exist. Heinlein and de Camp were doing it in *Astounding* every month. Huxley had already published *Brave New World,* and there was a legitimacy to the genre going back through Wells's *When the Sleeper Wakes* to Swift's *Gulliver* and beyond. But in my own work it was another decade or so until I got around to stories like—well, a couple of dozen, from *The Space Merchants* to *The Gold at the Starbow's End.*

The chaos of World War II did not merely throw the Communist Party into catatonic shock, it of course affected everybody, even before Pearl Harbor. It affected young men very directly; Congress passed the first peacetime draft laws ever, and any of us might be called any time.

Except that I, personally, seemed reasonably immune. Being married, I was automatically entitled to some deferment on the grounds of having a dependent. Moreover I lived in a high-rise housing development called Knickerbocker Village, in downtown New York, just up against the New York side of the Manhattan Bridge. The importance of that point lay in the fact that Knickerbocker Village was part of Selective Service Local Board No. 1's bailiwick, which also took in Chinatown. That made a difference. When war came and young men over America volunteered to fight the Japanese, in Chinatown they

† A little while later my friend had had it forever, too.

were *all* volunteering. I don't know if Local Board No. 1 ever had to draft anyone.

Doë and I had apartment BH8—Building B, Floor 8, Apartment H—with a handsomely large living room, small bedroom, tiny kitchen and almost invisible bath. We liked it a lot, and liked most of all the fact that Knickerbocker Village really was a village, almost a small city of its own. Restaurants, bars, a co-op supermarket, newsstands, drugstore—they were all in the building. We could get to them through the underground maze without ever setting foot out of doors. And we had our friends there. Dick Wilson and his pretty new wife Jessica were in apartment EE2, across the courtyard. We didn't have to waste money on phone calls; we could wigwag to each other from window to window. In the penthouse of our own building was Willard Crosby and his wife, child and Siamese cats; a couple of buildings away was Loren Dowst. Bill and Dusty were senior editors at Popular Publications, admirable, intelligent, droll people. Other old friends turned up as tenants, and we made new friends with some of the neighbors. KV was generally a nice place to be.

That was fortunate, because I spent a lot of time there.

Like most fan groups, the Futurians had schismed. The basic power struggle was between Don Wollheim and myself. I don't remember what we were fighting about. Probably everything. At one of our meetings there was some kind of vote. I claimed my side had won, Donald claimed it was his side, and so the Futurians split apart.

We still stayed on speaking terms, but the social life in Knickerbocker Village was beginning to appeal more than the social life of the Futurians anyway. I had discovered a few new interests. Doë had introduced me to the ballet: first the Ballet Russe de Monte Carlo, with Frederic Franklin taking sixty-four bars of music to die as the slave in *Scheherazade;* then Ballet Theatre, with Anton Dolin and Nora Kaye and Eglevsky and Toumanova and all of those other great dancers in marvelous three-part performances. The format was always the same: something classical, like *Sylphides;* a virtuoso piece like *Gala Perform-ance;* something modern, like the Tudor ballet with Nora Kaye to Schoenberg's *Verklaerte Nacht.*‡ Ballet led me to listen to the music

‡ I claim the autobiographer's privilege of special pleading. Ballet Theatre's classical performances were always abbreviated into one-act form. As God is my witness, they're better that way. One of the greatest present forces for dullness in dance is the movement to give the likes of *Swan Lake* in full, evening-long tedium. There is marvelous music and marvelous dance in *Swan Lake,*

the ballets were danced to, which led me to other music; slowly I began to accumulate records and even ventured out to concerts. Even opera, although I felt then (and am sure, now) that there aren't more than five operas that are really fun to watch, and when you've named *La Bohème* and *Don Giovanni* you have to start thinking pretty hard to find the other three.*

I also discovered chess, but that is a more complicated story.

I spent most of 1941 playing as much chess against human opponents as I could in the evenings, and devoting at least a couple of hours during every day in replaying master games out of the books, practicing end games like the two-bishop checkmate and inventing new opening gambits. I had the time to do it, because for six or seven months at the end of 1941 I was unemployed. Well, actually I was a free-lance writer. But when you are a free-lance writer and the checks are slow coming in it feels a lot like being unemployed.

What had happened was that I had gone brashly up against my boss, Harry Steeger, with a threat to quit unless I got a raise from $20 a week to something really lavish, like maybe $27.50. He said no. I am not exactly sure what happened then. Either I quit or he fired me. Anyway, when I walked out of his office I wasn't working there any more.

That wasn't so bad. I estimated I could make as much writing as I could editing.† I had already begun to sell a few stories to outside markets—not only outside my own magazines, but outside the science-fiction field. In fact, I guess I did earn about twice as much from my work in those months as I had averaged in the months before. There were, however, two problems. One was that writing a story and waiting for someone to buy it and send out a check is not very much like having a payday every Friday. All free-lance writers must learn this,

---

Giselle et al., but it all fits nicely into forty-five minutes. Stretching them out to full-length ballets necessitates padding with second-rate music and irrelevant dancing. Write your congressman.

* Is there some rude iconoclastic Bing who might start doing *operas* in abbreviated groups of three?

† I get a lot of questions about how much money writers make, so maybe it is worthwhile to put a couple of facts on record. For equal work and equal ability, writers make more than editors. In my own case, I have spent nearly twenty years, aggregate, living the double life of writer and editor at the same time. In every year, the time I spent at being an editor was much more than the time I spent at being a writer. Nevertheless, my income in all of those years was much more from being a writer than from being an editor. Writing is my living; editing is a hobby.

usually at great cost to their nervous systems. The other was that I had helped myself over a temporary financial problem by buying a couple of stories from myself that I hadn't quite written yet.

So I had to get them written real fast and turn them in; and *Daughters of Eternity,* which follows, was one of them. It was published in *Astonishing Stories* for February 1942.

Daughters of Eternity

JAMES MacCREIGH

What it finally boiled down to was Earth, Mars and Venus—against the Oberonians.

Oh, there were other planets and races represented at the Peace Conference. Every nation in the Solar System was there. But the little nations, the minor powers, didn't count for much. Whatever permanent peace terms came out of the conference, they would be made by Earth, Mars, Venus—and the Oberonians.

And the Oberonians were out for war.

The Great War was just over, leaving every race decimated. I was a press attache to the Terrestrial delegation—which is really only a nicer way of saying I was a reporter. The fact that I held any kind of newspaper job was, I am proud to say, due to my work alone. But my managing to wangle the career-making assignment of covering the First Interplanetary Peace Conference can probably be traced to the fact that I am the son of Eustis Durand, Earth's World President.

None of my associates on the other papers and news services ever seemed unduly respectful to me because of my father's high position. I didn't mind; I liked it that way. It gave me a chance to know them better. And one or two of them, such as Barbara King, the Radiovox correspondent, I wanted to know real well.

Barbara came into my room just as I was eating breakfast on the morning of the fifth day of the conference. She's tall, red-headed, and has a voice that reminds you of Braunzwich's electro-viol when he plays a Chopin nocturne.

She said, "Move over, Lower-order, and pour me some coffee."

Barbara King was liable to call you most anything, in that husky, smooth voice of hers, and make you like it. But "Lower-order" was something out of the usual line of affectionate insult.

"What do you mean, 'Lower-order'?" I asked. "I like me, even if you don't."

She smiled, showing teeth that were whiter than the rays of Sirius. "Then you haven't heard the news, I take it? Well, read this!" She flipped a news-transparency into my toast.

I fished it out, blotted it, and read: *"Strictly confidential.* Report to Terrestrial delegates. Do not file. Agents operating on Rhea, former colony of Oberonian Empire, report inflammatory speeches being made, seemingly with government approval, if not actual sponsorship. Oberonian racist theories are re-emphasized. Many references are made to Terrestrials and Martians as 'Lower orders of animate matter . . . unfit for rule, good only for slaves to the Oberonian Master race'. This is propaganda in direct conflict with the anti-nationalism clauses of the Armistice. If meetings are held under government approval, would seem to indicate that dissolution of Oberonian Empire was a fraud and that undercover reorganization work is being carried on."

I tried to keep my voice steady. "Where did you get this?" I asked. "And why are you showing it to me? Your outfit would like an exclusive story on a piece of news like this. Why cut me in on it?"

Barbara sighed. "Act your age, Lee," she said reprovingly. "You won't send that to your paper any more than I would. Do you think I would have showed it to you if I thought there was any chance of its getting out? I got it from a delegate—a guy who trusts me. Even if it didn't mean getting him in trouble, I still wouldn't send that. It's hot."

She was right, of course.

"Well—" I began—and stopped.

I drank the last of my coffee and lit a cigarette before I asked, "What are we doing about it?"

Barbara shrugged. "That I don't know. If the Oberonians are up to their old tricks, it means that this conference is a failure before it gets well started. And we're all wasting our time out here." She glanced at her watch and then rose hastily.

"I've got to get going," she said. "I've got to interview Madame Lafarge—Earth's only woman delegate. Human interest stuff. I just thought you ought to know about this. Keep your eyes open when you're around the Oberonian contingent—and remember this, you owe me a favor for letting you see this."

She waved the message at me, then struck a match and ignited it. When it was burned completely she broke up the ash and went out.

"So long," she called.

"So long," I echoed thoughtfully.

I leaned back in my pneumatic chair and drew a deep breath from my cigarette. The heavy Venusian tobacco smoke made excellent smoke rings. I blew one and stared at it, trying to see through it to what lay ahead for humanity.

The Oberonian Empire had started the last war. The five planets and moons which formed their empire had been the most potent military reservoir in the history of the Solar System. They'd made only one little miscalculation when they set off the fuse that plunged the nine planets into four years of carnage. They hadn't figured on Earth's immediate and decisive entrance into the war. Venus and Mars, the original targets for their attack, they could have vanquished within months. But Earth, the untapped reserve of man-power and industries; Earth, the most highly mechanized planet of all, had for once acted with courage and immediate decision.

The Oberonian drive had been stopped. Then the war had resolved itself into a contest of duration. The planet that could hold out the longest would win. Holding out meant building new rockets to replace those destroyed by enemy fleets; meant keeping up the morale despite constant attacks by raiders, despite occasional major defeats; meant diverting all of the planets' productive resources into the channels of war.

The Tri-Planet Confederation—Earth, Mars and Venus—had won. But at a terrific cost. Ten percent of the intelligent life of the Solar System was destroyed. Some planets suffered more than others—Mercury's frightful toll is too well known to mention. Others, such as the Oberonians themselves, lost comparatively little. But every planet, belligerent or not, felt the effects of that war economically at least. And the economic toll, in the long run, was perhaps even worse than the loss of life.

The war had ended finally through a palace coup in the Oberonian government. Faced with the inescapable fact that Tri-Planet production was increasing by leaps and bounds, the Oberonians had only one recourse: to stop the war. They stopped it for good and all, it seemed. Popular pressure forced the abdication of the War-minded emperor; no new king succeeded to the throne. The Oberonian Parliament proclaimed the independence of all the colonies, the end of the Empire, and the withdrawal of all the territorial claims that had inspired the war.

That move saved the skins of the Oberonians. For the traditionally sportsmanlike Earthmen, as was to be expected, showed quick willingness to forget old wounds and to give the new regime a place in the Peace Conference. Nor was that a wrong thing to do. For the Oberonian Empire had been potent only because it was so large. Split into five separate groups, it was considerably less formidable.

Only, according to the secret message I had seen, it wasn't split at all, but was united as ever—probably by secret treaties and agreements which might even have been concluded before the formal announcement of the end of the Empire.

I lit a new cigarette from the butt of the old and tried to follow the thing through. Why would the Oberonians be anxious for a resumption of hostilities? They'd lost the last war. A new one, so soon after the first, would be hopeless. Everything was the same—wasn't it?

No! It wasn't the same at all!

For I recalled with a sinking heart the fact that Earth, and to a lesser degree Venus, had already begun the demolition of certain munitions industries. Scores of private space-yachts and freighters, appropriated by the space-navies for the war, were being stripped of their armaments and returned to their owners. The armies and navies were being demobilized, their members returning to civilian life.

The thing that was different about the present situation was the Peace Conference itself. Where before it had been common knowledge that the Oberonian Empire was a rapacious, martial group of predatory nations, now people had dismissed that menace from their minds. A project of the Conference was to have been total disarmament. Earth's government had already begun on that. If the Oberonians should fail to follow suit, it would mean. . . .

It might mean almost anything—including a new war which Earth and its allies would lose.

I flipped my cigarette away and left for the press room. It was nearly time for the day's session to begin.

I had forgotten my pass and the Press Relations Bureau was very strict about things like that. They made me go back for the pass, which was also my identification. I couldn't blame them for taking every conceivable precaution to see that unauthorized persons were kept from the council room, but I still felt vaguely angry with someone as I arrived at my sealed-in booth ten minutes late.

A Martian delegate was speaking on the horrors of war. Purely platitudinous; just one of the things that a politician likes to get on the record. I made sure the recorder-tape was running so that I could send the text to my paper, then proceeded to forget the speaker.

The Council Hall was probably the largest and most magnificent enclosed room ever built anywhere. The Peace Conference couldn't meet on any major planet because of the gravity. For political reasons, it was advisable that it not meet on any planet, lest the government of the favored world feel that it was entitled to special favor. So an entire asteroid—Juno—had been hollowed out, fitted with special sealed chambers for the delegates from each world, equipped with the newest and best equipment of every sort of communication, relaxation, comfort and efficiency.

The representatives of forty-two supposedly sovereign powers were here. Each group had its own gas-tight chamber, as luxuriously furnished as could be, each in the proper style for the beings it contained. The ammonia-men from Jupiter and Saturn sat ponderously in their rotating cells of high-pressure methane gas. The rotation provided them with the gravity to which they were accustomed; by special stroboscopic lighting devices they were able to view the outside scene as well as if they had been motionless.

The great black metal delegates from the Robot Republic stood utterly motionless in a perfect vacuum. They had no special gravity-effects; high gravity or low it made no difference to these "descendants" of the intelligent robots that had been banished from Earth and Mars scores of years back.

The Venusian representatives—there were two groups of them, one from each polar civilization—swam restlessly about in murky, tepid water.

And the Oberonians were there too, as well as the lesser delegates.

The Martian had completed his speech with an appeal for disarmament. I kept the tape running, but opened up the switch which kept me connected in direct, automatically coded radio with my paper's office on Earth. If there were going to be speeches on disarmament, I wanted to be ready to make my commentaries on them. I knew, probably better than any but a half-dozen others, how important that question had suddenly become.

An Oberonian signalled that he wished the floor. The Chairman for the day, a lank, demon-black Callistan, yielded it to him and the mechano-translators clicked and buzzed as the switch from Martian to Rhean dialect of Oberonian was made.

The Rhea-Oberonian began to speak. I couldn't hear his voice, but I had a pretty good idea what it was like—a thin, whining twitter. That was Oberonian language, in whatever dialect. The mechano-translator, of course, made impeccable English of it.

The Oberonian, viewed in the synchronized stroboscopic lighting, was an impressive sight. That race runs to height, and this member of it was no exception. He was close to fourteen feet tall, and the light gravity of his home world had allowed him to spread out. On Earth he would have weighed close to a thousand pounds.

Except for the fact that they are a dozen times bigger, Oberonians greatly resemble lemurs. Their skin is furred—a necessity in their cold home worlds. The pattern of their fur reminds me of a North American animal, *mephitis mephitica*—skunk.

That's what their politics reminded me of, too.

I was all set to forget about diplomatic secrecy and send through a hot message to my office. The Oberonian, I was sure, would disregard what the previous speaker had said, and try to get the attention of the Conference fixed on some new topic. Disarmament would be something taboo with him—if that secret report had been correct. Perhaps he would talk about it in weasel-words, or he might even denounce it openly, though that wouldn't be at all in keeping with the Oberonian foreign policy. But it ought to prove interesting.

So I leaned forward in my chair, listening to the calm, metallic voice of the mechano-translator. . . .

And twenty minutes later, when the Oberonian had finished speaking, I was still leaning forward, in a tense expectation that had somehow gone sour.

For the Oberonian hadn't evaded the issue of disarmament. Nor had he denounced it. He had, instead, presented what seemed to be a complete, efficient, and workable plan for disarmament—*plus* a proposal for an interplanetary police force with full authority to investigate every part of every planet and use any measures necessary to insure that the disarmament agreement was kept.

There might have been loopholes in the proposal—loopholes that the Oberonians were planning to wriggle out of. There might have been, and by all the evidence I'd ever heard concerning the treachery of Oberonians, there should have been. But I, who was looking for any such loopholes, who knew things that were supposed to be Oberonian state secrets, couldn't find them.

It was enough to shake my faith in Oberonian nature. I had a strong impulse to go over and brave the sub-arctic cold of their section to shake the speaker's hand and ask his apology.

It was a good thing I didn't.

There were a lot of other speeches made that day, but none of them counted for much. I walked out on them, after sending my notes and commentaries—minus the secret item—to the paper. I went back to my room and sat down to think. But I didn't get a chance. Without the formality of a knock, the door opened and Barbara King walked in. She had a companion with her—and the companion was Mercurian!

Not a live Mercurian, of course. There aren't any of those; they were exterminated to the last one in the War. This was one of the Mercurian semi-robots, the metal creatures in whose skulls were planted living Mercurian brains. Such brains came from the very highest type of Mercurian—and that was a pretty high type of individual, for the Mercurians were a brainy lot. The honor of having your brains transferred to a metal body took away from you some of the pleasant bodily functions, but it carried some boons too. A life-expectancy of a thousand of Mercurian years, an average of about fifteen hundred Earth years, went with it, as well as complete freedom from aches, pains, diseases, and all other physical frailties.

The Mercurian "spoke" first—actually, he communicated by mental telepathy.

"I had not wished to come," he said gravely. "It is against the custom of the Conference for delegates of different powers to fraternize. But your young friend here has a certain claim on me, which she exercised."

Barbara flushed. "Not against your will," she reminded him aloud. "This will be to your interest as much as to ours."

The Mercurian made no visible motion, but I received an impression of judicious agreement, as though he had nodded his great, spined plastic head.

"True," he thought compellingly. "But it is not the habit of our race to violate custom—not even the customs of others."

I was still in the dark about the purpose of the visit.

He began to explain: "Have you noticed the wording of the resolution the Rhean delegate introduced today?" he asked. "No? I thought not. It was not intended to be noticed—one little phrase. The resolution, if enacted, would totally outlaw the construction of all existing types of warships. Those which are already built would be either destroyed or irrevocably converted to peace-use spaceships. And a very efficient policing system would prevent any power from disobeying that law. I have reason to believe that the Oberonians are willing to obey that law implicitly. To the letter of the law. But only that far, no farther!"

Barbara broke in there, her hazel eyes shaded. "What he is saying, Lee, is that there's a rider on that definition of a battleship." She dug in the pocket of her coverall. "I'll read it to you. The construction is outlawed of 'all ships constructed in whole or in major part of steel, iron, a similar ferrous metal, or an allotropic form thereof, excepting' —Well, I won't read the rest. The exceptions are small ships. Do you see the catch?"

"No," I said frankly. "You can make passenger and freight ships without steel, because they have pretty easy going. But a battleship needs ray-gun armor, and that has to contain iron alloys. Nothing else is strong enough; Earth has tried practically everything else."

"*Earth* has," she flashed back. "But does it occur to you that the Oberonian Empire is not Earth? It's a good deal different—and that difference is important. The Oberonians have developed an allotropic form of mercury. It's harder than any steel yet devised. It works perfectly for ray screens. It's lighter than most steel, and it seems to have every necessary quality for making battleships. There's only one thing wrong with it, from our standpoint. At normal Earthly temperatures it's a liquid."

That was the why of the Oberonian's actions.

"Can you prove what you say?" I asked tensely. "How do you know about it?"

The Mercurian answered that. "We of Mercury have a special power for reading thoughts," he said obliquely. "It is not used ordinarily, for it would not be courteous. But now and again a situation will call for it. You'll see the delicacy of trying to prove any such statement. It would be necessary first for me to admit that I had—infringed on the privacy of the Oberonian delegate."

And that would not be good. It looked as if the situation called for some tall thinking.

I was getting ready to try and fill that order when Barbara said, "There's one thing we haven't told you yet. Besides finding out about the new construction material, he found out that what we had deduced was true. There is a secret Oberonian Empire. It's run by a dictator, not the old emperor or any of his successors. The dictator is an army fanatic, one of the generals who forced the emperor into war. We couldn't get his name, but we found out one thing. He is in a warship of the new design, somewhere in space, not a hundred thousand miles from here."

We three discussed the question for an hour or more without coming to any particular conclusion. The Mercurian, whose intelligence was unquestionable, nevertheless did not seem to be up to the problem of doing anything constructive about our dilemma. He became gloomier and gloomier as the discussion went on. Finally he left, after taking precautions so that he would be unobserved as he went back to his own quarters. He told us not to worry. The intimation was that he would take care of things for us. But I couldn't see what he could do.

I said as much to Barbara. She, surprisingly, seemed to put a lot of confidence in him.

"Don't forget, Lee, it meant a fight against all his training to come here at all. He said he'd help us and he will. I don't know what he can do, but mark my words, he'll do something."

He did something, all right. The next morning the news of what he'd done was all over Juno. Sometime during the night he'd taken a helico-ray pistol and destroyed his metal brain-case and the almost immortal brain within.

Confronted with a problem, his answer had been suicide.

A special funeral ship brought his remains back to his native planet, and an alternate delegate filled his place in the Conference until a fully accredited one could be sent from Mercury.

In the three days that it took for the new delegate to arrive from Mercury, events moved rapidly. The proposal of the Oberonian had been adopted and implemented by codes and rules suggested by delegates from every planet. An interplanetary police force had already been authorized, to be paid for and staffed jointly by all civilized planets. An iron tracer, the military secret of Callisto, had been given to all, particularly to the policing agency mentioned before. With the aid of this device, it was possible to spot an iron-bearing ship within a distance of a half-million miles, and aim your guns at it without even seeing it.

The outlook for peace would have been rosy. . . . If the Oberonians hadn't managed to develop the new metal. For every bill for disarmament presented to the Conference was only an amplification of the first one drawn up by the Oberonians. And the definition of a warship remained the same.

I dropped hints right and left to all the Terrestrial delegates I could manage to buttonhole, but my hands were tied. Barbara had asked for and received a promise of secrecy in regard to everything she'd told me. As yet, it was not quite imperative that I act immediately. Full-scale disarmament, including the dismantling of all war rockets, wouldn't be begun by Earth until the Peace Conference was over and all the agreements signed. Before they were signed, there was no great need for action and I could keep my promise. If the actual signing became imminent without any encouraging sign, I'd have to tell the whole story to any Terrestrial diplomat I could convince.

I didn't see much of Barbara in those three days. I tried hard enough but she made herself scarce. And I was kept rather busy too, so I never had a really good chance to get her alone and find out what she was planning to do.

The new Mercurian delegate came and nothing happened. I was one of the crowd of newsmen of assorted shapes and races who met him at the entrance-porte to the Halls of the Delegates when his ship landed. He was nothing special, I thought, just a typical Mercurian— and probably, I thought bitterly, as worthless as the one before him. He didn't pause for much of a personal interview, just distributed printed statements to the reporters and went off to his chambers.

But that night I suddenly found cause to remember him vividly.

I woke to find someone in my room, rummaging through my things. I rose and was about to challenge the intruder when he whirled and stared at me. It was the new Mercurian delegate!

The mind-power of the Mercurian cannot be overrated. His metal-glass eyes seemed to shine with a weird inner fire as they stared into mine. They enlarged and became more brilliant, and I found myself swirling off to sleep again. . . .

Pure hypnosis, a type impossible for a human being to exercise. But the superior mentality of the Mercurian made it possible for him to dominate my lesser mind so completely that I had to obey his unspoken command to sleep.

But the command could not have any lasting effect. It wore off, probably in a matter of seconds. As I came to again, I heard the door to my room slide gently shut.

I leaped out of bed and examined my belongings. I quickly discovered what the Mercurian had been after: my photo-key to the Press Relations Bureau.

Hastily I climbed into my one-piece coverall and followed.

No one was in sight in the corridors. I made my way quickly to the Press Relations room. I found the door open, and the night attendant asleep within.

The hall was almost totally dark, and, except for the Mercurian and myself, empty. I stared through the blurring transparencies and tried to find him. I saw him moving—yes, it was he—walking rapidly through the Callistan section to the Oberonian one beyond.

I followed. I was totally unequipped for such a venture. The Callistan section, I knew, would be all right. The air pressure would be lower and the atmosphere would have a pungent reek of rare gases, but otherwise it would be much the same as Earth's.

But the Oberonian—this was the Rhean division—section would be considerably different. Cold—frightfully cold.

So I was forced to watch his actions from a distance. He seemed to be doing something—I couldn't tell what—to the mechano-translator, by the light of a small pocket-torch, to judge by the feeble glow. Then the light went out and I could see his gleaming form coming back.

I made myself inconspicuous and allowed him to pass.

I followed him through the door to the Bureau, slipped past the again unconscious night man, and went back to bed. I immediately fell asleep. When I awoke my light-key was in its accustomed place once more.

That was the morning of the day the Oberonian Empire died once and for all. . . .

Barbara King saw the blow struck. "I was on the way from my room," she said that night while we were celebrating. "I had a little time to spare and I had an idea of what was coming, so I walked along the promenade. Lucky the Earth-section happened to be facing the right direction then. It was a big, blue flare of light. It blotted out the stars, almost blinded me."

"And it killed the Oberonian dictator," I said. "But I'm still wondering about some of the details."

I turned to the steel-bodied Mercurian who stood by, mentally benign. "I realize you could find out everything that was going on in the minds of the Oberonians by thought-reading. That's how you knew they were in tight-beam radio connection with the dictator on their new allotropic-mercury ship. And when you rigged up that super-heterodyne gadget on their secret transmitter, it started a vibration in the receiver located on the ship. I'll take your word for it that a vibration of that certain special type is all that's necessary to destroy one of their ships, by destroying the complex arrangement of the mercury atoms. But what I want to know is—how did you happen to bring the gadget with you?"

The Mercurian's thoughts turned suddenly grave. "For that we owe a debt to my predecessor, the delegate who destroyed himself. Thought transmission is normally carried on only at short distances. But by a special intense effort, thought can be made to reach any individual to whom the sender is attuned, wherever he may be, within hundreds of millions of miles. The consequences of an effort like that cause insanity to the sender.

"My predecessor—who was also my intimate friend—deliberately forced his brain to destroy itself by working it too hard. His mind reached out to me on Mercury, told me all that had happened. Then, when the first symptoms of degeneration began to be felt, he killed himself. And that served a purpose too. As a substitute for a dead man, my coming aroused no curiosity. As a diplomat, my effects were inviolate. I was able to bring in the 'gadget' with impunity."

Barbara nodded. "I was pretty sure that the Mercurian would do something."

I leaned back and lit a cigarette, feeling good. These minor powers with their mental powers were mighty handy allies.

Early in 1942 I got a telegram from my former masters at Popular Publications offering to rehire me. It was not as elevated a job as I had had before. I would not be a Real Editor, with buy-or-bounce decision-making power over my very own magazines. I would be an assistant to Alden H. Norton on his group of pulps. On the other hand there were advantages. As a Real Editor I had earned $20 a week; as a lowly assistant they were willing to pay me $35.

It required no thought. The steady paycheck was irresistible. Besides, Al Norton was a good man to work for. He had come aboard in the first place as editor of the sports magazines, had accumulated titles in the fields of mystery, horror, Western and air-war, and had inherited my two sf magazines. I was helping on all of them.

It seems to me now that they were pretty awful specimens, considered as examples of American literature. Once in a great while there was some good writing. Surprisingly, some of it was in the sports magazines; even a little in the Westerns. A few individual writers—Joel Townsley Rogers in particular struck me as stunningly good, compared to the hacks he was usually surrounded with—seemed literate. But mostly editing the stories was about as much fun as repairing sewer pipes. You could take a certain amount of pride in the skill with which you did the job, but the end product was not noble.

Pulp writers in those days had very few recognized rights. The concept that an author, any author, had a certain privilege of control over the published version of his work did not apply to them. Mostly they didn't deserve it, being pretty poor writers, but whether they deserved it or not the idea of giving them such rights never crossed any of our minds.

It was not just at Popular Publications. My friend and colleague, Horace Gold, worked for Popular's chief competitor at the time, a firm known as the Thrilling Group. There each day's work by an editor was checked over by the boss. He didn't bother to read the stories. He did carefully assess the quantity of pencil markings on each page. If there wasn't a lot, the editor was called on the carpet. No one did that to us at Popular, but the stories provided an imperative of their own.

The air-war magazines were particularly awful; some of them were written entirely on contract, by single authors. Editing them was agony. When the two magazines written by contract authors were killed because of the paper shortage of World War II, the two authors each opined that they would have to find new markets. I'll try the *Saturday Evening Post,* said one of them, while the other decided he would change over to mystery novels, because he thought there would be money in the film rights. We snickered behind our hands—but the *Saturday Evening Post* did indeed buy everything the first author sent them, at about twenty times as high a rate as we had ever paid him; and the other's mysteries have, in fact, been made into at least two very successful films.

As John F. Kennedy was wont to remark, it is not a fair world.

With competition like the slop I was editing every day, I was emboldened to try to write for markets outside the science-fiction field, and it turned out that I could sell them without much trouble. The first sales I made were love poems. Like most literate teen-agers, I had put a few together to impress girls. It was a revelation to me that people would give me money for them. Other revelations were in store. I had sold a love poem which began:

> You never knew I waited for your footsteps in the spring
> Or counted fifty at your door before I dared to ring. . . .

I was paid about a dime a line for these things, which came, as you can see, to twenty cents for the sample above. Then the editor took pity on me. She was a stocky, good-natured ex-circus aerialist named Jane Littell, and she pointed out that the same poem could have been written:

> You never knew
> I waited for
> Your footsteps in the spring,
> Or counted fifty
> At your door
> Before I dared to ring. . . .

instantly tripling my income.

There wasn't much income in love poetry at best, though. I liked Janie, but I couldn't bring myself to write *stories* for her love pulps; nor, ever, have I been able to write a Western. But I tried all the rest. My card file for that period is laced with titles like *Cure for Killers* and *R.A.F. Wings East*. What the pulps demanded was tightness of plot, action and pace. I learned a lot about that; maybe more than was good for me. And I think some of that pulp tightness begins to show up even in the sf I wrote around that time, like *Earth, Farewell!*, which appeared in the February 1943 issue of *Astonishing Stories*.

Earth, Farewell!

JAMES MacCREIGH

1

Lords of the Vassal Earth

Collard came in to see me a while ago. He told me that they were nearly ready. I have an hour and a little; then it will be my turn.

I don't know what will happen. I think I will die when they put me under the rays of the machine and try to make me a creature of theirs, puppet to their renegade wills; when they try to make me flout the law and the wisdom of the Others. I want to die now, but the strength that the Others gave me forbids it. I can't die by my own hand. I tried poison. It doesn't work. I wish I could die.

But I have an hour yet. If at this eleventh hour something should happen and the rule of the masters be restored, I want to tell my story for those who will come after. Not for my own sake; for the sake of those who will be loyal to the Others.

I think it is deliberate, on Collard's part, that I can see the shadow of the machine from where I am. Through the transparency of the door that I cannot open I see a hall, and through a window in that hall leap in the lights from the flaming city around. And by coming close to the crystal door, peering to one side, I can see the machine, limned in the dancing lights of the flames. I can hear the whir of it, its ominous drone, as the others like me are brought to it—and shattered by its radiant strength, their brains warped.

I am the strongest, and that is some consolation. They are saving me for the last. I think they are letting me see the machine to weaken me.

I shall not be weakened. I have writing materials; I will use them. Listen—

To make sure there will be no sort of treachery, the Other People take full charge of the selection. The human governments on Earth are not strong and not well organized, but they are tricky enough to try to sneak someone into the Four and the Four who will not be entirely loyal to the masters. You know how the Earth governments are. It makes one ashamed he's an Earthman.

President Gibbs gave me the official send-off. I knew that I was to be selected as one of the Four and the Four, of course. I saw my marks on the honor list, and then the Other People's emissaries had been swarming all over the neighborhood for a couple of days, questioning my father and those who knew me. But it didn't seem real, somehow, until I got the sealed-channel wire that ordered me to zip down to Lincoln and see the President.

Things had been growing worse for a long time. There have always been troublesome crackpots on Earth, as long as we've had a history. Before the Others came, with their laws of science and sanity, it was even worse, of course.

But I'd never seen it as bad as this. In the tube to the rocketport I was accosted by a man, shabby and furtive, who seemed to know by my appearance and possibly by secret, underground ways, that I had been chosen. There was fierce urgency in his voice as he spoke to me. What he said was absurd—gibberish about the rights of humans to rule their own planet, about the intolerance and rigidity of the laws of the Others—but there was a certain strength in the way he said it.

I ordered him to leave me alone. Had there been a lawman around, I should have turned him in for speaking treason—though with the corruption of the human courts, beyond doubt he would have gone free. I told him what I thought of him and his demented kind. I tried to explain to him, reasonably, how much good the Others had done Earth. How they had ended the folly of war and international dispute; the absurdity of democracy and so-called free elections. . . .

Well, he was not moved, nor had I expected him to be. But he saw, I know, from the way I spoke and the positive assurance in my manner, that I was no weakling.

I thought there were the beginnings of tears in his eyes as he turned away. But all the way down to Lincoln, for the full two hours of the journey, I was conscious that I was being observed. It only ended when I presented my order-wire to the armed human guards at the door and was admitted to the Presidential Mansion.

And then I was too absorbed to think much about the almost open insurrection that was threatening Earth. For the guards conducted me to a door and I walked in.

I'm afraid I succumbed to a little emotion. One of the Other People was there—and an important one, too! You know that there are only seventy-seven of them on the Earth anyhow—never more, never less—and they keep pretty busy all the time. They have little time for humans, with their constant investigation into Earth's possibilities and resources and history—all, of course, for the good of humanity, despite Collard's lies.

It's a wonderful thing about the Other People—they always work, one hundred per cent of the time. Human beings are handicapped because they have to sleep, sure. But even their waking hours many of them spend in totally useless things—playing games, writing books, reading, talking—great Strength, how much talking they do! I'm human-born, I realize, and I shouldn't be flattering myself. But even the Other People have said that I am almost more like a member of their own race.

That is a proud thing to remember—though the mind machine may blank that memory out for me within the hour, or make me hate that memory. It may make me human again.

I fear that.

But there was an Other in President Gibbs' mansion. I'd seen the Others before, one or two of them. But this one was the first I'd seen that had the wide orange circles around his irises to show he was a member of the king class. Tall, gray-skinned, looking as though he were constantly overbalanced by the weight of the flapping, ponderous fat-wings that grew out of his spindly back, he was an absorbing sight. They say that the Others used to swim around in the water of their home planet, long ago. I don't know, but those fat-wings were not made to work in any atmosphere, even the thin one of their light, dying world. They look something like a seal's flippers, but rigidly muscular and utterly boneless.

As a member of the king class, the Other had a name. It was Greg. He said, "You are Ralph Symes. You have been chosen as one of the Four and the Four. Come up before me."

I made my feet move, and walked up to him. I stood before him and he looked at me out of his tawny, orange-rimmed eyes. He was seated in a crystal, thronelike chair, but it was on a pedestal and his eyes were level with mine. They looked deep inside me, dizzyingly deep. They penetrated—Strength, how they penetrated my innermost consciousness! There was a heavyness in those tawny eyes, and a sort of dark thing—a chill, cutting thing that had me swinging by my long, furry tail from some antediluvian tree, while my ape-brothers chattered and giggled around me.

Then I remembered that I was human only by the mischance of birth, and one of the Four and the Four by choice. Then I could look back at him. Not insolently. If I had been insolent to Greg I would have died at his hand then and there—or at my own. But I could look into his eyes and see that the darkness was the shadow of a mind so superior that I couldn't see into it, and that the heavyness was strength, harsh and raw, but still just to those who, like me, served it.

Then President Gibbs stood up. I hadn't seen him before, though he was an impressive figure for a human. He had wanted to be of the Four and the Four in his youth, and had almost succeeded. Only a physical weakness had prevented him from becoming of the elect. But he had become president later, which was something of a consolation.

He said, "Citizen Ralph Symes, you have been honored by selection as one of the Four and the Four. You have subscribed to the code of the Vassal Earth. You know the penalties if, as a member of the Four and the Four, you fail to carry out the wishes of Greg and his honored fellows. You will begin your course of training within the next half hour. One hundred days thereafter you will be given your instructions. What they will be I do not know, nor does any human save the Four and the Four." He handed me a large, ornate box, paused a moment before he went on, looking at me thoughtfully.

"This," he said at length, "is your crown. Cherish it. Now it is only a symbol of your status, but when it is attuned to your mind and the power is released at the end of the hundred days, remember—it is the most powerful shield and weapon ever conceived. Never use it carelessly."

Greg, always working, not taking part in the discussion just then, had been doing intricate and mysterious things with a small knobbed apparatus on the arm of his crystal chair. He looked up from it after a second and stared at me.

He said, "They are ready for you. Take him to the ship, President." He almost emphasized the "president," but not quite. It was with his thin-whiskered cheeks that he pointed it up, made it a humorous title that you might give a child. His lips quivered and drew together, almost in a smile.

The Others never quite smile, though. Not like humans, who laugh and laugh at nothing.

I would have gone wherever he commanded, but I'm afraid I hesitated. I looked around and was conscious of what I had missed in the quick excitement of this thing. Just the President, Greg and myself; no one else was in the great chamber.

"Pardon," I said. "Forgive me. I do not mean to question *you,* but when will the presentation—"

Greg's cheeks twitched again, then were abruptly still. "Presentation?" he said, so softly that I almost missed the note of steel in his voice. "What do you mean?"

"Why," I floundered, "the presentation—the investiture. When I am given my crown. My induction as one of the Four and the Four, when the assembly is held, and the rejoicings. Forgive me," I said, "but I had expected—"

President Gibbs interrupted, "Due to the unsettled conditions this year—" but Greg waved him aside.

"There will be no formal presentation," said Greg, and the steel was naked now. "None at all. You have your crown. Do you question me?"

Disappointment swarmed up inside me. It was what I had always dreamed of. I could hardly bear to have it taken from me. The crowds, the cheers, my father, excited, seeing me for the last time. . . .

But I was now one of the Four and the Four, and I couldn't have human emotions. I said, "Forgive me," for the third time.

That was all.

We left Greg there, sitting and fumbling with his chair-arm apparatus. The President escorted me out—and *he* opened the door for *me.*

I got into the zip-ship that was waiting, and was seated in a sealed compartment. I heard the rockets roar a second later. The ship zoomed off.

I fell asleep shortly. I think a hypnophone was planted in the chamber, for I woke up in a strange bed in a strange room. But before I slept, I was thinking, thinking of the strangeness of the fact that the Other People had permitted a break in their routine. The presentation ceremonies were a part of the whole business of the Four and the Four, part of the rule of the Other People over Vassal Earth.

The unsettled conditions that President Gibbs had mentioned must go even deeper than I thought.

I woke up in a strange room. . . . Well, I am no traitor, though I may be about to become one, here in this room with a city burning about me and an empire dying. They shall not make me one, whatever devilish—or human—torture they bring to bear on me. Even though Collard has turned renegade to the Four and the Four, even though I have added to his disgrace and mine by not killing him when I might have, I shall not betray what I have sworn to revere.

What I learned in those one hundred days I am bound by oaths on the linked triangles of the Other People not to reveal. I will not tell, though Collard may.

I learned much. I am no longer quite human, even in appearance. Great strength is mine now, and I, like the Others, need never sleep. Solid, tormented days we spent in the ray chambers, I and the other three young men who were chosen with me. Had you seen us before the one hundred days, seen the four of us together, you might have thought we were brothers. The rigid tests of the masters insured that, with their emphasis on great height, strength and vitality.

But when the hundred days were through—we were identical; stamped of the same mold, forged in the same fires of growth, milled on the same sharp edge of learning.

The animal pinkness of human flesh left us, and our skin took on a greenish cast, as chlorophyll cells were absorbed into us. We can swallow up pure light energy and convert it, like a plant, to heat and force. Our flesh was transmuted in other ways, to great tensile strength. Oh, we have to eat still. But the food is only for the replacement of cells which die and wear off, not for energy.

The one hundred days passed quickly. Collard and I, and two others who do not matter, being dead, were the four youths. The Four and the Four are not all trained together. The four maidens are taught and rebuilt to be simple recorders, animate libraries for the use of the Others.

They also are placed in ray chambers, but the rays that flood their bodies, tear them down and rebuild them, are of a different order. The retentive capacity of their brains is increased, and the other functions become lesser. Physically they are not changed, for they need not be. The wise Others do not tamper with what need not be changed.

This is what is done with the four maidens. I may tell it, for it is no secret. Collard will be on his way back to Earth soon, arrowing through the void at mind speed, the first human to make the trip in that direction.

I pray that the Others will be prepared for him. But whether they are or not this secret is out.

The Others on Earth are constantly studying, always learning. All men know what they study—the Earth, and its unexplored potentialities. What they learn is telepathically transcribed on to the ray-sensitized brains of the four maidens. The maidens learn to be telepathic in their one hundred days. They receive a burden of knowledge, four of them each year.

And when they have absorbed all that has been learned by the Others in their year, they are sent back to the green world from which the Others came.

The four youths bring them there; that is our destiny.

I shall not tell you how, for if Collard dies that must remain a secret. But the crowns we wear have much to do with it. They are, as Gibbs said, a perfect weapon and a perfect shield. They are also a perfect vehicle. With their aid we can spurn gravity, cast the Earth aside, cleave the thin air at light speed. Nor need we breathe, and so we can travel the space between the planets.

Enough of that. I can still see the machine in my mind's eye, and the flames still dance above the stricken city. My hour, too, is running short.

The one hundred days ended, and we were not men any more. We were gathered together, the four of us, plus the two Others who had supervised our training. One of the Others spoke, bid us take off the human garments we wore and dress in purple-red coveralls, ornamented with the linked triangles of the Others. Self-heating, perfectly insulated, these would prevent our absorbing too much energy from the naked rays of the sun while still in Earth's vicinity, yet would keep us warm when we attained outer space, en route to the far star around which spun the planet of the Others.

While he was talking, a zip-ship sighed into the air overhead and slowly settled down beside us, the wide purple fans of its underjets lighting up the darkness all around. Overhead the calm stars twinkled. There was no moon.

A couple of humans—special police, clad in tunics and emblems like ours, but without the crowns—were running the ship. One opened the port and stepped out. His companions inside handed limp white figures out to him—the four maidens. He deposited them gently on the ground. Then, without a word to any of us, he got back in the ship. The port closed and it lay quiescent, waiting for the girls to be removed so that its jets could flare without cremating them on the spot.

There were no last-minute instructions. We knew what we were to do. Collard and I and the other two walked over to the unconscious, unbreathing maidens, whose life-processes had been suspended by the science of the Others to fit them for the journey through airlessness.

We picked them up, clasped them under our arms. They were light burdens, for they were only girls. Attractive girls, surpassingly beautiful, even, for only superior physical and mental specimens get into the Four and the Four.

The Others stood and watched us, without words. There was nothing they needed to tell us. Collard was the leader, he with his strange streak of humanity in him, human strength that did not have the chill rigidity of the strength of the masters, but could bend and give way where their strength broke, and then return; Collard looked around at the remainder of us and saw that we were ready; Collard seized the leadership, and it was he who said the word of command.

And all of us, four youths and maidens, set out on an incredible journey. Each man of us raised up his arm. Each of us willed the pull of gravity to relinquish its hold, denied the existence of weight and Earth-pull. We rose into the air with gathering speed.

A moment, and we were shrieking through the dense air of the lower strata, not looking down or back, but conscious that the Earth was dwindling underneath. A moment after that and the air was a thin, weak thing that no longer held us back. Coldness began to seep in. Our lungs worked hard, until the soothing, tingling power of the crowns and the heat suits took hold, and warmth and air were luxuries we did not need.

And then, not abruptly, there was no air.

The trip may have been long; I have no way of knowing, for the time was not like the passage of hours or days on a planet. Onward we fled, faster until even the stars were crawling about in space, and we could see them slide slowly behind us. Their colors changed and disappeared. Behind us the stars were red; ahead, deep, smoky violet. And then, quickly, all the stars were ahead of us, with different colors being the only thing that showed where they really were, as we caught up with and passed the light rays that came from behind. Faster than light —infinitely faster—we went, while the stars crept slowly around and winked from violet to red as we fled past them.

Then we knew by the signs we had been taught to watch for that we had arrived. And our wills, greater than human and multiplied by the crowns we wore, changed their impulse and concentrated on slowing us, stopping us.

Picture us there in space, the Four and the Four. Four men whose only life was in the mind for that time, whose bodies might as well not have been. And the girls we carried across the void, unmoving and rigid as ourselves. . . .

But we slowed and slowed more, and a green planet detached itself from the twinkling cosmos of stars that again were beating at us with white rays and blue, and red and yellow and all of the normal colors. The green planet grew larger.

It might have been a dozen seconds, and it might have been a thousand years since our journey had begun. But there we were, standing on a strange blue-green earth, moving our arms and legs again, breathing once more. And unhurriedly there walked toward us one of the Others, moving without strain on this light world, looking at us as he came. He had been waiting. He had known when we would come. . . .

2

Green Planet of Madness

Collard looked in at me. I cannot have much time left, by the expression on his face. There was pity there, and a curious friendliness that frightens me. He must believe that his mind machine will warp my brain, make me betray the Others. Absurd! Why, his machine is compounded of the science of the Others and their superhuman artisanry. He stole it from them, as he stole the strength and intellect they gave him in his training for the Four and the Four. He—

It does not matter. I must be brief.

There were bad things even on the planet of the Others. I was prepared for that, for I knew that nothing was perfect, not even in the wisdom of the masters. Collard was not prepared for it, with his curious human optimism that could not be wiped out of him; with his impossible ideals.

The one who had been waiting for us when we landed asked no questions, made no remarks. He beckoned us to follow him, and we carried the girls into a strangely un-ornate building, that looked as though it had been poured in magenta glass around the thing it was built to house. It had odd shapes and angles, curious wavy buttresses cascading away from the main structure, but they were not for decoration. You could see that they were needful to the purpose of the building.

Inside—there were rows upon rows of slabs, many empty and waiting. But most were in use. At the head of each of them there was a mind machine, like the mind machine the Others used to read and mold thoughts in the tests for the Four and the Four, like the machine that Collard cannot wait to use on me. At the foot was a cylinder of crystal, and a box under each cylinder that droned and pulsed. And in the space between, on each slab, there lay the figure of a girl of the Four and the Four.

A hundred of them at least there were, in this one room. There are four each year, and the pick of Earth's young girls for a quarter of a century lay somnolent on plastic, molded slabs there before us.

Many of them were no longer beautiful. Some were no longer human.

Each cylinder of crystal at the slab-foot was filled with a bluish red fluid that was blood, and each cylinder had two flexible crystal tubes running out from it, sinking themselves at the ends into the flesh of the girls. That was what gave life to the girls who had been of the Four and the Four. That and nothing else, for they were unmoving, rigid. The eyes of each girl were closed, and only slowly did their bosoms rise and fall; only slowly did the pale veins pulsate in their throats.

The Other gestured, and we carried the girls in, put them on empty slabs at the end of the long row. We left them there, and another of the masters came in and opened a case that held sharp steel knives. He took one out, slowly, carefully, and walked over to the slabs with their new occupants. At the door Collard paused, turned, looked back. The little muscles under his cheeks were quivering and his jaw was rigid.

I touched his arm. He looked at me uncomprehendingly, then turned and walked out with the rest of us.

Two more of the Others passed us going in.

I did not look back to see what they did. But they wore mind-reading crowns, and I believe they were going already to tap the reservoir of knowledge we had brought them.

That first thing sowed a seed of doubt in Collard. It did not in me, for I was and still am aware that humans, even those of the Four and the Four, live only by the tolerance of the Others and at their disposal. Still, it was—not pleasant.

What hurt even me, and what turned Collard into the wretched creature of rebellion that he is now, was something that happened only slowly and took a long time to penetrate. It came to us gradually that we had done our job. We were no longer necessary. That for which we had been chosen and trained had been accomplished, and we were through.

Oh, the Others gave us work to occupy us. I tended a machine in a great hall where a thousand wheels revolved and shifted direction. It was work that was pleasant, and it was necessary for someone to do it, for even the best machine must have a brain to back it up.

Collard had work, too. With delicate, tiny spectroscopes and other miraculous tools he had to sort and analyze specimens of minerals from the deep subsurface regions of their own planet that the Others were still exploring. A machine could have done Collard's job, but there was no machine. And there were too few samples to warrant constructing one, while a human could do the work.

Those two who had come with us had work also. And we met more than a score of other men in that city to which we were taken, a short distance from the crypt where the dead-alive girls lay on their plastic slabs, their minds open to the probing of the Others. Only a little more than a score of men were there, though, and they could not tell us what had happened to the men who were missing.

Our jobs kept us busy. But they were—unsatisfactory. What we did could have been done by anyone on the human Earth.

Those who had been on the green planet for the longest time showed clearly that they had realized their unimportance, and were hurt by it. There were lines in their faces, bleakness in their eyes.

They would not talk much, those who had been longest on the green planet. Not to me. But Collard was with them whenever he and they were not working. Always they were talking in low tones that became silent when I came near.

A dozen weeks, in the green world's time, that went on. Collard spoke to me hardly at all, though often I saw him watching me as though he were about to say something. He never did.

Then he disappeared.

Five of the older men went with him. They walked out of our living quarters to work—and never returned.

The Others came around several times then to look us over, murmuring and clicking to themselves in their incomprehensible tongue. And I saw that other men were beginning to show lines curving around the corners of their eyes, to keep silent and look watchfully at everything that went on. For days it was clear that the Others were giving us unwonted attention. Wherever I went there were always one or two of them somewhere about, working at something but looking at me from time to time, almost speculatively, almost with apprehension. From the men I quartered with, I learned that they had the same experience. I could not understand—

Then I saw Collard again.

I was walking to work, as the Others preferred us to do. We could have flown by the telekinetic mind power our crowns gave us, but they thought it better that we walk always, to prevent our muscles from atrophying through disuse. My way lay by the great mausoleum where slept the girls of the Four and the Four, ready for the giving of information when the Others wanted it.

I had been resting for a while, an hour or two. It had been the first time in several days. It was about an hour before dawn. Still dark, I could nevertheless see a hint of the pure white rays of the green planet's sun silhouetting the mountains on the horizon, twenty miles away. I looked at them, without much interest. . . .

Then abruptly I did become interested. Half a dozen flickering, dodging black spots, winking with faint white flame now and again like monstrous fireflies, spun about in the sky somewhere between the mountains and me. As I watched they grew larger, bearing down on me at great speed. They were humans like myself. The lights they bore were the streams of force from their crowns, surging out as they drove themselves up in great bounds, then fell freely forward until they lost momentum and drove up again. They dared not, of course, use the full thrust of their crowns in the atmosphere.

What were five men doing, flitting about the sky in such haste, using their crowns against the wishes of the Others?

I watched. They drove on till they were directly overhead, then dropped at the end of one of their sweeping parabolas until they were almost on the ground. A faint thread of white flame leaped out from the outstretched arm of each, and they gently touched ground.

Quickly they scattered out, running. Three of them made for the great building that housed the unconscious girls, shining in the starglow dead ahead. Another stood where he was, staring around, dragging a thing from his belt that looked weaponlike, sinister. The fifth came pelting madly in my direction.

He saw me then and brought up short. "Symes!" he said.

It was Collard. I was speechless. I saw that he was holding one of the weapons. It was a blaster like those carried by the deputies of the Others on Earth, but larger and much more deadly-looking, glinting evilly in the starlight. It was not pointed at me, but dangled slackly from his hand. *What does he need one of those for?* I wondered. In his crown lay the seeds of greater destruction than a blaster could wreak. It did not occur to me that, against the Others who constructed them, the crowns were impotent. . . .

"Symes," he said. "Symes, I'm glad to see you. Are you one of us?"

"One of you?" I repeated. "I don't—"

His face fell. "I see," he said slowly. "I thought for a moment— Well, it was absurd. Symes," he said, and his hand swung up with the blaster leveled at me, "I'm going to have to inconvenience you. Take off your crown! And don't try to blast me with it—the gun will go off!"

Well, I know I should have made the effort. My life is nothing— much less than nothing, compared with what I might have saved had I hurled the destroying force of my intellect at Collard in that moment. I might have saved an empire if I had dared. I am willing to die at the command of the least of the Others, for any reason they care to give or for none. I should have died then, by willing Collard out of life and letting his weapon annihilate me. But I hesitated.

And then it was too late, for the other human with a gun had seen us, and came running up. With the two of them there I could not destroy either, for their crowns reinforced each other, made them invulnerable to my lone will.

Unwillingly, I reached up and took the crown from my head, handed it to Collard.

He stared at me a second, and his eyes held a hint of that curious expression I had seen there before that meant that he held a strange regard for me, would not willingly do me harm if he could avoid it. He was clearly speculating, coming to a decision. Then the light died out of his eyes and he dropped my crown abruptly to the ground, stamped it savagely into disintegration with one heavy foot.

I must have cried out, for Collard said swiftly, "This is too important, Symes. I can't take a chance that you might get the crown back. You've been indoctrinated too thoroughly, believe too firmly in the righteousness and perfection of the masters. You wouldn't believe me, even though I proved to you what I can prove. Even though I showed you that the Others are not the protectors and benevolent friends of humanity—but tyrants who plan to destroy us!"

I laughed, but there was no humor in this thing. Collard was dangerous and insane. I said sharply, "Don't be a fool, Collard. What you say is a lie, and I must report you for it. But even if it weren't, what difference would it make? The Others—"

"The Others are glorious and their will is beyond question," Collard finished for me. "Whatever they wish must be. . . . I knew it would do no good."

The other man, who had been watching us intently, said, "We're wasting time, Collard. They'll be ready soon, and the ship will be here."

Collard nodded. Still to me, he said, "You'll have to come with us, Symes. Either that, or I'll kill you now. I don't want to do that."

His eyes were hard as the vacuum between the stars, and I did not want to die. There might come a chance. . . .

"All right," I said. "I'll come along. Where?" There was no point in arguing with him, since he was mad.

With the gun he gestured toward the building ahead where slept the girls. To the other man he said, "Stay here. I don't think there will be any trouble. They must be nearly ready by now."

I walked ahead of him to the building. We went inside, and it took a moment for my eyes to adjust to the soft light inside, after the darkness of the night without. Then I saw that which was horrible.

A group of Others, three of them, stood in awful silence by the wall, facing it, their backs covered by a human with a blaster. The other two men were working busily at the blood-tanks that fed the unconscious maidens, opening them at the top and pouring into each a few drops of fluid from a crystal flask. Not all of the girls were so treated, the older ones being spared.

When they had finished this strange procedure, having doctored the plasma of forty maidens or more, they returned swiftly to the first. Not a glance did they spare for Collard or me, beyond a single incurious look as we entered. They must have had full confidence in him and his judgment, and they were obviously working against time. They totally ignored the savage, silent backs of the three Others.

One of the two raced into another chamber, returned wheeling a portable machine whose purpose I could not guess. Quickly I learned, though, for he dragged a tube ending in a sort of funnel from the interior of the machine, pressed it to the face of the first maiden in line.

His companion took a quick glance at the color of the blood-fluid in the tank—which was reddening, becoming more like the blood of a normal human—then leaped to the head of the slab and, with an abrupt motion, jerked the ends of the tubes from where they were imbedded in the girl's pale shoulders!

I might have jumped forward—I must have started involuntarily, and perhaps I cried out. It was too horrible, almost blasphemous! But Collard said sharply, "Hold on!" and I felt the muzzle of his blaster thrust into my back. I slumped back, knowing that this was not the time. I prayed that the Others beside the wall, with their superhuman senses, would know that I was not of this terrible conspiracy, that I was determined to do what I could to bring Collard and the others to punishment.

I saw at once what the wheeled machine was for. Just as the one human tore the blood-tubes from the girl's flesh, the other touched a stud on the machine, and it began to sigh and pulse rhythmically. I saw the girl's breasts rise and fall, spasmodically, then more regularly. The first man had a finger on her pulse, and after a second he nodded. They stopped the machine, wheeled it to the next girl, repeated the process.

It was frightful. Blasphemous. The Others, in their wisdom, had brought these maidens from Earth, with a mind full of knowledge in each, knowledge that they wanted and so should have. Here were members of the most sacred body of humans ever to exist—the Four and the Four, chosen by the Others to bring this knowledge to them—deliberately destroying the fruits of the mission for which they had been selected! My mind reeled; I thought desperately of a million things I might do to stop this madness. But there was nothing, not yet.

The awakened girls were sitting up, walking around, with dazedness in their eyes. They seemed afraid, but not of the two men who had awakened them. Always and always their looks went to the Others standing by the wall, motionless as three statues, even their fat-wings ceasing to ripple. There was terror in the eyes of the girls when they saw the Others, naked and unashamed terror.

I wondered at the Others, standing there so still. It was incredible that they should not make an effort to halt what was going on.

The timing of the renegades was splendid. What they had been given by the Others in the way of keen intellect and sharp sense, they put to full use in their revolt. Just as the last of the treated maidens was awakening there came a soft purring from overhead. I looked out the door just in time to see a great robot-operated cargo ship lowering itself gently to the ground on its jets. The cargo hatch swung open, and a man jumped out, came running over. The guard Collard had left came running too, and all five of the renegade humans—all but the one who guarded the Others and kept a watchful eye on myself—began herding the bewildered girls into the yawning hatch of the ship.

They were all in, and so was I, and so were the renegades, except for the one who guarded the three Others and was backing toward us watchfully, gun in hand, when—

The Others struck!

That was what the three masters had been doing, so stiff and rigid there against the wall. That was what had been their weapon and defense.

The brains of the Others are mighty. Without the aid of the crowns, with only the inborn intellect they possess, they can by a tremendous effort of will communicate directly, mind to mind, among themselves. It is a hard thing for even them, and it requires a concentration impossible except under the urgency of a great crisis.

They had done it—had summoned help!

Far above us, a cloud of wan stars appeared in the sky, so high that they were not even pinpoints but merely a blending glow of light. Collard, standing in the hatch, saw them first. It took a second for him to realize what they were; then he acted at top speed.

He shouted to the man backing toward us, who spun immediately and dashed into the ship. Collard swung the hatch shut and at once the man who had usurped the place of the robot pilot touched the cams that sent the ship into the sky. Vertically up for a couple of seconds, then flashing forward at immense speed, we fled.

"Zip-ships!" Collard yelled. "A whole flock of them—and they're diving down on us, trying to crash us! We'll have to get out of here!"

The ship was traveling at an incredible pace already, the plume of the rocket jets behind us stretching back for half a mile. And our speed was growing rapidly as the man at the controls ruthlessly jammed on every erg of power. But through the transparent skyport overhead I could see other jets flashing brighter as the robot pilots of the massed ships that followed swerved their course, arced around to follow us as we streaked along. They had the advantage of altitude; gravity was helping their straining jets to beat our speed—but we had a human brain to direct our ship. I cursed the man at the controls, planned a thousand ways to reach him and crash the stolen ship into the ground. But there was always the blaster in the hand of the guard, and it was pointed at me.

Collard tore his eyes from the ships that raced down on us from overhead and leaped to the side of the man at the controls. He spoke urgently, gesticulating, and the man nodded. A quick gesture of his hand on the levers, and our ship spun end-over-end, looped up and over and was backtracking in a split second. Again he touched the lever, and the ship spun about in a quarter turn, always going up. The robot mechanisms could never quite keep up to his hair-trigger reactions; each maneuver brought us up a little higher, then a little lower and farther behind. The ship reeled and bucked till I found my hard flesh bruised from being jolted against the unyielding walls, and always we were nearer to safety.

We had run a full circle, and were back above the sleep-palace again, plunging in the direction of the city of the Others when a new flight of ships appeared dead ahead, arrowing at us. Their jets were invisible now, in the gathering light of day, and only the dawnlight glinting off their polished hulls revealed them. Collard spun around and saw more ships behind, and still another flight racing over the horizon at us from one side.

We had a moment's grace, until the flights of robot-planes should coalesce. Then it would end.

With exultation I saw the inevitability of our destruction, without fear for my own life, which was surely doomed. But Collard saw what was ahead too—and Collard acted.

He lipped a word to the pilot, and there was instant comprehension in the man's eyes. Grimly he touched another lever, one that was not on the flight-control bank, one that had nothing to do with driving the ship.

The floor fell out from under us, and we were dropping, all of us, all but Collard and the pilot. The pilot had released the cargo compartment, let it drop from the ship, while the empty hulk raced on with a spurt of speed as the compartment ceased to drag at it. Under us the feeble flares of the braking rockets, designed for emergencies only, went into operation. But still we were falling, fifty of us in a thin-walled thing that was never meant for flight. Our speed was reduced, we had a chance to survive—but we were falling.

Through the open end of the compartment, where the air was whistling past as we fell, we could see the ship streaking onward, looking strangely skeletal with a section out of the middle of it. We saw it swerve in its course as the onrushing flight of robot ships stabbed at it. It dodged madly, fled almost through the midst of them. It got through the first wave of them, a dozen or more, and then it was over the city.

The end was there, for it was ringed by robot ships. It screamed up in a short zoom that broke as it nosed over and plunged for the ground, its jets blazing behind it. It was heading for one of the towers of the Others, the central tower in which lay great and mysterious mechanisms—for what purpose they operated, I did not know.

I thought I saw two tiny black figures, jetting white light of their own, flung away from the diving ship in mid-air.

Then it struck. A volcano of energy flared up from the stricken tower, dimming the light of the risen sun for a second of ultimate violence. As it settled, smaller lights of explosions puffed up all about, one at a time, then by dozens. The robot ships were crashing, plunging into the ground as if their automatic pilots had lost control!

I darted a glance below us, where we were coming down with too much speed in a plaza on the outskirts of the city of the Others. The ground was rushing up at us, too fast. I had a quick, insane glimpse of figures—figures that were not men, but the Others—huddled on the ground in distorted attitudes all over the square. Strangely, they made no attempt to rise, or to escape the down-plunging hulk we were in.

Abruptly, a group of jets on one side of our compartment spurted wildly, then were dead. The cubicle lurched wildly, then pinwheeled, the jets no longer keeping us up but spinning us end over end as we dropped to the closed ground. There was a splintering sound of cataclysm. My head struck against a wall and then there was blackness. We had come to earth.

3

Awakening in Hell

Collard was standing over me when I woke up, his eyes filled with that familiar mixture of anxiety and mistrust. His crown was not on his head, but a blaster was jammed negligently in his belt and his right hand was never far from the butt of it.

He said, "You're not hurt. You can thank the Others for that. Five of the girls were killed, but it takes a lot to bother a man of the Four and the Four. Just take a minute and rest up. I want to talk to you."

I felt like I'd been beaten with clubs, but I pushed myself up and looked around. What I saw was fantastic—absurd—frightful! All about there lay corpses, the bodies of the Others. They were dead, but without a mark on them, as though they had perished in some weird pandemic. I could not understand.

I looked at Collard. "You've killed them," I said, but it was not an accusation, for I simply could not believe that it had happened. I had never seen a dead master before; I had not known that they could die.

He shook his head. "No," he said cryptically. "The Others are still alive."

"Alive?" I gasped. "But—"

"Their bodies are dead," he said carefully. "At least, they're dead as any machine is dead, when the power is turned off. The Others themselves—their minds and egos—are . . . Well, look." He held out one hand to me, showed me a capsule of coppery metal. "This," he said solemnly, "is what you are so devoted to. This is one of the masters."

I reached up automatically, touched it. It was curiously chill, as though it had been in outer space for weeks. I fondled it, looked at it. . . . Then what Collard had said penetrated.

"You fool," I said. "What are you—"

He held up a hand, took back the coppery capsule.

"I'm not lying," he sighed, "but I didn't expect you to believe me. Well, let me tell you anyhow. The Others were robots. Where they came from, how they came into being, perhaps they could tell you, though I doubt it. Certainly, I can't. But all they were was clever machines—oh, made of organic materials, for the most part, yes. But a machine can be organic in composition. The robots were activated from without, supplied with energy from the central sending station that we crashed into and annihilated. When the power stopped—they stopped.

"They are unharmed. That is why we are removing these capsules—which contain the mind of the robot—from their bodies. You see, the power might be turned on by some of those who, like you, are still under the domination of the Others. We can't chance that."

I looked around, bewildered. For the first time I saw that the sending tower was still blazing furiously, sending up a tower of unbelievably thick white smoke. Other, lesser pyres all around marked where the robot ships had crashed. I looked back at Collard.

He was smiling at me. I wondered at his smile, open and sincere, warm. I wondered—until I understood.

I stood up. "You had me going," I admitted. "I understand now. All right. You killed these Others, and you dare not admit it to me. You are a rebel—a heretic—a renegade. You must be punished, and it seems that I am the only one who can do it. Collard," I said, "draw your gun. I'm going to kill you."

His smile faded, but he made no move for his gun. He looked at me for a long second. Then, just as I was about to spring for him, he said quietly, "Take him."

I had been a fool! Two pairs of arms grabbed me from behind, and pinioned me. I struggled, but I was weak and there were twice as many of them. I fought them all the way, but they brought me here, to this room. And there they left me.

Collard came back in a while ago to tell me that I had five minutes. He has been reading what I have written—I let him, because it does not matter. I have given up hope of getting this to those it should reach, even as I have given up hope of dying. Collard was too smart for me; he left his blaster outside when he came in with another like him. Otherwise I would have died at the muzzle of his blaster—and I might have taken him with me.

Collard has been talking to me as he reads. He says I am deliberately deceiving myself, omitting important things. He says that I should not refer to the machine he is going to use on me as a torture machine. He says that the Others used the same machine on me during the hundred days of training, repeatedly; that they indoctrinated me with it, very thoroughly, and that all he is going to do is to cancel out what they impressed on my mind.

That may be true. But I do not want it canceled out; I do not want to become a traitor to the Others. What Collard has said may be true, in part; it may be that the Others were robots, the mechanical descendants of some organic race that once lived on this green planet and disappeared without a trace. I don't know; it doesn't matter. The Others were—the Others. I swore to obey them and to serve them.

I do not want to be forced to change that.

They must be nearly ready for me. Almost all of those of the Four and the Four who were still loyal to the masters have been through the mind-molding machine already. They have been warped as Collard is warped, have degenerated to mere humans again, though with all the physical powers and mental keenness that the Others gave them still. But their emotions and their outlook have become human.

That was how it began. I think the Others could have prevented it, if they had thought ahead far enough, and cared enough. The mind is an elastic thing, and tends to return to its original shape. After a time on the green planet, even the most devoted of the Four and the Four began to question, to change back to humanity.

Yes, even I might have done so, in time. For it is true that the Others did not plan well what to do with us after we arrived; all that concerned them was getting us here, with the girls.

Collard claimed an absurd thing. He said that this planet of the Others is dying out, that it will soon be uninhabitable even for them. He said that that is why the Others have seventy-seven representatives on Earth. That, he said, is why the maidens of the Four and the Four were sent—to provide all information necessary. It may be, as I told him, true. And if so it does not matter, for the Others are beyond our questioning.

It might have been well if the three Others there in that great tomb-like structure where the maidens waited, somnolent, had been unable to send warning. All that Collard and his cohorts wanted was the girls themselves. Some insane idea they had of finding a hidden spot on this green planet, where they could live and have children and, after the Others had left for Earth, take over the green planet. The Others could have spared the maidens—they were important, but not vital—and the aerial duel over the city, with its frightful consequences, need never have been.

But it is too late to think of that.

Collard is getting impatient. If the mind operation is successful on me—if I become a traitor—he will want me to go back to Earth with him, to seek out the radio-power station that feeds the Others there and destroy it.

If the mind machine fails he will go alone.

I hope it fails.

Collard is opening the door, beckoning to me. The shadow of the machine is visible, flickering only slightly in the light of the flames that are finally beginning to die down. It is waiting for me, and I must go.

I pray that it will kill me—

But I have become sure that it won't.

I have just added up the prices I was paid for all the stories (and the one sf poem) included up to this point in this book. It comes in the aggregate to $283.50. Money was worth more a generation ago, but not *that* much more. The principal reason I wrote so much and earned so little from sf was that I was writing mostly for myself, at the rates I could afford to pay.

Partly that was because of lack of confidence. Partly it was lack of money. A terrible disadvantage in working cheap is that it condemns you to go on working cheap. You can't afford to take chances, even if they might pay off better. While I was my own editor I didn't pay much. But I paid fast, and I paid sure.

When Al Norton took over my magazines it was no longer quite as fast, because he had the quaint notion that he should read my stories before he bought them and that usually took a week or two. And, at least in my mind, it wasn't as sure. I don't remember Al ever rejecting a science-fiction story of mine. But it could have happened. And I reasoned that as long as I had to go back to being a civilian I might as well try a few other markets.

So I cast around for a new outlet. I found one in *Planet Stories,* which published *Conspiracy on Callisto* in its Winter 1943 issue.

Conspiracy on Callisto

JAMES MacCREIGH

Duane's hand flicked to his waist and hung there, poised. His dis-gun remained undrawn.

The tall, white-haired man—Stevens—smiled.

"You're right, Duane," he said. "I could blast you, too. Nobody would win that way, so let's leave the guns where they are."

The muscles twitched in Peter Duane's cheeks, but his voice, when it came, was controlled. "Don't think we're going to let this go," he said. "We'll take it up with Andrias tonight. We'll see whether you can cut me out!"

The white-haired man's smile faded. He stepped forward, one hand bracing him against the thrust of the rocket engines underneath, holding to the guide rail at the side of the ship's corridor.

He said, "Duane, Andrias is your boss, not mine. I'm a free lance; I work for myself. When we land on Callisto tonight I'll be with you when you turn our—shall I say, our *cargo?*—over to him. And I'll collect my fair share of the proceeds. That's as far as it goes. I take no orders from him."

A heavy-set man in blue appeared at the end of the connecting corridor. He was moving fast, but stopped short when he saw the two men.

"Hey!" he said. "Change of course—get to your cabins." He seemed about to walk up to them, then reconsidered and hurried off. Neither man paid any attention.

Duane said, "Do I have to kill you?" It was only a question as he asked it, without threatening.

A muted alarm bell sounded through the P.A. speakers, signaling a one-minute warning. The white-haired man cocked his eyebrow.

"Not at all," he said. He took the measure of his slim, red-headed opponent. Taller, heavier, older, he was still no more uncompromisingly belligerent than Duane, standing there. "Not at all," he repeated. "Just take your ten thousand and let it go at that. Don't make trouble. Leave Andrias out of our private argument."

"Damn you!" Duane flared. "I was promised fifty thousand. I need that money. Do you think—"

"Forget what I think," Stevens said, his voice clipped and angry. "I don't care about fairness, Duane, except to myself. I've done all the work on this—I've supplied the goods. My price is set, a hundred thousand Earth dollars. What Andrias promised you is no concern of mine. The fact is that, after I've taken my share, there's only ten thousand left. That's all you get!"

Duane stared at him a long second, then nodded abruptly. "I was right the first time," he said. "I'll *have* to kill you!"

Already his hand was streaking toward the grip of his dis-gun, touching it, drawing it forth. But the white-haired man was faster. His arms swept up and pinioned Duane, holding him impotent.

"Don't be a fool," he grated. "Duane—"

The P.A. speaker rattled, blared something unintelligible. Neither man heard it. Duane lunged forward into the taller man's grip, sliding down to the floor. The white-haired man grappled furiously to keep his hold on Peter's gun arm, but Peter was slipping away. Belatedly, Stevens went for his own gun.

He was too late. Duane's was out and leveled at him.

"*Now* will you listen to reason?" Duane panted. But he halted, and the muzzle of his weapon wavered. The floor swooped and surged beneath him as the thrust of the mighty jets was cut off. Suddenly there was no gravity. The two men, locked together, floated weightlessly out to the center of the corridor.

"Course change!" gasped white-haired Stevens. "Good God!"

The ship had reached the midpoint of its flight. The bells had sounded, warning every soul on it to take shelter, to strap themselves in their pressure bunks against the deadly stress of acceleration as the ship reversed itself and began to slow its headlong plunge into Callisto. But the two men had not heeded.

The small steering rockets flashed briefly. The men were thrust bruisingly against the side of the corridor as the rocket spun lazily on its axis. The side jets flared once more to halt the spin, when the one-eighty turn was completed, and the men were battered against the opposite wall, still weightless, still clinging to each other, still struggling.

Then the main-drive bellowed into life again, and the ship began to battle against it's own built-up acceleration. The corridor floor rose up with blinking speed to smite them—

And the lights went out in a burst of crashing pain for Peter Duane.

Someone was talking to him. Duane tried to force an eye open to see who it was, and failed. Something damp and clinging was all about his face, obscuring his vision. But the voice filtered in.

"Open your mouth," it said. "Please, Peter, open your mouth. You're all right. Just swallow this."

It was a girl's voice. Duane was suddenly conscious that a girl's light hand was on his shoulder. He shook his head feebly.

The voice became more insistent. "Swallow this," it said. "It's only a stimulant, to help you throw off the shock of your—accident. You're all right, otherwise."

Obediently he opened his mouth, and choked on a warm, tingly liquid. He managed to swallow it, and lay quiet as deft feminine hands did something to his face. Suddenly light filtered through his closed eyelids, and cool air stirred against his damp face.

He opened his eyes. A slight red-headed girl in white nurse's uniform was standing there. She stepped back a pace, a web of wet gauze bandage in her hands, looking at him.

"Hello," he whispered. "You—where am I?"

"In the sick bay," she said. "You got caught out when the ship changed course. Lucky you weren't hurt, Peter. The man you were with—the old, white-haired one, Stevens—wasn't so lucky. He was underneath when the jets went on. Three ribs broken—his lung was punctured. He died in the other room an hour ago."

Duane screwed his eyes tight together and grimaced. When he opened them again there was alertness and clarity in them—but there was also bafflement.

"Girl," he said, "who are you? Where am I?"

"Peter!" There was shock and hurt in the tone of her voice. "I'm—don't you know me, Peter?"

Duane shook his head confusedly. "I don't know anything," he said. "I—I don't even know my own name."

"Duane, Duane," a man's heavy voice said. "That won't wash. Don't play dumb on me."

"Duane?" he said. "Duane. . . ." He swiveled his head and saw a dark, squat man frowning at him. "Who are you?" Peter asked.

The dark man laughed. "Take your time, Duane," he said easily. "You'll remember me. My name's Andrias. I've been waiting here for you to wake up. We have some business matters to discuss."

The nurse, still eyeing Duane with an odd bewilderment, said: "I'll leave you alone for a moment. Don't talk too much to him, Mr. Andrias. He's still suffering from shock."

"I won't," Andrias promised, grinning. Then, as the girl left the room, the smile dropped from his face.

"You play rough, Duane," he observed. "I thought you'd have trouble with Stevens. I didn't think you'd find it necessary to put him out of the way so permanently. Well, no matter. If you had to kill him, it's no skin off my nose. Give me a release on the merchandise. I've got your money here."

Duane waved a hand and pushed himself dizzily erect, swinging his legs over the side of the high cot. A sheet had been thrown over him, but he was fully dressed. He examined his clothing with interest—gray tunic, gray leather spaceman's boots. It was unfamiliar.

He shook his head in further confusion, and the motion burst within his skull, throbbing hotly. He closed his eyes until it subsided, trying to force his brain to operate, to explain to him where and what he was.

He looked at the man named Andrias.

"Nobody seems to believe me," he said, "but I really don't know what's going on. Things are moving too fast for me. Really, I—why, I don't even know my own name! My head—it hurts. I can't think clearly."

Andrias straightened, turned a darkly-suspicious look on Duane. "Don't play tricks on me," he said savagely. "I haven't time for them. I won't mince words with you. Give me a release on the cargo now, before I have to get rough. This is a lot more important to me than your life is."

"Go to hell," Duane said shortly. "I'm playing no tricks."

There was an instant's doubt in Andrias' eyes, then it flashed away. He bent closer, peered at Duane. "I almost think—" he began.

Then he shook his head. "No," he said. "You're lying all right. You killed Stevens to get his share—and now you're trying to hold me up. That's your last chance that just went by, Duane. From now on, I'm running this show!"

He spun around and strode to the door, thrust it open. "Dakin!" he bellowed. "Reed!"

Two large, ugly men in field-gray uniforms, emblazoned with the shooting-star insignia of Callisto's League police, came in, looking to Andrias for instructions.

"Duane here is resisting arrest," Andrias said. "Take him along. We'll fix up the charges later."

"You can't do that," Duane said wearily. "I'm sick. If you've got something against me, save it. Wait till my head clears. I'm sure I can explain—"

"Explain, hell." The dark man laughed. "If I wait, this ship will be blasting off for Ganymede within two hours. I'll wait—but so will the ship. It's not going anywhere till I give it clearance. I run Callisto; I'll give the orders here!"

II

Whoever this man Andrias was, thought Duane, he was certainly a man of importance on Callisto. As he had said, *he* gave the orders.

The crew of the rocket made no objection when Andrias and his men took Duane off without a word. Duane had thought the nurse, who seemed a good enough sort, might have said something on his behalf. But she was out of sight as they left. A curt sentence to a gray-clad official on the blast field where the rocket lay, and the man nodded and hurried off, to tell the rocket's captain that the ship was being refused clearance indefinitely.

A long, powerful ground car slid up before them. Andrias got in front, while the two uniformed men shoved Duane into the back of the car, climbed in beside him. Andrias gave a curt order, and the car shot forward.

The driver, sitting beside Andrias, leaned forward and reached a hand under the dashboard. The high wail of a siren came instantly from the car's roof, and what traffic was on the broad, straight highway into which they had turned pulled aside to let them race through.

Ahead lay the tall spires of a city. Graceful, hundreds of feet high, they seemed dreamlike yet somehow oddly familiar to Duane. Somewhere he had seen them before. He dragged deep into his mind, plumbing the cloudy, impenetrable haze that had settled on it, trying to bring forth the memories that he should have had. Amnesia, they called it; complete forgetting of the happenings of a lifetime. He'd heard of it—but never dreamed it could happen to him!

My name, it seems, is Peter Duane, he thought. *And they tell me that I killed a man!*

The thought was starkly incredible to him. A white-haired man, it had been; someone named Stevens. He tried to remember.

Yes, there had been a white-haired man. And there had been an argument. Something to do with money, with a shipment of goods that Stevens had supplied to Duane. There had even been talk of killing. . . .

But—murder! Duane looked at his hands helplessly.

Andrias, up ahead, was turning around. He looked sharply at Duane, for a long second. An uncertainty clouded his eyes, and abruptly he looked forward again without speaking.

"Who's this man Andrias?" Duane whispered to the nearest guard.

The man stared at him. "Governor Andrias," he said, "is the League's deputy on Callisto. You know—the Earth-Mars League. They put Governor Andrias here to—well, to govern for them."

"League?" Duane asked, wrinkling his brow. He had heard something about a League once, yes. But it was all so nebulous. . . .

The other guard stirred, leaned over. "Shut up," he said heavily. "You'll have plenty of chance for talking later."

But the chance was a long time in coming. Duane found himself, an hour later, still in the barred room into which he'd been thrust. The guards had brought him there, at Andrias' order, and left him. That had been all.

This was not a regular jail, Duane realized. It was more like a palace, something out of Earth's Roman-empire days, all white stone and frescoed walls. Duane wished for human companionship—particularly that of the nurse. Of all the people he'd met since awakening in that hospital bed, only she seemed warm and human. The others were—brutal, deadly. It was too bad, Duane reflected, that he'd failed to remember her. She'd seemed hurt, and she had certainly known him by first name. But perhaps she would understand.

Duane sat down on a lumpy, sagging bed and buried his head in his hands. Dim ghosts of memory were wandering in his mind. He tried to conjure them into stronger relief, or to exorcise them entirely.

Somewhere, some time, a man had said to him, *"Andrias is secretly arming the Callistan cutthroats for revolt against the League. He wants personal power—he's prepared to pay any price for it. He needs guns, Earth guns smuggled in through the League patrol. If he can wipe out the League police garrison—those who are loyal to the League, still, instead of to Andrias—he can sit back and laugh at any fleet Earth and Mars can send. Rockets are clumsy in an atmosphere. They're helpless. And if he can arm enough of Callisto's rabble, he can't be stopped. That's why he'll pay for electron rifles with their weight in gold."*

Duane could remember the scene clearly. Could almost see the sharp, aquiline face of the man who had spoken to him. But there memory stopped.

A fugitive recollection raced through his mind. He halted it, dragged it back, pinned it down. . . .

They had stopped in Darkside, the spaceport on the side of Luna that keeps perpetually averted from Earth, as if the moon knows shame and wants to hide the rough and roaring dome city that nestles in one of the great craters. Duane remembered sitting in a low-ceilinged, smoke-heavy room, across the table from a tall man with white hair. Stevens!

"Four thousand electron rifles," the man had said. *"Latest government issue. Never mind how I got them; they're perfect. You know my price. Take it or leave it. And it's payable the minute we touch ground on Callisto."*

There had been a few minutes of haggling over terms, then a handshake and a drink from a thin-necked flagon of pale-yellow liquid fire.

He and the white-haired man had gone out then, made their way by unfrequented side streets to a great windowless building. Duane remembered the white-hot stars overhead, shining piercingly through the great transparent dome that kept the air in the sealed city of Darkside, as they stood at the entrance of the warehouse and spoke in low tones to the man who answered their summons.

Then, inside. And they were looking at a huge chamber full of stacked fiber boxes—containing nothing but dehydrated dairy products and mining tools, by the stencils they bore. Duane had turned to the white-haired man with a puzzled question—and the man had laughed aloud.

He dragged one of the boxes down, ripped it open with the sharp point of a handling hook. Short-barreled, flare-mouthed guns rolled out, tumbling over the floor. Eight of them there were in that one box, and hundreds of boxes all about. Duane picked one up, broke it, peered into the chamber where the tiny capsule of U-235 would explode with infinite violence when the trigger was pulled, spraying radiant death three thousand yards in the direction the gun was aimed. . . .

And that memory ended.

Duane got up, stared at his haggard face in the cracked mirror over the bed. *"They say I'm a killer,"* he thought. *"Apparently I'm a gunrunner as well. Good lord—what am I not?"*

His reflection—white, drawn face made all the more pallid by the red hair that blazed over it—stared back at him. There was no answer there. If only he could remember—

"All right, Duane." The deep voice of a guard came to him as the door swung open. "Stop making eyes at yourself."

Duane looked around. The guard beckoned. "Governor Andrias wants to speak to you—now. Let's not keep the governor waiting."

A long, narrow room, with a long carpet leading from the entrance up to a great heavy desk—that was Andrias' office. Duane felt a click in his memory as he entered. One of the ancient Earth dictators had employed just such a psychological trick to overawe those who came to beg favors of him. Muslini, or some such name.

The trick failed to work. Duane had other things on his mind; he walked the thirty-foot length of the room, designed to imbue him with a sense of his own unimportance, as steadily as he'd ever walked in the open air of his home planet.

Whichever planet that was.

The guard had remained just inside the door, at attention, Andrias waved him out.

"Here I am," said Duane. "What do you want?"

Andrias said, "I've had the ship inspected and what I want is on it. That saves your life, for now. But the cargo is in your name. I could take it by force, if I had to. I prefer not to." He picked up a paper, handed it to Duane. "In spite of your behavior, you can keep alive. You can even collect the money for the guns—Stevens' share as well as your own. This is a release form, authorizing my men to take four hundred and twenty cases of dehydrated foods and drilling supplies from the hold of the *Cameroon*—the ship you came on. Sign it, and we'll forget our argument. Only, sign it now and get it over with. I'm losing patience, Duane."

Duane said, without expression, "No."

Dark red flooded into Andrias' sallow face. His jaws bunched angrily and there was a ragged threat of incomplete control to his voice as he spoke.

"I'll have your neck for this, Duane," he said softly.

Duane looked at the man's eyes. Death was behind them, peeping out. Mentally he shrugged. What difference did it make?

"Give me the pen," he said shortly.

Andrias exhaled a deep breath. You could see the tension leave him, the mottled anger fade from his face and leave it without expression. He handed the paper to Duane without a word. He gave him a pen, watched him scrawl his name.

"That," he said, "is better." He paused a moment ruminatively. "It would have been better still if you'd not stalled me so long. I find that hard to forgive in my associates."

"The money," Peter said. If he were playing a part—pretending he knew what he was doing—he might as well play it to the hilt. "When do I get it?"

Andrias picked up the paper and looked carefully at the signature. He creased it thoughtfully, stowed it in a pocket before answering.

"Naturally," he said, "there will have to be a revision of terms. I offered a hundred and ten thousand Earth-dollars. I would have paid it—but you made me angry. You'll have to pay for that."

Duane said, "I've paid already. I've been dragged from pillar to post by you. That's enough. Pay me what you owe me, if you want any more of the same goods!"

That was a shot in the dark—and it missed the mark.

Andrias' eyes widened. "You amaze me, Duane," he said. He rose and stepped around the desk, confronting Duane. "I almost think you really have lost your memory, Duane," he said. "Otherwise, surely you would know that this is all the rifles I need. With them I'll *take* whatever else I want!"

Duane said, "You're ready, then. . . ."

He took time to think it over, but he knew that no thought was required. Already the hands that he had locked behind him were clenched, taut. Already the muscles of his legs were tensing.

"You're ready," he repeated. "You've armed the Callistan exiles—the worst gutter scum on nine planets. You're set to betray the League that gave you power here. . . . Well, that changes things. I can't let you do it!"

He hurled himself at Andrias, hands sweeping around to grapple for the dark man's throat. Andrias, off-balance, staggered backward. But his own hands were diving for the twin heat guns that hung at his waist.

Duane saw his danger, and reacted. His foot twisted around Andrias' ankle; his hands at the other's throat gripped tighter. He lunged forward, slamming the hard top of his head into the other's face, feeling flesh and cartilage give as Andrias' nose mashed flat. His own head pinwheeled dizzily, agonizingly, as the jar revived the pain of his earlier accident.

But Andrias, unconscious already, tumbled back with Duane on top of him. His head made an audible, spine-chilling thud as it hit the carpeted floor.

Duane got up, retrieving the two heat guns, and stared at him.

"They tell me I killed Stevens the same way," he thought. *"I'm getting in a rut!"*

But Andrias was not dead, though he was out as cold as the void beyond Pluto. The thick carpeting had saved him from a broken head.

Duane stepped over the unconscious man and looked around the room. It was furnished severely, to the point of barrenness. Two chairs before Andrias' ornate, bare-topped desk and one luxurious chair behind it; a tasseled bell cord within easy reach of Andrias' chair; the long carpet. That was all it contained.

The problem of getting out was serious, he saw. How could one—

III

Methodically he ransacked the drawers of Andrias' desk. Papers, a whole arsenal of hand guns, Callistan money by the bale, ominously black-covered notebooks with cryptic figures littering their pages—those were the contents. A coldly impersonal desk, without the familiar trivia most men accumulate. There was nothing, certainly, that would get him out of a building that so closely resembled a fortress.

He tumbled the things back into the drawers helter-skelter, turned Andrias over and searched his pockets. More money—the man must have had a fortune within reach at all times—and a few meaningless papers. Duane took the release he had signed and tore it to shreds. But that was only a gesture. When Andrias came to, unless Duane had managed to get away and accomplish something, the mere lack of written permission would not keep him from the rocket's lethal cargo!

When Andrias came to. . . .

An idea bloomed in Duane's brain. He looked, then, at unconscious Andrias—and the idea withered again.

He had thought of forcing Andrias himself to front for him, at gun's point, in the conventional manner of escaping prisoners. But fist fights, fiction to the contrary notwithstanding, leave marks on the men who lose them. Andrias' throat was speckled with the livid marks of Duane's fingers; Duane's head, butting Andrias in the face, had drawn a thick stream of crimson from his nostrils, turned his sharp nose askew.

No guard of Andrias' would have been deceived for an instant, looking at that face—even assuming that Andrias could have been forced to cooperate by the threat of a gun. Which, considering the stake Andrias had in this play, was doubtful. . . .

He stood up and looked around. He had to act quickly. Already Andrias' breath was audible; he saw the man grimace and an arm flopped spasmodically on the floor. Consciousness was on its way back.

Duane touched the heat gun he'd thrust into his belt; drew it and held it poised, while he sought to discover what was in his own mind. He'd killed a man already, they said. Was he then a killer—could he shoot Andrias now, in cold blood, with so much to gain and nothing to lose?

He stood there a moment. Then, abruptly, he reversed the weapon and chopped it down on Andrias' skull.

There was a sharp grunt from the still unconscious man, but no other sign. Only—the first tremors of movement that had shown on him halted, and did not reappear.

"No," Duane thought. *"Whatever they say, I'm not a killer!"*

But still he had to get out. How?

Once more he stared around the room, catalogued its contents. The guard would be getting impatient. Perhaps any minute he would tap the door, first timorously, then with heavier strokes.

The guard! There was a way!

Duane eyed the length of the room. Thirty feet—it would take him a couple of seconds to run it at full speed. Was that fast enough?

There was only one way to find out.

He walked around the desk to the bell cord. He took a deep breath, tugged it savagely, and at once was in speedy motion, racing toward the door, his footsteps muffled in the deep, springy carpet. Almost as he reached it, he saw it begin to open. He quickly sidestepped and was out of the guard's sight, behind the door, as the man looked in.

Quick suspicion flared in his eyes, then certainty as he saw Andrias huddled on the floor. He opened his mouth to cry out—

But Duane's arm was around his throat, and he had no breath to spare. Duane's foot lashed out and the door slammed shut; Duane's balled left fist came up and connected with the guard's chin. Abruptly the man slumped.

Duane took a deep breath and let the man drop to the floor. But he paused only a second; now he had two unconscious men on his hands and he dared let neither revive until he was prepared.

He grasped the guard's arm and dragged him roughly the length of the room. He leaped on top of the desk, brutally scarring its gleaming top with the hard spikes of his boots. His agile fingers unfastened the long bell cord without causing it to ring and, bearing it, he dropped again to the floor.

Tugging and straining, he got the limp form of Andrias into his own chair, bound him with the bell cord, gagged him with the priceless Venus-wool scarf Andrias wore knotted about his throat. He tested his bindings with full strength, and smiled. Those would hold, let Andrias struggle as he would.

The guard he stripped of clothing, bound and gagged with his own belt and spaceman's kerchief. He dragged him around behind the desk, thrust him under it out of sight. Andrias' chair he turned so that the unconscious face was averted from the door. Should anyone look in, then, the fact of Andrias' unconsciousness might not be noticed.

Then he took off his own clothes, quickly assumed the field-gray uniform of the guard. It fit like the skin of a fruit. He felt himself bulging out of it in a dozen places. The long cape the guard wore would conceal that, perhaps. In any case, there was nothing better.

Trying to make his stride as martial as possible, he walked down the long carpet to the door, opened it and stepped outside.

His luck couldn't hold out forever. It was next to miraculous that he got as far as he did—out of the anteroom before Andrias' office, past the two guards there, who eyed him absently but said nothing, down the great entrance hall, straight out the front door.

Going through the city had been easier, of course. There were many men in uniforms like his. Duane thought, then, that Andrias' power could not have been too strong, even over the League police whom he nominally commanded. The police could not all have been corrupt. There were too many of them; had they been turncoats, aiding Andrias in his revolt against the League, there would have been no need to smuggle rifles in for an unruly mass of civilians.

Duane cursed the lack of foresight of the early Earth governments. They'd made a prison planet of Callisto; had filled it with the worst scum of Earth. Then, when the damage had been done—when Callisto had become a pest-hole among the planets; its iniquities a stench that rose to the stars—they had belatedly found that they had created a problem worse than the one they'd tried to solve. One like a hydra-beast.

Criminality was not a thing of heredity. The children of the transported convicts, most of them, were honest and wanted to be respectable. And they could not be.

Earth's crime rate, too, had not been lowered materially by exiling its gangsters and murderers to Callisto. When it was long past time, the League had stepped in, and set a governor of its own over Callisto.

If the governor had been an honest man a satisfactory solution might have been worked out. The first governor had been honest. Under him great strides had been made. The bribe-proof, gun-handy League police had stamped out the wide-open plague spots of the planet; public works had been begun on a large scale. The beginnings of representative government had been established.

But the first governor had died. And the second governor had been —Andrias.

"You can see the results!" Duane thought grimly as he swung into the airfield in his rented ground car. Foreboding was stamped on the faces of half the Callistans he'd seen—and dark treachery on the others. Some of those men had been among the actual exiled criminals —the last convict ship had landed only a dozen years before. All of those whom Andrias planned to arm were either of the original transportation-men, or their weaker descendants.

What was holding Andrias back? Why the need for smuggling guns in?

The answer to that, Duane thought, was encouraging but not conclusive. Clearly, then, Andrias did not have complete control over the League police. But how much control he did have, what officers he had won over to treachery, Duane could not begin to guess.

Duane slid the car into a parking slot, switched off the ignition and left it. It was night, but the short Callistan dark period was nearly over. A pearly glow at the horizon showed where the sun would come bulging over in a few minutes; while at the opposite rim of the planet he could still see the blood-red disc of mighty Jupiter lingering for a moment, casting a crimson hue over the landscape, before it made the final plunge. The field was not flood-lighted. Traffic was scarce on Callisto.

Duane, almost invisible in the uncertain light, stepped boldly out across the jet-blasted tarmac toward the huge bulk of the *Cameroon*, the rocket transport which had brought him. Two other ships lay on the same seared pavement, but they were smaller. They were fighting ships, small, speedy ones, in Callisto for refueling before returning to the League's ceaseless patrol of the System's starlanes.

Duane hesitated briefly, wondering whether he ought to go to one of those ships and tell his story to its League commander. He decided against it. There was too little certainty for him there; too much risk that the commander, even, might be a tool of Andrias'.

Duane shook his head angrily. If only his memory were clear—if only he could be sure what he was doing!

He reached the portal of the ship. A gray-clad League officer was there standing guard, to prevent the ship taking off.

"Official business," Duane said curtly, and swept by the startled man before he could object. He hurried along the corridor toward the captain's office and control room. A purser he passed looked at him curiously, and Duane averted his face. If the man recognized him there might be questions.

For the thousandth time he cursed the gray cloud that overhung his memory. He didn't know, even, who among the crew might know him and spread the alarm.

Then he was at the door marked, *Crew only—do not enter!* He tapped on it, then grasped the knob and swung it open.

A squat, open-featured man in blue, the bronze eagles of the Mercantile Service resting lightly on his powerful shoulders, looked at him. Recognition flared in his eyes.

"Duane!" he whispered. "Peter Duane, what're you doing in the clothes of Andrias' household guard?"

Duane felt the tenseness ebb out of his throat. Here was a friend.

"Captain," he said, "you seem to be a friend of mind. If you are—I need you. You see, I've lost my memory."

"Lost your memory?" the captain echoed. "You mean that blow on your head? The ship's surgeon said something . . . yes, that was it. I hardly believed him, though."

"But were we friends?"

"Why, yes, Peter."

"Then help me now," said Duane. "I have a cargo stowed in your hold, Captain. Do you know what it is?"

"Why—yes. The rifles, you mean?"

Duane blinked. He nodded, then looked dizzily for a chair. The captain was a friend of his, all right—a fellow gun-runner!

"Good God," he said aloud. "What a mess!"

"What's happened?" the captain asked. "I saw you in the corridor, arguing with Stevens. You looked like trouble, and I should have come up to you then. But the course was to be changed, and I had to be there. . . . And the next I hear, Stevens is dead, and you've maybe killed him. Then I heard you've lost your memory, and are in a jam with Andrias."

He paused and speculation came into his eyes, almost hostility.

"Peter Duane," he said softly, "it strikes me that you may have lost more than your memory. Which side are you on? What happened between you and Andrias? Tell me now if you've changed sides on me, man. For friendship's sake I won't be too hard on you. But there's too much at stake here—"

"Oh, hell," said Peter, and the heat gun was suddenly in his hand, leveled at the squat man in blue. "I wish you were on my side, but there's no way I can tell. I can trust myself, I think—but that's all. Put up your hands!"

And that was when his luck ran out.

"Peter—" the captain began.

IV

But a sound from outside halted him. Together the two men stared at the viewplates. A siren had begun to shriek in the distance, the siren of a racing ground car. Through the gates it plunged, scattering the light wooden barrier. It spun crazily around on two wheels and came roaring for the ship.

Andrias was in it.

Peter turned on the captain, and the gun was rigidly outthrust in his hand.

"Close your ports!" he snarled. "Up rockets—in a hurry!"

"Listen, Peter," the captain began.

"I said, hurry!" The car's brakes shrieked outside, and it disappeared from the view of the men. There was an abrupt babble of voices.

"Close your ports!" Peter shouted savagely. "Now!"

The captain opened his mouth to speak, then snapped it shut. He touched the stud of a communications set, said into it, "Close ports. Snap to it. Engine room—up rockets in ten seconds. All crew—stand by for lift!"

The ship's own take-off siren howled shrilly, drowning out the angry voices from below. Peter felt the whine of the electrics that dogged shut the heavy pressure doors. He stepped to the pilot's chair, slid into it, buckled the compression straps around him.

The instruments—he recognized them all, knew how to use them! Had he been a rocket pilot before his mind had blanked—before embarking on the more lucrative profession of gun smuggler? He wondered. . . .

But it was the captain who took the ship off. "Ten seconds," Peter said. "Get moving!"

The captain hesitated the barest fraction, but his eyes were on the heat gun and he knew that Duane was capable of using it. "The men—" he said. "If they're underneath when the jets go, they'll burn!"

"That's the chance they take," said Duane. "They heard the siren!"

The captain turned his head quickly, and his fingers flashed out. He was in his own acceleration seat too, laced down by heavy canvas webbing. His hands reached out to the controls before him, and his fingers took on a life of their own as they wove dexterously across the keys, setting up fire-patterns, charting a course of take-off. Then the heel of his hand settled on the firing stop. . . .

The acceleration was worse than Peter's clouded mind had expected, but no more than he could stand. In his frame of mind, he could stand almost anything, he thought—short of instant annihilation!

The thin air of Callisto howled past them, forming a high obligato to the thunder of the jets. Then the air-howl faded sharply to silence, and the booming of the rockets became less a thing of sound than a rumble in the framework of the *Cameroon*. They were in space.

The captain's foot kicked the pedal that shut off the over-drive jets, reducing the thrust to a mere one-gravity acceleration. He turned to Duane.

"What now?" he asked.

Duane, busy unstrapping himself from the restraining belts, shook his head without answering. What now? *"A damn good question!"* he thought.

The captain, with the ease of long practice, was already out of his own pressure straps. He stood there by his chair, watching Duane closely. But the gun was still in Duane's hand, despite his preoccupation.

Duane cocked an ear as he threw off the last strap. Did he hear voices in the corridor, a distance away but coming?

The captain, looking out the port with considerable interest, interrupted his train of thought. "What," he asked, "for instance, are you going to do about—those?"

His arm was outstretched, pointing outward and down. Duane looked in that direction—

The two patrol rockets were streaking up after his commandeered ship. Fairylike in their pastel shades, with the delicate tracery of girders over their fighting noses, they nevertheless represented grim menace to Duane!

He swore under his breath. The *Cameroon,* huge and lumbering, was helpless as a sitting bird before those lithe hawks of prey. If only he knew which side the ships were on. If only he knew—anything!

He couldn't afford to take a chance. "Stand back!" he ordered the captain. The man in blue gave ground before him, staring wonderingly as Duane advanced. Duane took a quick look at the control set-up, tried to remember how to work it.

It was so tantalizingly close to his memory! He cursed again; then stabbed down on a dozen keys at random, heeled the main control down, jumped back, even as the ship careened madly about in its flight, and blasted the delicate controls to shattered ashes with a bolt from his heat gun. Now the ship was crippled, for the time being at least. Short of a nigh-impossible boarding in space, the two patrol cruisers could do nothing with it till the controls were repaired. The *Cameroon,* and its cargo of political dynamite, would circle through space for hours or days.

It wasn't much—but it was the best he could do. At least it would give him time to think things over.

No. He heard the voices of the men in the corridor again, tumbled about by the abrupt course change—luckily, it had been only a mild thing compared to the one that had killed Stevens and caused his own present dilemma—but regaining their feet and coming on. And one of the voices, loud and harsh, was Andrias! Somehow, before the ports closed, he'd managed to board the *Cameroon!*

Duane stood erect, whirled to face the door. The captain stood by it. Duane thrust his heat gun at him.

"The door!" he commanded. "Lock it!"

Urged by the menace of the heat gun, the captain hurriedly put out a hand to the lock of the door—

And jerked it back, nursing smashed knuckles, as Andrias and four men burst in, hurling the door open before them. They came to a sliding, tumbling halt, though, as they faced grim Duane and his ready heat pistol.

"Hold it!" he ordered. "That's right. . . . Stay that way while I figure things out. The first man that moves, dies for it."

Dark blood flooded into Andrias' face, but he said no word, only stood there glaring hatred. The smear of crimson had been brushed from his face, but his nose was still awry and a huge purplish bruise was spreading over it and across one cheek. The three men with him were guards. All were armed—the police with hand weapons as lethal as Duane's own, Andrias with an old-style projective-type weapon—an ancient pistol, snatched from some bewildered spaceman as they burst into the *Cameroon.*

Duane braced himself with one arm against the pilot's chair and stared at them. The crazy circular course the blasted controls had given the ship had a strong lateral component; around and around the ship went, in a screaming circle, chasing its own tail. There was a sudden change in the light from the port outside; Duane involuntarily looked up for a moment. Dulled and purplish was the gleam from the brilliant stars all about; the *Cameroon,* in its locked orbit, had completed a circle and was plunging through its own wake of expelled jet-gases. He saw the two patrol rockets streak past; then saw the flood of rocket-flares from their side jets as they spun and braked, trying to match course and speed with the crazy orbit of the *Cameroon.*

He'd looked away for only a second; abruptly he looked back.

"Easy!" he snapped. Andrias' arm, which had begun to lift, straightened out, and the scowl on the governor's face darkened even more.

Clackety-clack. There was the sound of a girl's high heels running along the corridor, followed by heavier thumps from the space boots of men. Duane jerked his gun at Andrias and his police.

"Out of the way!" he said. "Let's see who's coming now."

It was the girl. Red hair fluttering in the wake of her running, face alight with anxiety, she burst into the room.

"Peter!" she cried. "Andrias and his men—"

She stopped short and took in the tableau. Duane's eyes were on her, and he was about to speak. Then he became conscious of something in her own eyes, a sudden spark that flared even before her lips opened and a thin cry came from them; even before she leaped to one side, at Andrias.

Peter cursed and tried to turn, to dodge; tried to bring his heat gun around. But a thunder louder than the bellowing jets outside filled the room, and a streak of livid fire crossed the fringe of Peter's brain. Sudden blackness closed in around him. He fell—and his closing eyes saw new figures running into the room, saw the counterplay of lashing heat beams.

This is it—he thought grimly, and then thought no more.

<h1 style="text-align:center">V</h1>

Duane was in the sickbay again, on the same bed. His head was spinning agonizedly. He forced his eyes open—and the girl was there; the same girl. She was watching him. A cloud on her face lifted as she saw his lids flicker open; then it descended again. Her lips quivered.

"Darn you, Peter," she whispered. "Who are you now?"

"Why—why, I'm Peter Duane, of course," he said.

"Well, thank God you know that!" It was the captain. He'd changed since the last time Peter had seen him. One arm was slung in bandages that bore the yellow seeping tint of burn salve.

Peter shook his head to try to clear it. "Where—where am I?" he asked. "Andrias—"

"Andrias is where he won't bother you," the captain said. "Locked up below. So are two of his men. The other one's dead. How's your memory, Peter?"

Duane touched it experimentally with a questing mental finger. It seemed all right, though he felt still dazed.

"Coming along," he said. "But where am I? The controls—I blasted them."

The captain laughed. "I know," he said briefly. "Well— I guess you had to, in a way. You didn't trust anyone; couldn't trust anyone. You had to make sure the rifles wouldn't get back to Callisto too soon. But they're working on installing duplicates now, Peter. In an hour we'll be back on Callisto. We shut the jets off already; we're in an orbit."

Duane sank back. "Listen," he said. "I think—I think my memory's clearing, somehow. But how—I mean, were you on my side? All along?"

The captain nodded soberly. "On your side, yes, Peter," he said. "The League's side, that is. You and I, you know, both work for the League. When they got word of Andrias' plans, they had to work fast. To move in by force would have meant bloodshed, would have forced his hand. That would have been utterly bad. It was too dangerous. Callisto is politically a powder-keg already. The whole thing might have exploded."

Peter's eyes flared with sudden hope and enlightenment. "And you and I—" he began.

"You and I, and a couple of other undercover workers were put on the job," the captain nodded. "We had to find out who Andrias' supporters were—and to keep him from getting more electron rifles while the commanders of the Callisto garrison were quietly checked, to see who was on which side. They've found Andrias' Earth backers—a group of wealthy malcontents who thought Callisto should be exploited for their gain, had made secret deals with him for concessions. You, of course, slowed down the delivery of the rifles as long as you could. They lay in the Lunar warehouses a precious extra week while you haggled over terms. That's what you were doing with Stevens, I think, when the course change caught you both."

"You've had him long enough," the nurse broke in. "I have a few words to say."

"No, wait—" Duane protested. But the captain was grinning broadly. He moved toward the door.

"Later," he said over his shoulder. "There'll be plenty of time." The door closed behind him. Duane turned to the girl.

He shook his head again. The cloud was lifting. He could almost remember everything again; things were beginning to come into focus. This girl, for instance—

She noticed his motion. "How's your head, Peter?" she asked solicitously. "Andrias hit you with that awful old bullet-gun. I tried to stop him, but all I could do was jar his arm. Oh, Peter, I was so afraid when I saw you fall!"

"You probably saved my life," Peter said soberly. "Andrias struck me as a pretty good shot." He tried to grin.

The girl frowned. "Peter," she said, "I'm sorry if I seemed rude, before—the last time you were here. It was just that I. . . . Well, you didn't remember me. I couldn't understand."

Peter stared at her. Yes—he *should* remember her. He did, only—

"Perhaps this will help you," the girl said. She rummaged in a pocket of her uniform, brought something out that was tiny and glittering. "I don't wear it on duty, Peter. But I guess this is an exception. . . ."

Peter pushed himself up on one elbow, trying to make out what she was doing. She was slipping the small thing on a finger. . . .

A ring. An engagement ring!

"Oh—" said Peter. And suddenly everything clicked; he remembered; he could recall . . . everything. That second blow on his head had undone the harm of the first one.

He swung his legs over the side of the bed, stood up, reached out hungry arms for the girl.

"Of course I remember," he said as she came into the circle of his arms. "The ring on your finger. I ought to remember—*I put it there!*"

And for a long time after there was no need for words.

Meanwhile World War II continued. I was not too pleased about it.

My dissatisfaction was partly with the war itself, in which the bad guys seemed to win all the battles, partly with myself for not being part of it.

Around the office we told each other that we were, after all, contributing very significantly to the war effort. We were supplying morale-boosting relaxation to our brave boys on the combat fronts, not to mention Rosie the Riveter and the other heroes and heroines of the aircraft plants. Every issue we put out was jam-packed with gung-ho exhortations to buy war bonds, keep military secrets ("Loose Lips Can Sink a Ship"), lay off the black market and avoid unnecessary traveling ("Is This Trip Necessary?"). I doubt any of us really believed it.

Paper was getting short. There was plenty of it at the mills, but the mills were in Canada. All the transportation that would normally have brought it to our presses was otherwise engaged. Every month we killed a couple of titles on the Popular list.

Futurians were disappearing into the armed services and returning on leave, looking quite different in uniform. Dirk Wylie became an M.P. David A. Kyle was a sergeant in the Armored Corps. Jack Gillespie went off into the Merchant Marine. I felt I, personally, should be doing *something,* and so I joined a paramilitary thing called the City Patrol Corps. The object of the exercise was to produce hardened combat troops to guard the New York docks against spies and saboteurs. We were promised real .45s to wear on our hips, even uniforms. I never got quite that far. All I did was close-order drill, from 7 to 8:30 every Tuesday night, for a couple of months during the nice weather.

I had another problem, which was that my marriage to Doë had come apart.* When our lease expired in Knickerbocker Village we split up, Doë back to her parents' home, me to a hotel near Times Square. It was all getting pretty complicated, and so around the end of 1942 I decided to go to be a soldier.

It turned out not to be as easy as that.

The War Department had decided to regulate the flow of warm bodies into uniform by suspending voluntary enlistments. You had to be drafted. You could volunteer to be drafted—in my case, to be reclassified 1A—but I was still in Local Board No. 1, where the hunger for fresh meat was still being met by youngsters from Mott Street and Pell.

In some ways I think of the next couple of months as my finest hour. First I requested reclassification. Then I demanded it. Then I went down to my draft board, week after week, and pounded on the table and *insisted* they take me. All over America young men were being remorselessly torn from their studies, their jobs and their families. And here was I, desperate to go, and they wouldn't let me. I felt myself a spokesman for all the reluctant heroes . . . and besides, I was enjoying it.

My father was getting rapidly rich as the owner of several small machine shops making aircraft parts. He tried to talk me out of it. Brooklyn Tech had taught me all about machine tools; he could have given me a job that would have kept me a civilian forever, at three or four times the pay Popular was giving me. But that wasn't where the action was. I had been talking against fascism since I was sixteen years old, and I didn't like my own image of myself as long as I let it stay talk.

When I consider my military career, I am sure I could have damaged Hitler at least that much by remaining a civilian. But it didn't *feel* that way.

Moreover, there were additional psychosexual complications. I had become interested in a pretty young assistant editor at Popular named Dorothy LesTina.† When I told her of my intention to join up she decided she would join the WACs. That seemed very fitting and nice; but then it turned out that the WAC was blood-hungry for her and snatched her away in no time at all, while Local Board No. 1 was still dawdling over me. So I escorted her to Penn Station and kissed her

---

* The first such experience for me, but not the last. I have been married a *lot*. Cyril Kornbluth used to say, "Everybody does it, but Fred marries them."

† We were married in Paris, just at the end of the war.

good-by under the big Buy War Bonds sign, where the troops bade their final farewells—only she was the troops. I was the sorrowing civilian left behind her. Then Dick Wilson went off, and shortly thereafter his wife Jessica joined the WACs, and in her turn I escorted Jessica to Penn Station and kissed *her* good-by . . . I tell you, it was enough to make a hog weep.

But finally they got around to me, and I was sworn in—on April Fools' Day, 1932.

As a sort of going-away present Popular gave me a check for a new short story called *Darkside Destiny,* and the rate was a full penny a word. I would like to include it here. For that matter, I would like to read it. The magazines died right about that time, slain by lack of paper. The Canadian editions limped on for a few issues, and *Darkside Destiny* appeared in one of them. But I don't have a copy. The story has never been published in the United States at all.

The other day I had a visit from a young friend who has just completed his basic training, class of 1975. He reported that three men in his company had committed suicide and a batch had deserted. They must be doing something different these days. In the early part of 1943 it wasn't that way. I loved it.

It was not really all that lovable, I suppose, but I didn't mind even the chickenshit. The first few days were intermittently nasty. A lieutenant greeted us at Camp Upton, smiling falsely and promising us speedy classification and jobs worthy of our skills; whereupon they set me to cleaning latrines. The second day I got my AGCT score and the classification clerk allowed that it was real nice, and entitled me pretty much to pick my branch of service; whereupon they put me on night KP. The third day I turned in my choices. Send me anywhere but to the Air Force, I said, secure in my privilege. Field Artillery, Armored Corps—even the Infantry would be all right. Whereupon they sent me to the Air Corps.

Now that I think it over, they did me no harm. What I wanted was both combat and a commission, and as a glasses-wearer of long standing I didn't see how that could happen in the Air Force. It didn't. But if I had got my druthers I suspect that the other thing I would have got was killed.

Air Force basic training was in Miami Beach, not as glittery by far as it has since become but still full of resort hotels. None of them had any guests. Transportation priorities kept the tourists home. So the hotel owners made a deal with the Air Force, and we were in them, six or eight to a room, but with the pools and the beaches and the Florida sun thrown in free. We fell out at a quarter to five in the morning, with the stars still bright in the sky. We marched, our voices raised in obligatory song, all up and down the beach. Aircraft-recognition classes in preempted movie theaters on Lincoln Road. Physical training on a golf course. Obstacle courses and bivouacs up with the rattlesnakes on the sand dunes where Motel Row now stands. We learned to throw hand grenades, and fired thousands of rounds of small-arms ammunition out over the Atlantic. It lasted about two months, and the worst thing about it was that then I had to leave.

Why did I like it? Well, after you've edited *G-8 and His Battle Aces* for a year or two a lot of strange things begin to look good to you. But the big thing was that I had no responsibilities. I was told what to do at every step, when to get up, how to make my bed, when to eat, what to wear. It was a total vacation from responsibility, and now that I think of it about the only one I've ever had.

They sent me off to technical training as a weather observer, along with my good friend Joe Winters and a gaggle of other new PFCs. The place for that was Chanute Field, Illinois, an air base with a population of 30,000 attached to a town, Rantoul, Illinois, with a population of 1,500. I still felt I had found a home in the Army. I enjoyed learning about Bjerknes's air masses and isobars, and with the promotion I now had $54 a month to spend. Besides, wives were allowed at Chanute Field. I didn't happen to have one at the moment, but Joe did, and Dorothy Winters turned out to be a lovely lady with a quick brain and a marvelous sense of humor.

The other great thing about Chanute Field was that Jack Williamson was there too. Jack had already gone through the weather-observer class, served a year or two in the field and come back to take advanced training as a forecaster. I was impressed. I was also delighted. Jack Williamson is an old and dear friend with whom I have written a number of books, and hope to go on doing so indefinitely. I am always pleased to see him, but never more than at Chanute Field.

When I graduated from Chanute I was assigned to actual weather observing at a real flying field, in Enid, Oklahoma. That wasn't a bad place, either. Oklahoma City was only a light-year away by slow train. I got down there for an occasional weekend, saw my first oil well and my first Indian, and once in a while caught a road company ballet or opera performance. Between times there was the town of Enid, full of girls. The base was full of girls too, with a fine WAC detachment. One of them was a lovely blonde named Zenobia, also a weather observer, smart and funny. We spent a lot of time together, exploring the resources of Enid.

And I even found some time to write.

One of the stories I finished while at Enid was a novelette called *Highwayman of the Void*. It is not a collaboration—for better or worse, it is all mine—but for some reason I put Dirk Wylie's by-line on it. I had done that once or twice before by arrangement with Dirk, mostly to keep my masters at Popular from knowing how many stories I was buying from myself. That wasn't the reason this time, but I don't remember what the reason was, and Dirk is no longer alive to ask.

Anyway, I mailed it off to Malcolm Reiss at *Planet Stories*. I got his check in time for Christmas 1943, and he published it in his issue for Fall 1944.

Highwayman of the Void

DIRK WYLIE

Steve Nolan was three years dead, pyro-burned in the black space off Luna when a prison break failed. But Nolan had a job to do. Nolan came back.

Where the Avalon Trail bends across Annihilation Range, a thousand icy miles from Pluto's northern stem, Nolan stopped and closed the intake valve of his helmet. Count five seconds, and he unhooked the exhausted tank of oxygen; count ten more and it was spinning away, end over end over Pluto's frozen surface, and a new tank was already in place. He slipped the pressure valve and inhaled deeply of the new air.

He'd come ten miles by the phosphorescent figures on the nightstone markers beside the trail. Fifteen more miles to go.

His cold black eyes stared absently at the east, where the pseudo-life of the great Plutonian crystals rolled in a shifting, tinkling sea. He noted the water-avid crystals, and noted the three crablike crawlers that munched a solitary clump of metallic grass. You don't walk, talk and breathe after a Tri-planet Lawman has declared you dead unless you note everything around you and react to what may be dangerous.

But he was looking beyond the familiar Plutonian drear, to the eastern horizon where faint lights gleamed in the dark. That was Port Avalon. That was where Steve Nolan was bound.

Woller was in Avalon. The Alan Woller who had made him an outlaw, roaming the star trails from Pluto to the Satellites, never daring to return to the inner worlds where Tri-planet kept order.

There was a slow pulse mounting in Nolan's throat as he walked on, savagely kicking a crab-shelled crawler from his path. He'd seen the newssheet, months old, in a rickety old port on one of the Satellites—Io? Ganymede?—when he was down to forty credits and a friendly bartender. It hadn't been much of an item. The kind a country editor throws into his finance column when he unexpectedly loses an ad and has to fill space.

"The new shipping company, which expects to do much for improving commercial relations with the outer planets, is headed by Alan Woller, formerly with the Interplanetary Telenews Company. Woller is remembered as the prosecution's star witness in the trial of Steve Nolan, the Junta agent indicted for treason three years ago. Nolan, sentenced to life imprisonment in Luna Cave, was killed while attempting to escape.

The new company is capitalized at over a billion dollars, and has already taken options on bases in. . . ."

The drink had drained out of Steve Nolan when he saw that. And the bartender had been too friendly for his own good. He'd been a soft touch for five hundred credits.

That had been rocket fare to Pluto for Nolan.

He felt the drumming with the soles of his feet, a hard, grinding sensation against his metal boots. He jumped off the trail quickly and whirled to watch for the approaching skid.

It was moving slowly, chugging along on a single jet.

Clogged feeders, Nolan thought as he felt the uneven vibrations. *If he doesn't watch out he'll have a backblast.*

The skid faltered past him, no faster than he could run. He looked away from the incandescent flare of the one tail jet, then that stopped too. Tall as a man, a dozen feet long, the skid lay waiting on the trail.

Waiting for Steve Nolan?

Anything was better than walking. Nolan walked up to the skid, not fast, and kicked solidly at the entrance. It slid open with a creaking noise and he was in the tank, sealing the outer door behind him.

The inner door didn't open. A female voice from a speaker said, "Who are you?"

Steve waited till he saw the pressure and temperature gauges shoot up to normal, then swung open his faceplate. "Matthews is the name," he lied easily, out of three long years of practice. "I thought you were waiting for me. Say the word and I'll get out again if I was wrong."

"Oh, no." The girl's voice hesitated a second. "What are you doing out here?"

"I'm on my way to Avalon, out of Aylette. A skid bus took me across the Ice Plains, then I caught a lift on a prospector's skid. He turned off ten miles back and I decided to walk the rest of the way."

"Do you know anything about skids? Mine isn't working very well. I'll pay you if you can—"

"I'm not a mechanic," Nolan said wearily.

"Oh. Then you can't fix it."

"I didn't say that. You can't pay me for it. I'll take a lift to Avalon, though."

"A lift? But I don't know you from Adam."

Nolan sighed. "Lady, I don't know you either. Believe me, all I want is a ride. It'll take me four hours to walk to Avalon. I can't spare the time if I can help it." He waited a second. No answer. He shrugged and finished his speech. "I'll make you a proposition. Let me in and I'll fix your jets. We'll be in Avalon in twenty minutes, I'll get out and we'll never see each other again. Don't let me in and I'll tear these ignition wires right out of the lock. Then we'll both hitchhike."

The girl's voice came with controlled anger. "You win," she said. "Come in." There was a soft click, and the inner door yielded under Nolan's hand. He stepped in.

"No hard feelings," he said mildly. "I really wanted the ride. One thing you might remember in the future, though—there are no ignition wires in an air lock."

She was pretty, she was small, she was blue-eyed and brunette. But she didn't say a word to him. She kept to her seat at the controls, watching him lift the top off the distributing chamber, prod around in the gummy mess inside for a second, then replace it and nod.

"You can start it up now, lady," he said. He glanced over her shoulder through the plastic panel, to where Avalon's lights were glowing. Where Woller was. "And the quicker," he said, "the better."

The girl looked at him curiously but said nothing. She turned and fingered the controls. The song of power that came out of the skid's jets brought a quick, slight smile to her lips. Nolan caught a glimpse of her eyes reflected back at him from the plastic panel. Appreciative eyes.

He averted his look. Would there be another time when he could meet the gaze of a decent girl and answer it?

When Woller's dead, his subconscious answered him. *Until then you're not a man, Nolan. You're a weapon!*

The skid was climbing, hugging the side of one of the vast foothills to Annihilation Range itself, a hundred-foot chasm on one side and the cliff on the other. Nolan watched the girl's hands for a sharp second, then relaxed. She knew what she was doing. Unerringly the skid split the center of the trail, following its many turns as though on a track. But—

A sudden high sound escaped her lips. Her foot trod hard on the back-jet pedal. The skid slewed crazily, its side crunching against the cliff as it halted.

"What the—" snarled Nolan, hand leaping to the concealed pyro he wore under his shirt. Then he saw.

Ahead of them was an immense rounded bulk, dome-shaped, black as the frozen night. A crawler . . . but what a crawler! Its horny shell was half again the height of a man, filling the trail from cliff to chasm brink. There was no passing that beast. No wonder there had been no traffic from Avalon!

Mutely the girl turned to Nolan. He grinned sourly, then clambered into the heat suit he'd just put on.

He eyed the girl for a second. "I'm going to have to trust you. I have to get to Avalon, so I have to get this misbegotten monstrosity out of my way. And I have to leave the skid to do it. That gives you a fair, clear chance."

The girl shook her head. "I'll take you to Avalon. I owe you that much. But—but how—"

"Watch," Nolan said curtly, and climbed into the tank. Before he closed the door a thought struck him.

He poked his head out at her. "If anything should go wrong," he said, "and I find myself scattered all over that valley down there, you'd better stay put. Keep the crawler away with the brake jet. And wait for someone to come along. You're not the skidster to back this crate all the way down the trail, with just a brake jet."

Then he slammed the inner door, sealed his helmet, pushed his way out.

The crawler was even bigger than he'd thought. Standing within ten feet of it, he felt tiny and weak, a toy before this massive brute. Like ancient Earth dinosaurs, the crawlers kept growing as long as they lived. Tiny as the palm of a man's hand, foot-high creatures like those Nolan had kicked out of his way an hour before or monstrosities like the one before him—all three types existed side by side. Only seldom did they grow as great as this. Invulnerable though they were, they perished of starvation, when their bulk grew too much for their thousands of tiny legs to carry.

Out of the ebon hulk of the thing came poking a minute head, goggle-eyed, with a luminous halo of green tendrils surrounding it. It blinked weakly at Nolan. He waited patiently. If the thing was convinced he was harmless.

It was. Recovering from the shock of the skid's arrival it began to prepare for motion again. The head poked out toward the skid on a long, scrawny neck, examined it minutely. The big carapace shivered and rose slightly off the ground as the multitude of tiny legs took up the task of carrying it forward.

Nolan stood motionless. The creature moved ponderously toward him, ignoring him. In the dull mind of the creature an object as tiny as a man was nothing. Even the skid was merely another sort of boulder, against which it could lean, send it hurtling over to destruction, out of its way.

It moved forward till the hard horn almost touched him. Then Nolan leaped.

This was the moment of decision. He circled the long neck with one lashing arm, clamped on it all the pressure he could bring to bear. It was the one sensitive spot the creature had—and protected, normally, by armor battleship-thick.

Nolan strained the muscles of his arm, cursing the cushion of air inside his suit that made a pillow for the beast. The slippery flesh coiled and writhed in his grip; the beast exhaled a great, whistling screech of agony and the snakelike neck curved around. The popeyed head darted in at him, tiny mouth distended to show raw, red flesh inside. It battered ineffectually against the heavy plastic faceplate of his suit.

The crawler vented its whistling sigh again and staggered drunkenly away. Away from the remorseless pressure on its sore spot, away from the agonizing weight of him. Its tiny legs carried it rocking sidewise.

Then abruptly they tried to halt it, gave sharp warning to the tiny brain. It was too late.

The scrambling legs flailed for a foothold and found vacuum. Nolan gave a final heave, felt the thing slide away from him, leaped back. Just in time. He himself was teetering on the brink of the chasm as the crawler, tiny head darting frantically, soundlessly around, slid over and disappeared.

He didn't look down. The clattering and crashing vibrations from below told what happened. He turned, shook himself and headed for the skid.

The girl was waiting for him. Nolan was mildly surprised. She looked at him curiously as he entered.

"A dirty job," she offered tentatively.

He shrugged. "Yes," he said. "Let's get moving."

She turned without a word. All the way back to Avalon, her back was a silent reproach. Friendship, it said, had been offered—and rebuffed.

Nolan had his private thoughts, and dwelt in them. Except for the muffled blast of the rockets there was no sound in the skid until they'd jetted into the great cargo lock in Avalon's crystal dome and the handlers had come to slide the skid into a parking space.

Then, as they got out, she smiled suddenly.

She said, "I guess I misjudged you, Mr. Matthews. I'm sorry I was discourteous, but a girl can't be too careful. Let me take you to dinner for an apology."

Nolan paused and stared at her soberly. Then, "No, thanks," he said. "I meant it when I said I wasn't interested in you. I have things on my mind already." He ignored her outstretched hand, turned to leave, then stopped. "Oh, yes," he said. "Thanks for the ride."

He walked cumbrously over to a storage cubicle without looking back. He stripped off his heat suit and checked it with a stout man in Pluto-city green.

It was time to plan his next move. There was a pilot's hangout, he remembered, a saloon called the Golden Ray. He took a worn notebook from his shirt pocket, thumbed it to the forgotten address and held the page up for the checking attendant to see.

"How do I get there?"

The man's eyes widened a fraction as he took the address in. He shrugged imperceptibly. "Any slidewalk going north," he said. "Get off at the Hub and you'll be within a couple blocks of it."

Nolan nodded and headed for a moving slidewalk. The notebook went back into the pocket of his open-necked black shirt, and the hand that put it there paused a second to touch reassuringly the weight of a slim-barreled pyro that swung beneath his armpit, out of sight. It was nice to know it was there, even though he didn't need it—yet.

He paused in a robot restaurant to eat. Saloons like the Golden Ray don't sell much food—particularly to those who have tasted it once. It was getting on toward night.

The slidewalks were fast, and the first man he stopped at the Hub told him all he needed to know to find the saloon. Once he got within a block of it, it all began to come back. It had been years since he'd been there, but the place hadn't changed.

A blast of sound struck him as he clawed his way through thick tobacco smoke and sweet Martian hop-incense fumes to the bar. He nodded his head, and the short motion yanked a fat bartender to him.

The man's slitted eyes peeped surprisedly through the surrounding tallow.

"Gunner!" he whispered, amiable but hoarse. "Thought you were somewhere around Jupe. What'll it be?"

"It'll be nothing right now," Nolan said. "I thought Petersen might be here. I want to see him."

"Oh, sure," the bartender said. "He's dealin' red-dog at one o' the tables in the back."

Nolan was called "Gunner" by those who knew him by his alias— He'd never taken the trouble to think up a first name for "Matthews." He nodded and stepped away.

It wasn't hard to find Petersen when you knew his habits. The wrinkled little man always sat in the noisiest spot he could find. This time it was a table right behind the four-piece orchestra, pride of the proprietor's heart.

Nolan stood silently for a moment behind the little man's chair to watch the play. He marveled at the ease with which Petersen's gnarled fingers handled the flying pasteboards. As usual, Petersen's pile of chips was low, and the set of his back was discouraged.

Nolan grinned. It was part of Petersen's stock-in-trade to look like the tail end of a losing streak. The sucker trade stays away from a winning gambler. But they flocked to Petersen—and his pockets were always clinking.

Petersen's gambler's sixth sense was functioning. He twitched his shoulders uncomfortably, then turned around, glaring up. "Say," he began, "who the hell are— Oh, Gunner!"

Nolan nodded. "Hey there, Peter," he said.

Petersen grinned and blinked. He looked with regret at his top card, then at Nolan. "No?" he asked wistfully.

Nolan shook his head. "No."

The little man shrugged and flipped his cards away. "Okay," he said cheerfully, shoveling his chips into his clanking pockets. "Lead on, Gunner."

Nolan led on, to a more secluded corner where the clamor of the alleged orchestra was less deafening. He sent a waiter off for a bottle of sealed Terrestrial Scotch, then turned to Petersen.

"Where's Woller?" he asked.

Petersen scowled. "Listen, Steve," he begged, "stay out of trouble. Woller's big here."

"Don't call me Steve," Nolan said mildly. Two living men knew that Nolan and Matthews were the same. Petersen was one of them— Nolan himself the other. "I manage my own affairs. I want to see Woller."

"Okay," Petersen groaned. "He's at the Elena. The big hotel near South Lock."

Nolan nodded. "Good enough," he said. "I'll take care of my business with him right away."

The greasy-aproned waiter came back with the Scotch. Nolan inspected the seal critically, then broke it and poured two generous slugs. "How!" he said. "What've you been doing with yourself, Pete?"

Petersen swallowed his Scotch, grimaced non-committally. "Following the prospectors," he said. "Making money and losing it. It's been a long time since you were here."

Nolan ignored the implied question. "Pretty long," he agreed. "I wasn't figuring on coming, but I heard Woller was here."

Petersen nodded his head sadly. "You're aching for trouble," he observed. "Woller's no man to buck up against. He's got money behind him."

"Whose money?"

"I dunno. Some Martian syndicate, they say. He's come a long way since he was your boss at Telenews."

"Not so long I couldn't follow him."

Petersen cocked an eyebrow, then poured another round. "You followed him into a bad spot," he said slowly. "This whole town is be-jittered. He's doing about what he likes and nobody says boo."

"Why?"

Petersen frowned. "'Cause they're scared, it looks. Scared of the Junta. Talk is there are Junta men around. I wouldn't have to remind you, I guess, of what Woller can say about you if he sees you."

Nolan nodded. "He won't see me—in time for it to do him any good."

Petersen shivered. "You're building up trouble," he repeated. "Woller's pretty near running this place."

"'A louse,'" Nolan quoted, "'enthroned in luxury, will still a loath-some insect be.' That's Woller."

Petersen's wizened little troll-face gaped at him. "Lice bite," he said succinctly.

Nolan said soberly, "Live ones do. After tonight Woller may not be able to bite anybody. Dead lice have no friends."

II

Steve Nolan was deceptively slender in his open-necked, black military shirt and trim khaki slacks. In the half-hearted illumination thrown by Avalon's old gasglow lights, he looked almost boyish.

But he didn't look like the pale youth he'd been three years before. The good-natured roundness of his face had contracted to show the hard bone underneath. There was the ghost of a scar close to an eye, and the seared mark of pyro burn where neck joined his right shoulder. The long fingers that once had twirled the toggles of a field newscaster's walky-talky now were better acquainted with the grooves of a pyro butt.

"For the last time," he said, "you're better off home in bed. I think there may be trouble."

Petersen looked sour. "Good thinking," he said. "I have a hunch that way, too. I'm going to stick around."

Nolan shrugged. He eyed the Hotel Elena, towering almost up to the crystal dome, directly across the street from him. "It's your neck," he said. "You can catch me when I fly out." He glanced quickly at a wrist-chrono. "A quarter after four," he said. "If I'm not out in half an hour don't wait up. I may be detained."

Before Petersen could answer he was crossing the street, entering the hotel. The Elena was large, and the night clerk couldn't be expected to know every guest. He glanced up as Nolan entered, then went back to nodding over his magazine. Nolan walked to the gravwell and stepped in.

Nolan let the curiously soothing grav-currents flow over him, carrying him up till he'd ascended twelve floors. That was where Woller was, by the best information Petersen had been able to give him. He reached out a hand and swung himself out of the flow, into a silent corridor.

Not quite silent. Nolan listened and smiled. There was a party somewhere overhead; a vise-box blared briefly in one of the rooms on this corridor as a sleepless guest hunted music. From the grav-well came the low humming of the generators.

That was fine. If it were necessary to make any noise it might be confused with the vise-box, or the singing from overhead.

Woller's door was locked, of course. Nolan bent over the keyhole for a second. There was a tinny, springy *click,* and the door drifted open under the slow pressure of his hand.

The room was large and empty. A library, perhaps, as well as he could judge by the intermittent blood-tinted light that filtered in from an advertising stereolume across the street. Nolan flipped his cigarette lighter out, held it aloft and pressed the button. In the dim glow it shed he saw twin doors. After a moment's hesitation, he chose one, opened it gently, slipped through into a bedroom.

A night light glowed softly on the wall, revealing nothing. Nolan sniffed the air curiously, then wrinkled his nose. Perfume! Woller had added a new vice to his character. Nolan grimaced contemptuously, then moved toward the indistinct figure on the bed. His right hand dipped inside his shirt, came away with the slim pyro protruding from his fist.

"Woller," he said. "Wake up. You've got company."

There was a rustle from the bed, a gasp, a metallic click. Nolan jumped back, cursing. He flung an arm over his head as the overhead lumes burst into blinding light. But he'd caught a quick, stunning glimpse of what was on the bed and, quicker than starflight, his pyro jutted toward the lumes, flared wickedly. All lights died as the blast shorted the wires.

It had been a girl in the bed, blinking up sleepily, mouth a taut line of surprise. *The* girl—the one from the skid, the one he'd encountered in Annihilation Range! She had no more of a look at him than he at her, and she had been sleep-dazed, staring up at the light. Perhaps she hadn't recognized him—

"Hold still," he hissed—there is no personality to a whisper. "Where's Alan Woller?"

"Who are you?" the girl's voice came, a trifle unsteady. Good—she hadn't recognized him!

Nolan laughed voicelessly. "I'm the man with the gun," he replied. "I ask the questions. Where's Woller?"

"None of your business," the girl said. There was a note of confidence in her voice, and suddenly Nolan felt a furtive movement from the bed. Was there an alarm—a bell to summon servants?

"Hold it!" he whispered sharply. "One wrong move and I'll kill you. I mean business—and I want an answer."

The girl's voice was even now. "I won't give one."

Nolan's brows drew down over his eyes. What was this girl to Woller? Whatever the connection was, by rights he should take no chances. The girl was a danger to him—and the life of no woman on Woller's string should be permitted to stand between him and the chance for vengeance on the man who had framed him.

"I'll give you ten seconds," he whispered harshly.

But already he was stepping silently backward, concealed in the abyss-black gloom of the chamber. He reached noiselessly behind him for the knob of the door. He was being a fool and he knew it. But he had seen honesty in her eyes, back on the skid, and even the yearning for revenge couldn't make him blot that out with pyro-flame.

He opened the door, slid out, closed it softly behind him. The girl said nothing, perhaps had not known he had gone. Nolan cast a quick longing glance at the other door, but there was no time. In seconds the girl would discover she was alone. There would be an alarm, surely.

A dim thread of light showed him the door to the hall. Catlike he crossed to it, then halted, petrified. Men were coming down the hall, several of them by the voices. He caught a snatch of a rasping complaint: *"Old man Woller's tin soldiers, that's us. Who the hell does he—"*

Nolan swore lividly under his breath. The end of the trail had come.

But he stepped back a pace and stood there, pyro up-tilted and ready. He would have a split-second's advantage. If only there were no more than two or three of them—

And then the sound was drowned out. A sharp, moaning screech came from outside. A harsh metallic wail that climbed for the frigid heavens above, louder than the screaming trumpets of Ragnarök.

The alarm sirens! There was a break in the crystal dome that held the life of Avalon!

Meteorite, accident or simple fatigue—the dome had cracked. Air and heat would vanish. Death would tenant the city.

There was a sudden, sharp babble from the men outside, then the pounding of footsteps, halting as they dove into the grav-shaft. Nolan's chance! But he froze in his tracks, then whirled. He ran to the door behind him and wrenched it open.

"Get a heat suit!" he bawled to the girl on the bed. "Dome's cracked! You've got maybe twenty minutes—less, if it's a bad break!"

His voice was a bellow—there was no time for whispers. No time, and perhaps no need. If the dome had gone, Avalon might be a city of corpses, heat suits or none, before help could arrive with fresh oxygen tanks from far-away Aylette. Disguise would hardly matter then.

But he wasted no time in thought. He was out the door, down the hall and dropping into the cushioning grav-web of the descending shaft in seconds. Guests were waking in their rooms. The corridors were filling with shouting men and women. The shriek of emergency trucks filtered in from the street, and the hoarse bellow of the alarm sirens multiplied the havoc done to the peace of the night.

If he could get to a ship—?

But the slidewalks would be jammed with panicky humans, all with the same thought. A heat suit was his only chance. And the nearest ones he knew of were at South Lock, at the base of the dome itself!

He swung himself out of the shaft, raced across the lobby, which was already beginning to fill with people intent on escape. He was out the door with the van of them, racing across a still empty street toward South Lock.

A slim, pale figure darted across in front of him. He moved to dodge past, then slowed momentarily as he saw who it was.

"Steve!" Only one man knew that name—Petersen!

"Pete! What are you waiting for? Come on—get a suit!"

Petersen sighed, touched Nolan's shoulder to halt him. "There's no hurry, pal," he said mildly.

"No hurry! The dome alarm—"

Petersen shook his head. "Forget it," he said. "I turned the alarm in myself."

Toward what passed for morning in Avalon, the confusion died down. The emergency cars were off the streets, the sirens had long since stopped wailing and the last irate citizen had retired for what remained of a night's sleep.

Petersen came back from the window of his shabby little one-room apartment and reported on progress to Nolan.

"All quiet," he said. "Sure you won't change your mind and lie down for a while? You'll be needing sleep pretty soon."

Nolan swallowed the rest of his coffee, stubbed out a cigarette and shook his head. "No time," he said. He glanced at his chrono. "I figure on leaving in twenty minutes. You're sure Woller's going to be on that ship?"

Petersen grinned. "Pretty sure," he said. "I have my ways."

"You looked good on the deal last night," Nolan said. "You and your hammy ideas. I would have got out without all that."

Petersen was serious. "Not alive, no. When I saw those apes coming down the street I was pretty sure something was up. So I got on a phone—I got a friend works for Woller's company, and he reads the boss's mail—and that's what he told me. Woller has to get back to the Inner Planets in a hurry. He's sent a bunch of his company guards to pick up some stuff at his apartment. The only thing I could think of was to turn in the alarm and hope you'd get out in the confusion. You're a smart boy, but you ain't Deadeye Dick, friend. You couldn't of fought it out with five of Woller's finest."

Nolan inclined his head. "Maybe you're right. You say something big seems to be up?"

"What else? He gets a red-hot sealed teleflash from Aylette. Sealed, mind you—my friend can't listen in. He cancels the orders of the only ship his new company has in Avalon—cancels all the cargo contracts—and takes off in it in the middle of the night for Aylette. He'll be back here this morning, they say, to pick up those papers. Then they're off again, deep space, this time. The clearance says Mars."

Nolan nodded. His face was impassive, but a slight crinkling of the lines around his lean nose showed thought. What was Woller up to?

It was curiously difficult to concentrate on Woller. Absently, he found himself saying, "And you don't know who the girl was?"

"My information don't go that far," Petersen admitted. "He has a daughter some place, but she ain't supposed to be here now. But what's your guess about this she?"

"My guess is you're right," Nolan agreed reluctantly. There was something about soft blue eyes and silk-fine black hair that did not fit in the same picture with Woller.

Peterson was looking at him shrewdly, with a dim light of understanding glowing in his eyes and a hint of pity. As Nolan looked at him, Petersen looked away, began fumbling inside his waistband.

"What're you doing?" Nolan asked curiously.

"You'll need money," said Petersen. He finished unbuckling and dragged out an oiled-silk money belt. Without opening it, he tossed it to Nolan. "Here. You'll have to bid high to get passage on Woller's ship. This'll help."

Nolan nodded. "Thanks," he said. "Look, I—"

Petersen waved a hand airily. "Forget it. As long as there's enough radium on Pluto for prospectors to find, I'll have plenty money."

"Sure," said Nolan. "But the thanks still goes." He closed his eyes for a second, rubbed them. Then he blinked rapidly, took out his pyro and checked it. Full clip, save the one shell he'd used on the light last night. Twenty-three shots. He deftly slipped another cartridge in to make the full two dozen, then replaced the gun in its shoulder holster.

"You're going to get into trouble with that thing," Petersen prophesied.

Nolan shrugged. "I've got a name to live up to. A gunner has to have a gun—and I kind of think I'm going to need this one." He glanced at the chrono again and stood up, stretching.

"Well, good-by," he said casually. "I owe you a bunch of favors. You won't have to remind me."

"Course not," Petersen agreed. "Wouldn't do much good. But I'll sort of mention it to your heirs."

At the Operations lock of the Avalon spaceport Nolan opened the money belt Petersen had given him for the first time. He peered inside and whistled.

The cards had been with Petersen, all right. The little man had carried a young fortune around with him. He tucked the belt in a pocket with a mental resolve to pay it back some day, if he lived long enough, and went into the observation room.

Through the crystal dome he could see the ship, the only one on the field. It was a beauty—brand-new and glistening. By the look of her, she was the latest type. Pure gravity drive, the rocket jets used only for landing. It had a name, limned phosphorescent on a dark panel in the glittering hull: *Dragonfly*.

He turned and walked over to the port clearance officer. "I have to get to Mars," he said. "I hear this ship's bound there. Who do I see about booking passage?"

The port official scratched his bony head. "It's an unscheduled run," he said, "and I dunno if they're taking any passengers. But over there—" he waved a hand—"is the second mate. He might help you."

"Thanks." Nolan walked over, eyeing the pallid, short-bodied Venusian indicated. The man was staring glumly out of the observation panel.

"You the second on the ship out there?" Nolan asked.

The man turned slowly and looked him up and down. "Yeah," he said finally. "What about it?"

Nolan allowed his eyes to narrow conspiratorially. "I hear you're bound for Mars," he said, lowering his voice. "Any chance of taking a passenger?"

"No."

Nolan tapped a pocket. "Listen," he said, "it isn't just that I want a ride. I have to get to Mars. I'll pay."

The Venusian laughed sharply and Nolan thought, not for the first time, how superior environment is to heredity. The Venusians, like most of the System's intelligent life, were descended from Earthmen all right, but the adjective that described them best was "fishy."

The second said, "Pay? You haven't got enough money to get you into the lock of that ship."

"Oh, I don't know," Nolan said easily. He took the money belt out of his pocket, flashed the contents for a second. "I meant it," he said. "I have to get to Mars. Name your price—I've got it."

The Venusian's eyes widened. Nolan saw, from the corner of his eye, a skid rocketing across the field. It halted by the *Dragonfly,* and the ship's lock opened. Two bulky, heat-suited figures hurried out of the skid, into the ship.

"What do you say?" Nolan persisted, accelerated by the sight of the figures. One of them would be Woller's thug with the apparently vital papers. That would be the big one—the smaller might be a clerk from his office.

"Okay," the mate capitulated. "Tell you what. It'll cost you ten thousand credits. If it's worth that to you, all right."

Nolan shrugged wryly. "It's worth my neck," he grinned confidentially.

The Venusian grinned moistly back. "Payable in advance," he specified. "Now give it to me and I'll go out and arrange the deal with the captain."

Keeping a percentage of course, Nolan thought; but he only nodded and silently counted out the money. The Venusian grabbed it without checking the count. He said, "Okay, I'll be back in a minute," and left.

Nolan watched him struggle into his suit and clamber across the frigid soil of the field. The lock opened for him, then closed again. Nolan sensed a sudden uneasiness. He almost jumped when the port officer came up behind him and said:

"Wouldn't take you, huh?"

Nolan turned. "Sure," he said. "He had to go arrange it with the captain. I'll go out with him when he comes back for his clearance papers."

"Clearance papers!" the official barked. "Good Lord, man, they've had those for hours. That man isn't coming back!"

III

Nolan, swearing incandescently, flung his heat-suit voucher at the officer, grabbed the first suit in the rack and was in the main lock, waiting for the inner door to close, before he put it on. He had already sealed the suit and stepped out on the field when he noticed what the excited hammering of the port official on the lock door should have told him.

The suit had only a single oxygen tank in its clip—and the gauge showed "empty"!

He hesitated only a moment. His eye caught a glimpse of the *Dragonfly,* etched sharply against the black horizon by the field's blazing floodlights. Its smooth lines were suddenly blurred and indistinct. The grav-web was building up around it. In a moment it would be gone!

"Damn!" yelled Nolan, to the sole detriment of his own eardrums. Already the slight amount of air in his suit was nearly used up. But as soon as the web reached full focus the *Dragonfly* would blast off and Woller would be beyond reach for a long time!

Nolan swore fervently, then sealed his writhing lips to save air. He set off in a slow, heavy trot for the shimmering spaceship. He was breathing pure carbon dioxide and staggering nicely by the time he pushed his way through the thickening resistance of the grav-web to the massive outer door of the lock.

His bulging eyes caught the lever that opened the lock, guarded by a scoop-shaped streamshield. He yanked it blindly, saw the heavy panel roll aside, stumbled in.

Some member of the crew must have been watching—someone with compassion, unexpected enough in a ship of Woller's. The lock door clanged shut behind him and clean air hissed in. Nolan tore frantically at his faceplate and gulped deeply, dizzyingly.

The metal flooring shuddered. He felt an intolerable weight drag at his water-weak body as the ship took off. He hadn't made it by much, at that. A couple of seconds more and he would have been left.

"Boy!" Nolan gasped. "Somebody sure doesn't want me along on this ride."

The inner door was sliding open. Nolan stepped out into a well lit corridor, almost colliding with the flabby bulk of the Venusian.

The mate glared at him darkly, the hand on his waist poised suggestively above the butt of a pyro.

Before he could speak, Nolan said mildly, "You're a thieving louse. But I'm on the ship, and I won't hold it against you. Only—don't try that again."

The mate flushed. "The captain didn't want to take you," he mumbled. "I was going to send your dough back soon's we touched ground."

"Sure," Nolan agreed. "Having my full name and address the way you do, it'd be easy. Well, skip it. Where's my cabin?"

You wouldn't call it exactly hospitable, the way the mate stalled as long as he could, obviously trying to cudgel his feeble Venusian brain into some plan for getting rid of the unwanted passenger. But Nolan finally got his cabin.

It was the smallest and worst on the ship, of course, but the ship was a beauty. Nolan smiled in real appreciation when he saw the room. The furniture was glow-tinted plastic; the bed was covered with Earth silk.

"Beat it," he told the mate, and watched the door close behind him. Then he sat down to chart a course.

Woller might recognize him.

That was the first danger. True, Nolan had been reported dead and Woller knew nothing to the contrary. It was only a miracle that Nolan wasn't dead, in fact. Only the incredible chance of his being picked up in midspace, where he floated helplessly, one shoulder brutally pyro-scarred and half the air gone from his suit, had saved him then.

That had been one miracle, for even the ranging, avid patrol boats hadn't been able to find him after his mad leap from a lock of the ship that was carrying him to the moon.

But that miracle had occurred. And the second miracle was that the pleasure craft that saved him was piloted by a man who lived outside the law but had an iron-clad code of honesty—who wouldn't turn Nolan in for the bounty money on fugitives. Pete Petersen's scrawny shoulders bore no wings, but he'd seemed like an angel to Nolan that desolate day, when he'd seen the flare of Nolan's desperate signal rocket and swung round in a wide arc to pick him up, eventually to take him to the lawless safety of the Belt.

To everyone but Petersen, Steve Nolan was dead. And the little shots of gray now running through Nolan's dark hair, the scar that crossed one tanned cheek, gave him a new personality. He looked slender and dangerous as a lunging rapier, and every bit as cold.

But Woller would have good cause to remember Nolan. Woller had sat there in the courtroom, back on Earth. He'd sat there the whole dragging week of the trial, with Nolan's eyes on him every minute. He looked directly at Nolan, even while he was in the chair, telling the lies that linked Nolan with the Junta—the secret, revolutionary group of outer-planet malcontents that sought to overthrow Tri-planet Law's peace and order.

Nolan's lips contorted savagely as he recalled that. A traitor! His sole crime had been that he knew too much about Woller, his boss!

Woller had been clever about it. The law itself had removed Nolan, a menace to his lawless schemes. When Nolan, on his own initiative, had talked and bribed his way into seeing a confessed and condemned saboteur of the Junta for an interview, he'd found to his sick astonishment that the man was one he had seen in Woller's own office, not two months before.

He'd been childishly simple about it, had confronted Woller and demanded an explanation. Woller had put on his friendliest face and promised one—later. . . .

And then Woller had turned the dogs loose.

Within an hour Nolan was in jail for the bribery of the prison officials. The next morning came the incredible indictment: Sabotage for the Junta!

Nolan grimaced, recalled the careful, hideous network of lies and forgeries, the distorted evidence, the perjuries. But he had been one man, and Woller represented vast power.

Then abruptly there was a knock on the door. Jolted out of his thoughts, Nolan started, then called: "Just a minute."

This was the moment—and he had no plan. His pyro slid out into his hand. He broke it, stared at the twenty-four potent heat charges. They would be plan enough for him, if he got a clear shot at Woller. But if he should be disarmed, if Woller should suspect.

A moment later, the pyro hidden beneath his shirt again, he opened the door. It was the Venusian second, as before.

"Captain wants to see you," he growled. "Come on."

The *Dragonfly* was a single-deck craft, the captain's cabin located topside of the deck and amidships. Nolan looked around curiously, despite his internal tension, as he followed the Venusian along. The plastic keel panel underfoot showed an infinity of stars. There was one, large and bright, outstanding among the lesser stars. Nolan recognized it—the Sun, parent star to the farflung planet they'd just left. Now it was dim and feeble, but by the time they got within sight of the Inner Worlds it would be a ravenous thing, reaching out to destroy them with lethal radiations.

Out of curiosity, he asked, "When are you going to opaque?"

"Huh?" The Venusian looked startled for a second; then his blubber-drowned little eyes became shrewd. "Oh, about Orbit Saturn, I guess."

Nolan suppressed a sudden frown. He asked carefully, "Say, how do you do it on these new-type ships anyhow? All the ones I've been on, you had to have the panels filter-shuttered before they lifted gravs."

"Paint," the mate said curtly. "Okay, here we are."

He stood aside, pointed to a door with a glowing golden star embossed on it. Nolan nodded and entered, but his thoughts were racing.

Paint the panels! It would take the whole crew, and they'd never get it off. If they opaqued with paint the ship would be blind for weeks. The filter shutters—great strips of polarized colloid—were the only solution to the problem of keeping out the worst of the sun's dread radiations, but admitting enough light to guide the ship. But they had to be put on externally, before the ship took off. Mars? This ship, ports transparent as they were, would never dare approach the sun's blinding energies closer than Jupiter!

No wonder they didn't want me, Nolan thought grimly. *They're not going within a hundred million miles of Mars!*

The thought froze in Nolan's mind as he entered the captain's cabin. First he saw the captain, a tall, demon-black Martio-Terrestrial, standing before his own desk. Then his eyes flicked past, toward the florid-faced man who sat behind the desk, fumbling with a cigarette lighter.

And then, for the first time in three years, he was face to face with Alan Woller.

Nolan might have showed a flicker of emotion in his face. Heaven knows, the blast of iron hatred that surged up through his body was powerful enough. But Woller was lighting a cigarette. The second that it took him to finish it and look up was time enough for Nolan to freeze.

"Vincennes is my name," the captain was saying. "What's yours?"

"Matthews. I'm sorry to have forced my way onto your ship, but I had to get to Mars."

Woller looked up then, and a sudden trace of consternation flashed into his eyes. It died away, but a doubt remained.

He stared intently at Nolan, then said: "Why?"

Nolan smiled easily. "A lot of reasons—all of them personal. Who are you?"

Woller stood up. "I own this ship," he said coldly. "I didn't ask you aboard. Now that you're here, you'll answer my question or get off."

The time for a showdown had arrived. *Well,* Nolan thought, *it had to come some time.* He was strangely relaxed.

He shrugged. "You've got a point there," he admitted. "Well—"

He frowned and raised his hand as though to scratch his head, changed the motion in mid-air. And with the speed of a hopped-up *narcophene* smoker, the thin-snouted pyro was in his fist, slowly traversing a lethal arc that covered both men.

His voice was taut as he spoke. "It's your ship, Woller, but I'm taking it over. Woller—Alan Woller—look at me. *Do you know who I am?*"

Woller stared deep into the icy eyes confronting him. The doubt flared again in his own. His jaw dropped slack. His brows lifted and he whispered, "Nolan!"

Nolan didn't bother to nod. He said grimly, "Your hands—hold them where they are. You, too, Vincennes. I've come a long way for this and I don't mind killing. You taught me that, Woller. A man's life is nothing. Mine was nothing to you, when it endangered the dirty little treacheries you were working."

The life seemed to have gone out of Woller and left only a hulking, pallid carcass, propped up by the internal pressure of its own fear. There was murky horror crawling in his eyes.

Steve Nolan looked at him and his thin lips curled into a snarling grin. But those were only his lips. Strangely, there was no triumph in his heart, none of the fierce pleasure he'd dreamed of all those dreary years. There was only dull disgust, and the hint of a long-dead hope for rest again. Rest, and the common things of life on the Earth which was forbidden to him.

Woller could die before him now, and he would be avenged. But Woller alive could say the words that would wipe out the banishment, would return him to the green star that was home. Woller could be made to confess—

"I ought to blast you now," he said in a soft, chill tone that was like a whip to Woller, jerking him upright. "I ought to, and I will if I must. But you can live if you want to."

Woller was licking his lips, his face a mask, only his panic-stricken eyes alive.

"You can live," Nolan repeated. "A full statement about the Junta frame, in writing. Write it out and thumbprint it, and we'll telestat it to the nearest TPL station. Then you can have the lifeboat, Woller, and as much of a start as TPL gives you. Are you willing to pay that much for your life, Woller?"

Woller's lips were stiff but he forced the words through. "Go to hell."

Nolan nodded, and the deadly weariness settled down over him again. "I see your point, of course," he said slowly. "Tri-planet doesn't come out here much and a man is reasonably safe from them. But you, Woller—power's your life blood. And a man on the run can't have much power. I know."

His finger curled on the trigger of the pyro and Woller, staring avidly, desperately, whitened at the mouth. His lips moved as though about to form words—

Nolan's trigger-sharp senses caught a hint of movement behind him. *Fool!* he thought desperately. *The door!* He tried to hurl his body aside, out of the way of the door that opened behind him. But he couldn't do that and keep the pyro leveled on the two men at the desk. He saw Woller, exultant hatred leaping into his purpled face, plunging for a drawer of the desk; saw the door opening and someone stepping through. Then, just as he was leveling the gun on Woller again, he saw the flashing swing of the other man in the room. Forgotten Vincennes —with a heavy nightstone paperweight held bludgeon-like in his hand, leaping in at him! He had no chance even to try to turn. The weight was coming down on the side of his head. All he could do was try to roll with it.

But the momentum was immense and the heavy weight struck him down to the floor, drove him headlong into unconsciousness. . . .

Somebody was kicking him. Nolan groaned once, then compressed his lips as he remembered where he was.

He opened his eyes and rolled over. The blubbery Venusian second was standing over him, face sullen but eyes glinting with perverse pleasure. He raised his heavy spaceman's boot again—

"Hold it," said Woller from the desk. They were still in the cabin.

Woller got up, came over, looking down at Nolan. His bearing was confident again; he exuded an aura of brutal power.

"You should have killed me, Nolan," he said. "You only get the one chance, you see."

Nolan silently pushed himself erect. His ribs were agonized where the second had booted them, and a blinding throb in the skull reminded him of the captain's blow. He was conscious that his armpit holster hung light. The pyro was gone.

Vincennes had left. Only Woller and the Venusian second were in the cabin with him. "My only doubt," Woller was saying, "is whether to blast you now or save you for a little later, when I'll have more time."

"Sure," said Nolan tonelessly. "If you want my vote, it's for now. Get it over with."

Woller nodded. "That would be much pleasanter for you. I think I'll save you." He nodded slowly. Then, to the mate, "Take him below!"

Back down the corridor, the mocking stars still bright through the crystal underfoot. Back and down, till they came to the grav room, where the pulsing, whining generators spun their web of antigravitational power.

"We don't have a brig," the mate apologized. "But I think this will hold you in."

Eyes warily on Nolan, he circled him and opened a round metal door. It was an unused storeroom, bare except for rows of vacant metal shelves.

"In you go," said the Venusian, and Nolan complied. The door slammed behind him and was bolted.

There was a whine in the air, he noticed. The singing of the grav-generators. It was not unpleasant . . . at least, not unbearable, he corrected himself. But how it persisted! It was constant as the keening of a jammed frequency-modulator, high as the wail of a banshee.

He let his aching body slip to the floor, lay there without even trying to think. He raised his head for a searching second, but there was nothing to see. Bare walls, bare shelves.

He was helpless. His chance might come when the second let him out. Till then, he would sleep.

When had he slept last? Save for the few minutes of unconsciousness, it was easily thirty hours. He pillowed his head on his arm. . . .

He moved his head uncomfortably, burrowed his ear deeper into his biceps. That damned keening! He shifted restlessly, stopped his exposed ear with his other hand. That movement racked the beaten ribs, but the shrilling, soft and remorseless, kept on. It was enough to drive a man mad! It was—

He sat bolt upright, eyes flaring angrily. That was what Woller had planned!

It was torture—subtle, undramatic, simple. But pure, horrid torture.

Nolan's face was gray with strain. It was incredible that a sound, a noise, could become a threat. He'd heard the same sound a million times before, though never at such close range, or from such titanic generators. But now—

He began trying to fill his mind with other things, but there was no room for thought in a brain that was brimming with naked sound. Snatches of school-days poetry, long columns of multiplication tables— They jumbled in his brain. The lines ran together and muddled, were drowned out by the wail of the generators. He gave up and sat there, forcing himself to be still, while the sound hovered in the atmosphere all around him, his jaw muscles taut enough to bite through steel, a great pulse pounding in his temples. . . .

Flesh could stand only so much. After a while—he didn't know when—he was mercifully unconscious.

A volcano erupted under him and awoke. His whole body was a mass of flame now, head throbbing like the jets of a twenty-ton freight skid, chest and ribs as sore as though they were flayed. A sickening weight held him crushed against the metal floor.

The roaring from without was the sound of the rockets, loud enough to drown out the whine that had nearly killed him. The ship was landing. And at once there was a gentle jar, then a dizzying vertigo as the grav-web was cut off abruptly. The rockets died down and were silent.

Everything was silent. The change was fantastic, a dream. Nolan, lying there, thought the silence was the finest thing he had ever heard.

It didn't last. There were footsteps outside, and the Venusian second mate entered. "On your feet," he said curtly. "The boss is ready for you."

Nolan stood up cautiously. His feet were shaky, but he could use them. He stepped over the rounded sill and followed the Venusian's directions. There were men in the corridor, some of them in heat suits. Nolan wondered where they were. Neptune was on the other side of the sun—could they be as far in as Uranus? How long had he been unconscious!

"Get moving," repeated the second, and Nolan moved.

The blessed stillness! He was grinning to himself as he walked along the corridor, listening for the lethal whine that wasn't there any more. When they got to where Woller, space-suited and bloated, was directing a crew of men in the moving of a bulky object, Woller noted the grin. He was not pleased.

"Enjoying yourself, Nolan?" he asked, unsmiling. "That will have to stop."

A grin stayed on Nolan's face, but it was not the same one. It was a savage threat. Woller looked at it, and looked hastily away.

"Stand him over in the corner," he said to the Venusian second. "I'll attend to him right away. Business first."

The second jerked a thumb at the corner formed by the airlock door and the wall of the corridor. Nolan looked in the direction indicated, and a sudden tic in his brows showed a thought that had come to him. The red signal light winked out as he watched; the inner door had closed.

He stared through the transparency at what was beyond. Darkness was all he could see—darkness, and the light-dotted outline of buildings in the distance. Just beyond the lock was something that looked like a skid, with men's figures around it. His forehead puckered, and his eyes returned to the signal light, now dark—

The Venusian second watched Nolan limp slowly over to the indicated position. His eyes narrowed. "Hey, what's the matter?" he asked surlily.

Nolan shook his head. "Something in my shoe," he said. He halted and balanced himself on one foot, poking into the offending footgear. "A button, I guess," he said as he drew out, concealed, something that he knew quite well was *not* a button.

He breathed a silent prayer, and it was answered. The Venusian grunted and turned away. Nolan walked quickly over to the wall, by the lock light, turned and stood surveying the scene without interest. His hands apparently were linked idly behind him—but behind his back they were moving swiftly, dexterously. A *clink* of glass sounded, and Nolan winced as a sharp sliver cut his thumb. Then he stood motionless, waiting.

The men were shock-wrapping a long, casket-like object. To judge by the care they were using, the contents were delicate and the handling would be rough, Nolan noted absently. Explosives, perhaps?

The last loop of elastic webbing went around it, and the Venusian second pulled it taut. "All right," he grunted. "Take it away."

"Lock!" bawled Woller as the men picked up the bundle. That was Nolan's signal.

As slowly as he could manage he stepped idly away from the lock, away from the signal light, hugging the wall.

A deckhand, not troubling to look at the warning light across the corridor—Nolan mentally thanked his gods—touched the release that opened the lock door. And—

Ravenous flame lashed out from the wall.

IV

Nolan was in motion before the incandescent gases had died. The half-dozen men who had been in the corridor were either down on the floor or blindly reeling about. Even without a proton-reflector behind it to focus its fierce energies, a pyro charge exploded on unarmored men can do a lot of damage.

Nolan blessed the hunch that had warned of trouble, the remembrance of an old spacer's trick that had led him to hide a pyro charge in his shoe, back there in the stateroom. Still it had been luck, pure and simple, that gave him the chance to open the signal light socket, take out the lume and put the pyro pellet between the contacts. When he'd got out of range and the automatic warning as the lock opened had touched it off—

Catastrophe. He'd known when to close his eyes, where to stand for safety. The others hadn't. And so the others were blind.

He grabbed a pyro from a writhing wretch on the floor—there was horror in him as he saw the seared face that had once been that of the Venusian second. He picked a heat suit out of the cubby, and was into it and in the lock before the blinded men who had escaped the full flare could recover themselves.

The lock doors took an eternity to work, but at last he was out in the cold, black open. A hasty glance at the landscape told him nothing. Uranus or Pluto—it had to be one of them. That was all.

A man was just coming out of the skid, perhaps twenty feet away. Nolan clicked on his radio, waited for the inevitable question—but it didn't come. The man's transparent faceplate merely turned incuriously to Nolan for a second, then bent to examination of the fastenings of the skid's lock. Nolan turned calmly and strode off along the side of the ship. When he rounded the stern he broke into a run, heading straight out across charred earth to a chain of hummocks that promised shelter.

How long would pursuit be delayed? Late or soon, it would come. Nolan realized that he had no plan. But he had life, and freedom.

He topped the first of the hummocks, scrambled down into the trough behind it. He was relatively safe there, as he cautiously elevated his head to examine the ship and what lay behind it.

Already—it had been scant minutes since the carnage in the lock corridor—the search for him had begun. He saw a perfectly round spot of brilliance fall on the side of the ship, then dance away. Through the ice-clear Plutonian night he could make out the figure of a man with a hand light scanning the belly of the ship, looking to see if Nolan had hidden himself there. They would quickly learn the answer to that—and know what he had done.

Beyond the ship were a few dim lights, distorted by a crystal dome.

It was another city—or not quite a city, but a domed settlement out here in the wilderness.

Without warning a sun blossomed on the side of the ship. Nolan stood frozen for a split second, then dropped, cursing. They'd seen him, somehow, had turned the ship's powerful landing beam on him. But how?

A soundless bolt of lightning that splashed against a higher hill behind him drove speculation out of his mind. Nolan frowned. The ship was armed—he hadn't known that. Installation of pyros in interplanetary craft was the most forbidden thing of the starways. But there was no time for wonder.

As another blast sheared off the crest of a hill, Nolan, keeping low, scuttled away behind the shelter of the hummocks. His only safety was in flight. Armor he had none. The frozen gases that comprised the hummocks would never stop the dread thrust of a properly-aimed pyro.

He fled a hundred yards, then waited. Silence. He risked a quick look, saw nothing, retired behind the shelter of the hill to consider. They'd suspended fire—did they think him dead? Did they know he had escaped?

Or was there a hidden danger in this? It might be a ruse. They could be waiting for him to move, to show himself. . . .

Nolan shivered, and absently turned up the heat control of his suit. He felt suddenly hopeless. One man against—what? His thoughts, unbidden, reverted to the girl he had left in Avalon, and to the sordid fear that she might be what she seemed. Nolan's cheek muscles drew tight, and his face hardened. Woller, partly protected by his heat suit, undoubtedly had lived through the instant inferno when the pyro charge went off. That was one more thing against him—the girl. Nolan sighed.

And a faint reverberation on the soles of his feet brought him stark upright, staring frantically over the sheltering mound of ice. A skid was racing down on him.

Before he could move its light flared out, spotted him.

And a tiny voice within his helmet said, "Don't move, Nolan. You can't get away now. You'll die if you try. Next time you play hide-and-seek with me, Nolan—don't leave your helmet radio on!"

If Woller had burned with rage before, now he was frozen. He was a blind man there before Nolan, his eyes swathed in thick white bandages. But the hulking Earthman with the pyro who stood by his side, and lean black Captain Vincennes at the controls, were eyes enough for him.

"But I wish I could see you myself," Woller said softly, his fingers drumming idly against the wide fabric arm of his cushioned passenger's chair. "The ship's surgeon says it may be weeks before I see again. If I could afford to keep you alive that long—" He sighed regretfully. "No, I can't afford it," he concluded. "There are more important things, though nothing—" his voice shook but kept its chill calm—"that would give me more pleasure than to see you die."

"We could save him, Woller," Vincennes said. "Pickle him in a sleep-box like—"

"Be still, Vincennes!" Woller's voice was sharp. "I'll ask for advice when I want it!"

A sleep-box—Nolan remembered suddenly what they were. Small coffins, large enough for a man, equipped with an atomic-powered generator that kept the occupant in a sort of half-death, not breathing or able to move, but capable of existing almost indefinitely without food.

Nolan wondered absently what they were doing with sleep-boxes, then gave it up. It didn't matter. He cursed the carelessness that had led him to leave the radio on in his suit. It had been simple for the *Dragonfly*'s radio-man to tune in on its carrier wave, get a radio fix on his position.

The skid swerved abruptly in a sloppy turn, and the surly Earthman at the controls halted it and looked around. "Okay," he grunted. "Here we are."

Woller nodded. "Take me out," he ordered. "Nolan, too."

Nolan peered out the window. Absorbed in self-recrimination, he hadn't paid attention to their trip. He was surprised to find gleaming metal all around the skid. They were in a heat lock—they had come to the domed settlement.

The Martian Vincennes went first. As soon as the pressure gauge showed he was safely outside the Earthman gestured to Nolan. He wedged himself wearily into the air chamber, closed the door. He was ready for a break when the outer portal opened . . . but there was no break. Not with Vincennes and his ready pyro there.

Woller, stumbling and cursing, followed, and the Earthman. Vincennes opened the main lock and they went into the dome.

There were two great ships inside, dimly lighted by a string of pale lumes overhead. Nolan looked at the mass of them, at the rodlike projections clustered around the nose, and knew them for what they were: Warships!

Scaffolding was still around them. They were not yet ready for launching, not ready for whatever mission of treason Woller had planned them for. But by the look of them the day was close. And Nolan was—awaiting execution.

One look at Woller's iron countenance under the tape showed that. Vincennes' hand, tight-knuckled around the butt of his gun, was ample confirmation.

But the moment had not yet come. Woller said, "Are they waiting?"

Vincennes' glance sped to a lighted door at the far side of the hangar. "Looks that way," he said. "Shall I attend to Nolan first? He's tricky—"

Woller laughed softly. "He's used up all his tricks. We'll take him with us, alive. He might come in handy. He's been out of sight for three years now. I'm just a bit curious where he's been. Perhaps it's somewhere we should know about."

He groped for Vincennes' arm, found it. "Let's go," he said. "We can't keep the chief waiting."

Nolan was first through the door. He was in a small room where four or five ordinary-looking people were sitting around at ease. One was in uniform, the others the perfect example of quite successful businessmen.

"Is he here yet?" whispered Woller. The Martian looked around the room before he answered.

"Not yet. Cafferty—Lieutenant Brie—Searle—Vremczyk. That's all."

The dumpling-shaped soldier in the gray-green of Pluto's militia stared at Woller. "What the devil's the matter with your face?" he spluttered.

Woller answered before Vincennes could. "I had an accident, Brie," he snapped. "Keep your fat nose out of it."

The dumpling turned purple. But he said nothing, and Nolan realized Woller's importance in this gathering. This gathering of—what?

Nolan looked around quickly, and the answer raced to his brain. An officer of Pluto's defense forces—two or three well-dressed men, apparently wealthy, with something about them that shrieked "politico" —and Woller, once overlord of the System's greatest news-dissemina-

tion agency, still a man of vast influence. It looked like the back room
of a political convention—or the gathering of a cabal.

The Junta!

It had to be the Junta.

What they were saying began to make sense. A tall man in dove
gray was speaking.

"We're not satisfied, candidly," he was saying. "Woller, you've had
more money than our resources can afford. Everything you've asked
for you got. And what have you to show for it? Three ships—not one
of them fit to fly."

Woller laughed contemptuously. "Candidly, Cafferty," he mim-
icked, "I don't care how you feel. My money's gone right along with
yours. Warships cost money."

"So do thousand-acre Martian estates," shot the little lieutenant.
"How much of your money is in these ships—and how much of ours is
in your pockets?"

Woller turned his blind eyes toward the lieutenant and stood motionless for a second. Then, softly, "Once again, Brie—keep your fat
face shut. You are not indispensable."

The pudgy soldier glared and opened his mouth to speak—but an in-
terruption halted the quarrel. The door opened without warning, and
another man entered.

What he looked like Nolan could not guess. He wore a heat suit
with the helmet down. The polar-plastic faceplate was set for one-way
vision. Even his voice was muffled and distorted as he spoke.

"Are we all here?" he asked. The others seemed to note nothing
odd about his incognito—did he always disguise himself, Nolan wondered? "Where's Orlando?"

Brie answered. "He was on Mars, on the other side of the sun. He's
on his way."

The mirror-faced helmet bobbed as its owner nodded. Then it
turned toward Nolan. "What's this?" he asked, advancing.

Vincennes gestured with the pyro. "His name is Nolan," he said.
"He tried to get rough with Mr. Woller. He's dangerous."

"Dangerous!" The blurred voice was angry. "Then why is he here?
We have enough danger as it is. Give me that pyro!"

This was it, Nolan knew, and he tensed his body for the leap he had
to attempt, though he knew it was useless. The man in the heat suit
reached for Vincennes' pyro. In the moment while the gun was passing
from hand to hand there might be a chance. . . .

There were shouts from outside, and the sound of running feet. The man in the heat suit whirled. "Bolt that door!" he shouted. "Bolt it! Now!"

Brie, dazed for a second, sprang to obey. Then he turned, his plump, pale face damp with sudden sweat. "What is this, Chief?" he asked. "Are we—is there trouble?"

Chief! thought Nolan. So this hooded stranger was the leader of the conspiracy. Masked, disguised like the bandit chief of a flamboyant operetta.

The Chief was laughing. "Lots of trouble," he answered. The dull shouting from outside continued, rising to a crescendo as whoever was without pounded against the door and found it locked. Then abruptly it subsided. The huge telescreen on the desk buzzed sharply. The solid little man seated beside it automatically clicked the switch that turned it on.

"Turn it off!" bellowed the man in the heat suit. But it was already working. The prismatic flare on the screen showed no vision impulses were coming in, showed that whoever was calling was using a sound transmitter only—a portable set like those in a heat suit. A voice said sharply:

"Attention, Junta! The man who claims to be the Chief is a masquerader. Kill him! This is the Chief speaking now!"

V

Doubt sprang into the eyes of every man present. It lasted only a second—for the masquerader's action proved the charge against him.

He grappled the pyro from dazed Vincennes, sprang back, fired a warning blast that smashed the telescreen.

"Don't move, anybody!" he ordered. "Nolan—take their guns!"

Nolan threw questions to the winds, sped to obey. He found a business-like little heat pencil in the inner pockets of the chunky man, a pearl-handled burlesque of the service pyro in the gaudy gemmed holster Lieutenant Brie dangled from his belt. Nothing else—and his search was thorough.

"All set," he reported.

"Good enough. Searle—are there heat suits in this room?"

The chunky man looked stricken. He nodded. "In that locker," he said dizzily, pointing to the wall.

"Get them out, Nolan. Give one to every man and put one on yourself. Those outside will take their chances."

Nolan raced to comply. The stillness outside the door was menacing. While he was dragging the suits out, throwing them at the men, while they were putting them on, the man called Searle was staring at the masquerader with dawning comprehension.

"What are you going to do?" he whispered. "Are you—"

The man in the heat suit laughed sharply. "Get your suit on," he said. "You know what I'm going to do. All set?" Every man was garbed, helmets down. "Ten seconds to seal them. One, two, three—"

He counted slowly and Nolan watched him with fascination. At *five* the gauntleted left hand came up to the butt of the pyro, worked the tiny chambering lever half a dozen times. Nolan gasped in spite of himself. There were seven lethal pyro charges in the chamber of that gun—enough to blast down a mountain!

The count was finished. Through Nolan's helmet radio, automatically turned on, the man's calm voice ordered, "All right, Nolan. Open the door and let them in!"

Nolan moved. As his hand was on the lock, just as it turned and the door swung loosely inward—

Blam! the impostor swung and fired the massive charge in his pyro at the thin wall that kept air and life in the dome.

They were running over icy ground. At most there was a minute or so of advantage—less, if the men they'd left in the room had other weapons concealed somewhere. And still Nolan didn't know who his savior was.

"All right, now," he panted over the helmet phone. "Give. Who are you?"

The answer was a chuckle, mixed with gasping as the smaller man strove to match his speed. "Tell you later," he panted.

"Hold it!" Nolan broke in, suddenly recalling the oversight that had been so disastrous before. "Don't tell me. Show me—and turn off your radio. They've got tracers."

There was a snort of sudden comprehension from the phone, then silence. Nolan looked to see the figure spurt into the lead, gesture ahead. They were rounding the dome. The bulk of the *Dragonfly* appeared, with a big cargo skid drawn up beside it. The gesticulating arm of the other man pointed directly at it.

Nolan glanced around. There was no one following—yet.

The men hadn't had weapons, then—and those who had been out-side would not be pursuing anybody. He tried to thrust from his mind the recollection of what had happened when the sucking rush of escap-ing air had thrown wide open the door he had unlocked, and the tug of naked vacuum gripped the men behind it. A dozen of them there had been, hulking brutes from the flight sheds of a system's blowsiest ports, and one man in a heat suit, faceplate mirrored like that of the man Nolan ran beside. It is not pleasant to see a strong man try to shriek in agony, and fail because the air has bubbled from his lungs.

The outer door of the skid was open, and the impostor trotted in. When Nolan was beside him he leaned on the lock control. Ever so slowly, the outer door closed; slowly the inner opened.

They burst into a chamber where a man was just rising from a telescreen, face contorted with consternation and hate, hand bringing up a pyro from a drawer in the chart table.

The pseudo-chief's gun spoke first, and the head and shoulders of the other disappeared in a burst of flame and sickening smoke. There was no time for delicacy. Ruthlessly shoving the seared corpse away, the stranger dove for the controls, touched the jet keys.

The ungainly skid shuddered, then drove forward. The stranger opened all jets to the limits of their power. Creaking and groaning, the skid responded. The dial of the speed indicator showed mounting ac-celeration, far beyond what the ship was designed for.

Nolan, clinging with one arm to a floor-bolted chair, threw back his helmet and yelled: "I'm ready any time! What's the story? Who the devil are you?"

The impostor waved a hand impatiently. His muffled voice came: "Take a look in there. There may be more aboard!"

Nolan grimaced and nodded. He picked his way over the jolting floor, blaster out, to the threshold. His groping hand encountered the lume switch, flooded the cargo hatch with light. It was almost empty. A few crates, the long casket-like object he had seen in the ship. Nothing behind which a man could hide.

Nolan turned to see the masquerader unzipping the folds of his heat suit with one hand while he guided the careening skid with the other. He brought out a tiny black box, opened it to show a key and a lever. He thumbed the lever open, braced the box between his knees, began tapping the key rhythmically. A curious shrill staccato came from the box. *Dee dideedeedit didideedit deedeedit deedeedee didee didididit—*

After a second he stopped, waited. Then faintly an answer came back from the box. *Deedeedee dideedidit—*

And silence. Satisfied, the man closed the box, slowed the skid to a point where its guidance no longer required complete attention. They had reached the ring of ice hummocks that surrounded Woller's dome. The skid bounded over the first rise, zoomed through that trough and the next; then the man kicked the rudder jets. It spun along the trough to where the hummocks were highest; then he cut the jets.

He turned to Nolan, threw back his helmet.

"My God," gasped Nolan. "Pete!"

Petersen grinned. "You called it, boy," he admitted. "Don't I get around though?"

Nolan closed his eyes and tightened his grip on the back of his chair. "The story," he said. "Quick."

Petersen shrugged. "How can I tell it quick? It's long. . . . Maybe if I tell you one thing you can fill in the details."

"What's the one thing?"

"I work for TPL."

TPL—Tri-planet Law! That explained—

Nolan exhaled slowly. "I begin to see," he said. "I always did think you knew too much for a guy that made his living at cards."

Petersen laughed. "My biggest trouble," he said wryly. "I can't win at cards. Whatever I do. It's been quite a drawback to my career. You can see how people would get suspicious of a professional gambler who always loses. I had to keep on the move."

Nolan's brain was beginning to work again. "But listen," he said. "How come you didn't turn me in when you picked me up—right after I escaped? If you worked for the Law—"

Petersen's face grew serious. "Boy," he said, "you gave us a lot of trouble. You and your escapes. We weren't planning to keep you in jail, Steve. Any fool could see you were being framed—fixed court, semi-pro witnesses. But TPL couldn't step in, out in the open. We didn't know enough for a showdown. So you were going to be summoned to Mars for further questioning. When we found out all you knew you were to be taken care of some way or other. Given a new identity, kept undercover until we were ready to move."

"And I jumped the gun."

Petersen nodded. "I was in the neighborhood, heading for Earth. The TPL man on the ship called Earth Base; they called me. The ship had you spotted, but they decided not to pick you up. Base figured that if you thought you were being hunted you'd keep yourself under cover and we wouldn't have to bother. And if I picked you up I could pump you myself."

Nolan grinned. "How did you do?"

"Fine. You talked more than a ventriloquist with a two-tongued dummy. . . . Then you turn up on Pluto, just when things are getting hot."

"After three years of hiding in third-grade ratholes for fear of the law." There was no bitterness in Nolan's voice. Just a calm statement of an unpleasant fact.

Petersen's voice was level, too, but his eyes were alert as he watched Nolan. "That couldn't be helped, Steve. You know what was at stake."

Abruptly the grin returned. "The whole damned System, that's all," Nolan said a little proudly. "Well . . . go ahead with your story."

Petersen shrugged. He looked a little relieved as he spoke. "You know most of it. Oh—one part you don't know. Woller's daughter—her name's Ailse—knew about what he was doing. She just found out about it. We had a maid working in her home in Aylette—she didn't generally stay with Woller; they didn't get along."

Nolan's brows lifted. "Oh?"

"Yep. Ailse was worried silly. She even talked to the maid—not much, just enough that we could figure out what was happening. It seemed she was going to confront Woller with what she knew, try to talk him out of treason."

"A real good idea," Nolan remarked. "Knowing Woller—"

"That's how we knew where this base was. She told the maid. Oh, you do know where you are, don't you? On Pluto. The wildest section there is, north of Annihilation Range."

"How about this cockeyed disguise of yours? Who is this Chief you were supposed to be?"

Petersen frowned. "Don't know, exactly," he admitted. "There are three men it could be—they're all connected with the Junta, we're pretty sure. They're all on Saturn, and we got word that they were rendezvousing here. We knew the boss kept his identity hidden by wearing this get-up, so I was detailed to cut in."

Nolan nodded. Then, his thoughts reverting, he said, "Where's the—where's Ailse now?"

Petersen looked unhappy. "Uh—I don't know. After you left we sent for her, just to see what she knew that might help. The maid went after her—and couldn't find her. She'd gone out of town, wasn't expected back for some time. We couldn't wait. All the leaders of the Junta meeting here—it was too big a chance."

Nolan said, "Well, what are we doing about it? They're all there, and they're warned. And we're out here, parked on the edge of nowhere, waiting for them to get up a scout party and grab us."

Petersen turned to look out the window in the direction of the dome. He scanned the skies carefully, then pursed his lips.

"Well, no, Steve," he said, pointing. "Take a look."

Arrowing lines of fire were swooping down from far into the blackness. Three trails of white flame showed where three ships were plummeting to the surface. Nolan turned to Petersen with a startled question in his eyes.

"Watch," Petersen advised. "This'll be worth seeing!"

Down and down they drove, faster than meteor ever fell. A mile above the ground the jets behind died, and yellow flame burst ahead of them, flaring quickly to white. They slowed, poised, and then, in perfect unison, spun off to one side. They came around in a great circle and dived at the ground again. And repeated the operation, over and over.

And abruptly Nolan saw what was happening. He was witnessing the systematic annihilation of the domed settlement! Immense bursts of fire from ship-sized pyros were blazing into the ground. The hummocks prevented a clear view, but Nolan could see from the reflected glare on the mountainsides behind that the destruction was frightful.

"I called them," Petersen said softly. "You saw me call them. That black box—it's a telesonde."

Nolan didn't turn, fascinated by the sight. "What's a telesonde?" he asked absently.

"A radio that carries neither voice nor vision. Only one note short or long depending on how long the key is held down. Your great-great-grandfather knew about it. It was the first method of wireless communication. Now it's so completely forgotten that when TPL researchers dug it up it was adopted as the most secret method of communication available."

Nolan nodded his head. The ships came around again, and down. This time the forward jets were delayed. When they flared out they persisted, while the ships dropped gently out of sight. They were landing.

The destruction of the dome was complete.

Nolan turned away. "Quite a sight," he said slowly. "They deserve to die, of course. . . ."

"Steve."

Nolan's eyes narrowed suddenly. He looked at Petersen. "Yes?"

Petersen, for once, seemed almost at a loss for words. He licked his lips before he spoke. "Steve—there are one or two other things. Did you know that Ailse wasn't Woller's daughter by blood?"

Nolan looked at him unbelievingly. "Not his daughter?"

Petersen shook his head. "Woller married a widow. A wealthy one, with a daughter. They didn't get along too well. The woman died. Some people thought it might be suicide."

The quick joy flooded up in Nolan. Petersen saw it and his face grew somber. "That's one of the things, Steve," he said. "The other one— Hell, this is hard to say."

Nolan stood up and the joy was gone from his face. "Damn you, Pete," he said emotionlessly. "Don't break things gently to me."

Petersen shrugged. "Ailse wasn't anywhere we could find her—and we know a lot of places to look in. The ship left to come here. She was at Woller's home till just before then. Woller sent men to bring something from his apartment to the ship. I thought it was papers at the time—but it could have been a girl. So—where does that leave Ailse?"

Where? Nolan stood rocklike as the thought trickled through the automatic barrier his mind had set up. Where did it leave Ailse?

A charred fragment of what had once been beauty. A castoff target for TPL's searching pyros.

"I'll say it again, Steve. You know what was at stake. If the Junta had time— Well, we didn't know what kind of weapons they had there. That was one reason why I was sent ahead in that crazy disguise. If I had had time to scout around it might have been possible to do things less bloodily. I didn't have time. We couldn't take chances."

There was no anger in Nolan, no room for it. He sat there, waiting for Petersen to start the jets and send them back to the dome. He knew how he would scour the ashes, hoping against hope. And he knew what he would find.

It would have been better, he thought, almost to have died under Woller's pyro, or the TPL ships'. If he'd stayed behind—if Woller had put him in the sleep-box as Vincennes had suggested, and he had shared obliteration with her. . . .

The sleep-box! The casket!

It took Petersen a full second to recover from his surprise when the frozen face of Nolan suddenly glowed with hope, when he leaped up and dashed into the cargo hatch. It took him minutes to follow him. Minutes spent in making the difficult decision of whether or not he should prevent a man from taking his own life.

The decision was wasted, he found. Behind the scattered boxes of pyro shells, wedged into a corner of the hold, Nolan knelt beside a long, narrow casket. Fiber shock-wrapping was scattered about. Nolan's fumbling fingers were working the latch of the casket, lifting the lid. . . .

The shout that left his lips was deafening in the small hold. Petersen looked closer, tiptoed up—

And all the way back to the waiting ships of the TPL Petersen was grinning to himself. Though his hands guided the ship skillfully as ever, though his gaze was outward at the flowing terrain beneath, he saw but one thing.

The tableau as he had approached the casket and seen Nolan, face indescribably tender, shutting off the sleep currents, reaching for the ampoule of stimulant that would revive the unconscious dark-haired girl within.

The trouble with Enid was that once again I was beginning to feel guilty about being safe and warm in Oklahoma, while people I knew were getting killed in Italy, North Africa and the Pacific. When the final battle came along, I wanted to be in it. My 201 file bulged with letters requesting reassignment overseas. My CO kept forwarding them with approving endorsements, and higher echelons kept ignoring them.

So in the early part of 1944, when a circular came through asking for volunteers for Arctic service, I signed up instantly. Shortly thereafter I was on my way to Buckley Field, Colorado, for training.

Buckley Field was just outside of Denver, the home of a science-fiction writer named Willard E. Hawkins. Denver was also where the Colorado Writers' Association was about to have their annual dinner, and Willard was pleased to invite me to be their featured speaker. I accepted with pleasure.

Unfortunately the Air Force had other plans. I was a non-com by then, but Buckley Field was thick with non-coms. Stripes carried no exemption from shit details, and I was put on KP for the night I was supposed to speak.

It seemed to me that there was a way out of that. I went hunting for the base Public Relations Officer, in order to let him know what bad public relations it would be to disappoint the Colorado Writers because their featured speaker was pushing tin trays through the steam jets.

He saw the argument at once and got me off. However, he could not do that until I found him, and that took all day. By the time I had got off KP I had just seconds to change into ODs and catch the bus to Denver. By the time I reached the banquet hall dinner was over and Willard Hawkins was just rising to introduce me. He said a few gracious words. I got up in front of all those friendly, expectant faces. And it occurred to me right then, for the very first time, that in all the turmoil I hadn't got around to thinking of anything to say to them.

I don't know how long I stood there in silence, stolid and stunned, brother to the ox. It may have been a week. It felt longer. At some point Willard perceived I was in trouble, so he rose to ask me a question. I answered that easily enough, and then I was going.

But those first endless minutes are burned into my brain. I've talked to a lot of audiences in the thirty-odd years since and there have been disasters now and then—but, after that, nothing ever seemed really bad again.

A nice thing about Buckley Field was that it was easy to get a weekend pass to Denver. I used the weekends mostly for writing. I checked into a hotel with my lavender Remington #5 portable that I carried all through the war.* I would get up in the morning, call for coffee and orange juice from room service, set up the typewriter and start banging away. It didn't always work out. In one hotel I was kept awake all night by raucous noises from the other rooms. It wasn't until dawn that I got to sleep, and not until I got back to the base that I discovered the hotel was a full-scale whorehouse. God knows what the desk clerk thought I was there for, with my lavender typewriter and my innocent face.

* It was a twelfth-birthday present from my mother and I didn't retire it until I was in my thirties. Whatever became of typewriters like that?

Double-Cross was written in one of those hotel rooms. It appeared in *Planet Stories* for Winter 1944.

The Colorado interlude didn't last very long. What I remember most about it was interminable discussions with Air Force shrinks about the perils of isolation on the icecaps. That, and one long, evil day in a dentist's chair, while they pulled out all the old fillings in my teeth and replaced them with new ones, scientifically designed to be proof against the Arctic cold.

Then they sent me to Italy.

Double-Cross

JAMES MacCREIGH

The Officer of the Deck was pleased as he returned to the main lock. There was no reason why everything shouldn't have been functioning perfectly, of course, but he was pleased to have it confirmed, all the same. The Executive Officer was moodily smoking a cigarette in the open lock, staring out over the dank Venusian terrain at the native town. He turned.

"Everything shipshape, I take it!" he commented.

The OD nodded. "I'll have a blank log if this keeps up," he said. "Every man accounted for except the delegation, cargo stowed, drivers ready to lift as soon as they come back."

The Exec tossed away his cigarette. "*If* they come back."

"Is there any question?"

The Exec shrugged. "I don't know, Lowry," he said. "This is a funny place. I don't trust the natives."

Lowry lifted his eyebrows. "Oh? But after all, they're human beings, just like us—"

"Not any more. Four or five generations ago they were. Lord, they don't even look human any more. Those white, flabby skins—I don't like them."

"Acclimation," Lowry said scientifically. "They had to acclimate themselves to Venus's climate. They're friendly enough."

The Exec shrugged again. He stared at the wooden shacks that were the outskirts of the native city, dimly visible through the ever-present Venusian mist. The native guard of honor, posted a hundred yards from the Earth ship, stood stolidly at attention with their old-fashioned proton-rifles slung over their backs. A few natives were gazing wonderingly at the great ship, but made no move to pass the line of guards.

"Of course," Lowry said suddenly, "there's a minority who are afraid of us. I was in town yesterday, and I talked with some of the natives. They think there will be hordes of immigrants from Earth, now that we know Venus is habitable. And there's some sort of a paltry underground group that is spreading the word that the immigrants will drive the native Venusians—the descendants of the first expedition, that is—right down into the mud. Well—" he laughed—"maybe they will. After all, the fittest survive. That's a basic law of—"

The annunciator over the open lock clanged vigorously, and a metallic voice rasped: "Officer of the Deck! Post Number One! Instruments reports a spy ray focused on the main lock!"

Lowry, interrupted in the middle of a word, jerked his head back and stared unbelievingly at the tell-tale next to the annunciator. Sure enough, it was glowing red—might have been glowing for minutes. He snatched at the hand-phone dangling from the wall, shouted into it. "Set up a screen! Notify the delegation! Alert a landing party!" But even while he was giving orders, the warning light flickered suddenly and went out. Stricken, Lowry turned to the Exec.

The Executive Officer nodded gloomily. He said, "You see!"

"You see?"

Svan clicked off the listening-machine and turned around. The five others in the room looked apprehensive. "You see?" Svan repeated. "From their own mouths you have heard it. The Council was right."

The younger of the two women sighed. She might have been beautiful, in spite of her dead-white skin, if there had been a scrap of hair on her head. "Svan, I'm afraid," she said. "Who are we to decide if this is a good thing? Our parents came from Earth. Perhaps there will be trouble at first, if colonists come, but we are of the same blood."

Svan laughed harshly. "*They* don't think so. You heard them. We are not human any more. The officer said it."

The other woman spoke unexpectedly. "The Council was right," she agreed. "Svan, what must we do?"

Svan raised his hand, thoughtfully. "One moment. Ingra, do you still object?"

The younger woman shrank back before the glare in his eyes. She looked around at the others, found them reluctant and uneasy, but visibly convinced by Svan.

"No," she said slowly. "I do not object."

"And the rest of us? Does any of us object?"

Svan eyed them, each in turn. There was a slow but unanimous gesture of assent.

"Good," said Svan. "Then we must act. The Council has told us that we alone will decide our course of action. We have agreed that, if the Earth ship returns, it means disaster for Venus. Therefore, it must not return."

An old man shifted restlessly. "But they are strong, Svan," he complained. "They have weapons. We cannot force them to stay."

Svan nodded. "No. They will leave. But they will never get back to Earth."

"Never get back to Earth?" the old man gasped. "Has the Council authorized—murder?"

Svan shrugged. "The Council did not know what we would face. The Councilmen could not come to the city and see what strength the Earth ship has." He paused dangerously. "Toller," he said, "do you object?"

Like the girl, the old man retreated before his eyes. His voice was dull. "What is your plan?" he asked.

Svan smiled, and it was like a dark flame. He reached to a box at his feet, held up a shiny metal globe. "One of us will plant this in the ship. It will be set by means of this dial—" he touched a spot on the surface of the globe with a pallid finger—"to do nothing for forty hours. Then —it will explode. Atomite."

He grinned triumphantly, looking from face to face. The grin faded uncertainly as he saw what was in their eyes—uncertainty, irresolution. Abruptly he set the bomb down, savagely ripped six leaves off a writing tablet on the table next him. He took a pencil and made a mark on one of them, held it up.

"We will let chance decide who is to do the work," he said angrily. "Is there anyone here who is afraid? There will be danger, I think. . . ."

No answer. Svan jerked his head. "Good," he said. "Ingra, bring me that bowl."

Silently the girl picked up an opaque glass bowl from the broad arm of her chair. It had held Venus-tobacco cigarettes; there were a few left. She shook them out and handed the bowl to Svan, who was rapidly creasing the six fatal slips. He dropped them in the bowl, stirred it with his hand, offered it to the girl. "You first, Ingra," he said.

She reached in mechanically, her eyes intent on his, took out a slip and held it without opening it. The bowl went the rounds, till Svan himself took the last. All eyes were on him. No one had looked at their slips.

Svan, too, had left his unopened. He sat at the table, facing them. "This is the plan," he said. "We will go, all six of us, in my ground car, to look at the Earth ship. No one will suspect—the whole city has been to see it already. One will get out, at the best point we can find. It is almost dusk now. He can hide, surely, in the vegetation. The other five will start back. Something will go wrong with the car—perhaps it will run off the road, start to sink in the swamp. The guards will be called. There will be commotion—that is easy enough, after all; a hysterical woman, a few screams, that's all there is to it. And the sixth person will have his chance to steal to the side of the ship. The bomb is magnetic. It will not be noticed in the dark—they will take off before sunrise, because they must travel away from the sun to return—in forty hours the danger is removed."

There was comprehension in their eyes, Svan saw . . . but still that uncertainty. Impatiently, he crackled: "Look at the slips!"

Though he had willed his eyes away from it, his fingers had rebelled. Instinctively they had opened the slip, turned it over and over, striving to detect if it was the fatal one. They had felt nothing. . . .

And his eyes saw nothing. The slip was blank. He gave it but a second's glance, then looked up to see who had won the lethal game of chance. Almost he was disappointed.

Each of the others had looked in that same second. And each was looking up now, around at his neighbors. Svan waited impatiently for the chosen one to announce it—a second, ten seconds. . . .

Then gray understanding came to him. *A traitor!* his subconscious whispered. *A coward!* He stared at them in a new light, saw their indecision magnified, became opposition.

Svan thought faster than ever before in his life. If there was a coward, it would do no good to unmask him. All were wavering, any might be the one who had drawn the fatal slip. He could insist on inspecting every one, but—suppose the coward, cornered, fought back? In fractions of a second, Svan had considered the evidence and reached his decision. Masked by the table, his hand, still holding the pencil, moved swiftly beneath the table, marked his own slip.

In the palm of his hand, Svan held up the slip he had just marked in secret. His voice was very tired as he said, "I will plant the bomb."

The six conspirators in Svan's old ground car moved slowly along the main street of the native town. Two Earth-ship sailors, unarmed except for deceptively flimsy-looking pistols at their hips, stood before the entrance to the town's Hall of Justice.

"Good," said Svan, observing them. "The delegation is still here. We have ample time."

He half turned in the broad front seat next the driver, searching the faces of the others in the car. Which was the coward? he wondered. Ingra? Her aunt? One of the men?

The right answer leaped up at him. *They all are,* he thought. *Not one of them understands what this means. They're afraid.*

He clamped his lips. "Go faster, Ingra," he ordered the girl who was driving. "Let's get this done with."

She looked at him, and he was surprised to find compassion in her eyes. Silently she nodded, advanced the fuel-handle so that the clumsy car jolted a trace more rapidly over the corduroy road. It was quite dark now. The car's driving light flared yellowishly in front of them, illuminating the narrow road and the pale, distorted vegetation of the jungle that surrounded them. Svan noticed it was raining a little. The present shower would deepen and intensify until midnight, then fall off again, to halt before morning. But before then they would be done.

A proton-bolt lanced across the road in front of them. In the silence that followed its thunderous crash, a man's voice bellowed: "Halt!"

The girl, Ingra, gasped something indistinguishable, slammed on the brakes. A Venusian in the trappings of the State Guard advanced on them from the side of the road, proton-rifle held ready to fire again.

"Where are you going?" he growled. Svan spoke up. "We want to look at the Earth ship," he said. He opened the door beside him and stepped out, careless of the drizzle. "We heard it was leaving tonight," he continued, "and we have not seen it. Is that not permitted?"

The guard shook his head sourly. "No one is allowed near the ship. The order was just issued. It is thought there is danger."

Svan stepped closer, his teeth bared in what passed for a smile. "It is urgent," he purred. His right hand flashed across his chest in a complicated gesture. "Do you understand?"

Confusion furrowed the guard's hairless brows, then was replaced by a sudden flare of understanding—and fear. "The Council!" he roared. "By heaven, yes, I understand! You are the swine that caused this—" He strove instinctively to bring the clumsy rifle up, but Svan was faster. His gamble had failed; there was only one course remaining. He hurled his gross white bulk at the guard, bowled him over against the splintery logs of the road. The proton-rifle went flying, and Svan savagely tore at the throat of the guard. Knees, elbows and claw-like nails—Svan battered at the astonished man with every ounce of strength in his body. The guard was as big as Svan, but Svan had the initial advantage . . . and it was only a matter of seconds before the guard lay unconscious, his skull a mass of gore at the back where Svan had ruthlessly pounded it against the road.

Svan rose, panting, stared around. No one else was in sight, save the petrified five and the ground car. Svan glared at them contemptuously, then reached down and heaved on the senseless body of the guard. Over the shoulder of the road the body went, onto the damp swamp-land of the jungle. Even while Svan watched the body began to sink. There would be no trace.

Svan strode back to the car. "Hurry up," he gasped to the girl. "Now there is danger for all of us, if they discover he is missing. And keep a watch for other guards."

Venus has no moon, and no star can shine through its vast cloud layer. Ensign Lowry, staring anxiously out through the astro-dome in the bow of the Earth ship, cursed the blackness.

"Can't see a thing," he complained to the Exec, steadily writing away at the computer's table. "Look—are those lights over there?"

The Exec looked up wearily. He shrugged. "Probably the guards. Of course, you can't tell. Might be a raiding party."

Lowry, stung, looked to see if the Exec was smiling, but found no answer in his stolid face. "Don't joke about it," he said. "Suppose something happens to the delegation?"

"Then we're in the soup," the Exec said philosophically. "I told you the natives were dangerous. Spy-rays! They've been prohibited for the last three hundred years."

"It isn't all the natives," Lowry said. "Look how they've doubled the guard around us. The administration is cooperating every way they know how. You heard the delegation's report on the intercom. It's this secret group they call the Council."

"And how do you know the guards themselves don't belong to it?" the Exec retorted. "They're all the same to me. . . . Look, your light's gone out now. Must have been the guard. They're on the wrong side to be coming from the town, anyhow. . . ."

Svan hesitated only a fraction of a second after the girl turned the lights out and stopped the car. Then he reached in the compartment under the seat. If he took a little longer than seemed necessary to get the atomite bomb out of the compartment, none of the others noticed. Certainly it did not occur to them that there had been *two* bombs in the compartment, though Svan's hand emerged with only one.

He got out of the car, holding the sphere. "This will do for me," he said. "They won't be expecting anyone to come from behind the ship—we were wise to circle around. Now, you know what you must do?"

Ingra nodded, while the others remained mute. "We must circle back again," she parroted. "We are to wait five minutes, then drive the car into the swamp. We will create a commotion, attract the guards."

Svan, listening, thought: *It's not much of a plan. The guards would not be drawn away. I am glad I can't trust these five any more. If they must be destroyed, it is good that their destruction will serve a purpose.*

Aloud, he said, "You understand. If I get through, I will return to the city on foot. No one will suspect anything if I am not caught, because the bomb will not explode until the ship is far out in space. Remember, you are in no danger from the guards."

From the guards, his mind echoed. He smiled. At least, they would feel no pain, never know what happened. With the amount of atomite in that bomb in the compartment, they would merely be obliterated in a ground-shaking crash.

Abruptly he swallowed, reminded of the bomb that was silently counting off the seconds. "Go ahead," he ordered. "I will wait here."

"Svan." The girl, Ingra, leaned over to him. Impulsively she reached for him, kissed him. "Good luck to you, Svan," she said.

"Good luck," repeated the others. Then silently the electric motor of the car took hold. Skilfully the girl backed it up, turned it around, sent it lumbering back down the road. Only after she had traveled a few hundred feet by the feel of the road did she turn the lights on again.

Svan looked after them. The kiss had surprised him. What did it mean? Was it an error that the girl should die with the others?

There was an instant of doubt in his steel-shackled mind, then it was driven away. Perhaps she was loyal, yet certainly she was weak. And since he could not know which was the one who had received the marked slip, and feared to admit it, it was better they all should die.

He advanced along the midnight road to where the ground rose and the jungle plants thinned out. Ahead, on an elevation, were the rain-dimmed lights of the Earth ship, set down in the center of a clearing made by its own fierce rockets. Svan's mist-trained eyes spotted the circling figures of sentries, and knew that these would be the ship's own. They would not be as easily overcome as the natives, not with those slim-shafted blasters they carried. Only deceit could get him to the side of the ship.

Svan settled himself at the side of the road, waiting for his chance. He had perhaps three minutes to wait; he reckoned. His fingers went absently to the pouch in his wide belt, closed on the slip of paper. He turned it over without looking at it, wondering who had drawn the first cross, and been a coward. Ingra? One of the men?

He became abruptly conscious of a commotion behind him. A ground car was racing along the road. He spun around and was caught in the glare of its blinding driving-light, as it bumped to a slithering stop.

Paralyzed, he heard the girl's voice. "Svan! They're coming! They found the guard's rifle, and they're looking for us! Thirty Earthmen, Svan, with those frightful guns. They fired at us, but we got away and came for you. We must flee!"

He stared unseeingly at the light. "Go away!" he croaked unbelievingly. Then his muscles jerked into action. The time was almost up—the bomb in the car—

"Go away!" he shrieked, and turned to run. His fists clenched and swinging at his side, he made a dozen floundering steps before something immense pounded at him from behind. He felt himself lifted from the road, sailing, swooping, dropping with annihilating force onto the hard, charred earth of the clearing. Only then did he hear the sound of the explosion, and as the immense echoes died away he began to feel the pain seeping into him from his hideously racked body. . . .

The Flight Surgeon rose from beside him. "He's still alive," he said callously to Lowry, who had just come up. "It won't last long, though. What've you got there?"

Lowry, a bewildered expression on his beardless face, held out the two halves of a metallic sphere. Dangling ends of wires showed where a connection had been broken. "He had a bomb," he said. "A magnetic-type, delayed-action atomite bomb. There must have been another in the car, and it went off. They—they were planning to bomb us."

"Amazing," the surgeon said dryly. "Well, they won't do any bombing now."

Lowry was staring at the huddled, mutilated form of Svan. He shuddered. The surgeon, seeing the shudder, grasped his shoulder.

"Better them than us," he said. "It's poetic justice if I ever saw it. They had it coming. . . ." He paused thoughtfully, staring at a piece of paper between his fingers. "This is the only part I don't get," he said.

"What's that?" Lowry craned his neck. "A piece of paper with a cross on it? What about it?"

The surgeon shrugged. "He had it clenched in his hand," he said. "Had the devil of a time getting it loose from him." He turned it over slowly, displayed the other side. "Now what in the world would he be doing carrying a scrap of paper with a cross marked on both sides?"

Double-Cross was the last story I published during the war. By the time the war was over and I was back to civilian affairs again the world was a different place.

So this is a good place to close.

Yesterday I had lunch with Isaac Asimov, who was part of the Futurian scene in those ancient days and has been a good friend for pushing four decades. I told him what I was writing. It was only fair; after all, his *The Early Asimov* broke ground for this book. Sitting next to Isaac in the University Club in New York, along with Betsy Lester, Warren Preece, Carl Sagan and other admirable people, those teenage days of excitement and uncertainty seemed *very* remote. The luncheon was for contributors to the new Encyclopaedia Britannica,* the surroundings were plush . . . and none of us were seventeen any more.

* My own contribution was the essay on the Roman emperor Tiberius, in case you were wondering.

I thought of dedicating this book to Isaac. We have done so much of our growing up together (and listen, Isaac, I think we'll make it yet) that surely I should acknowledge so many years of close association, both as colleagues and as friends.

But in this book in particular it seems there are more debts incurred than I know how to pay. Not only Isaac Asimov. Not only all of the others who are mentioned here, the editors and the writers, the friends and the fans. Not only the entire membership of the Brooklyn Science Fiction League, the Independent League for Science Fiction, the International Scientific Association and of course the Futurians . . . not only editors, bookdealers, proprietors of secondhand magazine stores who endured my browsing for hours on end, and artists . . . but so many others that I cannot even count them.

And so there are only three names on the dedication page. They were all dear to me, and they all died too young.

Dear reader, at the end of this book let me level with you.

I'm not a particularly modest person, you know. It seems to me that I've had enough in the way of awards and money and celebrity to temper the agonies of adolescent ambition. And out of the large number of things I've written there are some stories—maybe a dozen, maybe not quite that many—that strike me as being about as good as anyone could ever have made those particular stories. Some were written decades ago. The most recent is one I am just finishing now. So in a sense I am not discontented with my life so far.

But everyone who spends his life trying to create something knows that there is no such thing as *enough* success or *enough* satisfaction. The story I am just finishing strikes me as very good. But I know perfectly well that after it is out of my hands and I start another, what will pass through my head is, "Okay, Pohl, *that* one was all right, but can you do it again?"

I know this is not just a personal hangup of mine. I've lived closely enough with other writers, and with artists and musicians and the more adventurous kinds of scientists, to know something of what happens in their heads, too. A couple of years ago I ran into some bad times and, for the first time in my life, visited a psychoanalyst. He was a pleasant, intelligent man. At one time he took me back into my early professional life—much the sort of thing I've been talking about in these notes—and asked me what I felt about myself. I said, "Well, the Futurians were a mighty bright, talented bunch. I feel pretty good about the fact that I've accomplished more than most of them—all but one, anyway." And Sigfrid von Shrink asked, "How do you feel about that one?" and quick as can be I said, "I hate his guts."

It happened that the next day I had lunch with that one ex-Futurian, who was Isaac Asimov. He mentioned that he had just sold a book for some kind of crazy money like a $50,000 advance, a lot more than *I* get, so naturally I told him the story about my conversation with my shrink. Isaac laughed and laughed. "When I signed the contract for fifty G," he said, "it was as ashes in my mouth, because I had just heard that Michael Crichton had signed one for half a million."

I don't *really* hate Isaac. He is my water brother, as long as we both live. But he will understand when I say that at the same time I really do, too.

W. H. Auden talked about that once. He said, "No poet or novelist wishes he were the only one who has ever lived, but most of them wish they were the only one alive, and quite a number fondly believe their wish has been granted." And I think that if with some part of your head you cannot believe that, at least for a moment now and then, then you really should not waste your time being a poet or a novelist, but get a job writing advertising copy or pick up the torch thrown down by Jacqueline Susann.

Reminiscing about the days when I was writing the stories in this volume has put me in a rueful, half-amused, half-sentimental mood. So I would like to say something sentimental at the end, an act of courage one seldom permits oneself in public.

Immodest as I am, I am also fifty-five years old. It's pretty clear that I've done more up to now than I am likely to do from now on. Not necessarily *better*. But, just in terms of the simple arithmetic of the calendar, more.

I spend a great deal of time with college audiences and fan groups. There is no such assembly that does not contain a few young people who want very much to write science fiction. Now and then you see some who clearly are going to do what they want, and do it very well.

They are my water brothers, too. When I can see how, I help them. When I can't, at least I wish them well. I admire them. I love them. And I also hate their guts a little bit, now and then.

For my sins, I have been elected president of the union of our trade, the Science Fiction Writers of America. I've always spent a good deal of my time with other writers. Now there are weeks when it seems I do nothing else. Most of the several hundred members of SFWA are still

G

learning the business. Some perhaps never will learn it. But among them are the Clarkes and the Heinleins of tomorrow. What I have found out over the years is that *all* science-fiction writers are water brothers. It has nothing to do with language, country of origin, age, talent or experience. The Bradburys help the beginners. The beginners know and trust the stars.

All of us are vain enough to believe that maybe we are the only ones who matter. But we are even vainer than that, in a way that Auden didn't mention. The agenbite of our inwits is such that we are not satisfied merely to compete. We have to give our competitors a helping hand from time to time, in order to make the competition fair.

Everything considered, the world of science fiction is not a bad place to live.

So if I could go back in time to that first meeting with Dirk Wylie at Brooklyn Tech in those grimy early months of 1933, and have the chance to do it over, knowing everything I know now about the pains and the problems, the disappointments and the slow-coming rewards . . . I would do it exactly the same way, and exult at the chance.

Frederik Pohl

Red Bank, New Jersey

January 1975